Bad Intentions . . .

"She wants to buy Crewel World," said Betsy.

"She'll have to find a new place for it," warned Mickels.

"Yes, I was afraid of that," said Shelly to Mickels, coming out of the kitchen. "Are you going to be okay, Betsy?"

"I think so, thanks."

"But I can make the store the talk of the country," said Irene, now arguing with all of them. "I've wanted to open my own store for years and years, you know that, Shelly; but Margot got hers started first, so there wasn't anything I could do 'til she got out of the way."

"That's a strange way of putting it, Irene," said Shelly. "She didn't exactly decide on her own to step out of anyone's way. She was murdered . . ."

Irene shrugged. "Well, it's how I think of it. She wouldn't let me become her partner, so what could I do?"

"What do you mean?" asked Betsy sharply.

MORE MYSTERIES FROM THE
BERKLEY PUBLISHING GROUP..

DOG LOVERS' MYSTERIES STARRING HOLLY WINTER: With her Alaskan malamute Rowdy, Holly dogs the trails of dangerous criminals. ''A gifted and original writer.''—Carolyn G. Hart

by Susan Conant

A NEW LEASH ON DEATH	A BITE OF DEATH
DEAD AND DOGGONE	PAWS BEFORE DYING

DOG LOVERS' MYSTERIES STARRING JACKIE WALSH: She's starting a new life with her son and an ex-police dog named Jake... teaching film classes and solving crimes!

by Melissa Cleary

A TAIL OF TWO MURDERS	SKULL AND DOG BONES
DOG COLLAR CRIME	DEAD AND BURIED
HOUNDED TO DEATH	THE MALTESE PUPPY
AND YOUR LITTLE DOG, TOO	MURDER MOST BEASTLY
FIRST PEDIGREE MURDER	OLD DOGS

SAMANTHA HOLT MYSTERIES: Dogs, cats, and crooks are all part of a day's work for this veterinary technician... ''Delightful!''—Melissa Cleary

by Karen Ann Wilson

EIGHT DOGS FLYING	COPY CAT CRIMES
BEWARE SLEEPING DOGS	CIRCLE OF WOLVES

CHARLOTTE GRAHAM MYSTERIES: She's an actress with a flair for dramatics—and an eye for detection. ''You'll get hooked on Charlotte Graham!''—*Rave Reviews*

by Stefanie Matteson

MURDER AT THE SPA	MURDER AT THE FALLS
MURDER AT TEATIME	MURDER ON HIGH
MURDER ON THE CLIFF	MURDER AMONG THE ANGELS
MURDER ON THE SILK ROAD	MURDER UNDER THE PALMS

PEACHES DANN MYSTERIES: Peaches has never had a very good memory. But she's learned to cope with it over the years... Fortunately, though, when it comes to murder, this absentminded amateur sleuth doesn't forgive and forget!

by Elizabeth Daniels Squire

WHO KILLED WHAT'S-HER-NAME?	WHOSE DEATH IS IT ANYWAY?
MEMORY CAN BE MURDER	IS THERE A DEAD MAN IN THE HOUSE?
REMEMBER THE ALIBI	

HEMLOCK FALLS MYSTERIES: The Quilliam sisters combine their culinary and business skills to run an inn in upstate New York. But when it comes to murder, their talent for detection takes over...

by Claudia Bishop

A TASTE FOR MURDER	MURDER WELL-DONE
A PINCH OF POISON	DEATH DINES OUT
A DASH OF DEATH	A TOUCH OF THE GRAPE
	A STEAK IN MURDER

CREWEL WORLD

Monica Ferris

BERKLEY PRIME CRIME, NEW YORK

This is a work of fiction. Names, characters, places, and incidents are either the product of the author's imagination or are used fictitiously, and any resemblance to actual persons, living or dead, business establishments, events or locales is entirely coincidental.

CREWEL WORLD

A Berkley Prime Crime Book / published by arrangement with the author

PRINTING HISTORY
Berkley Prime Crime edition / March 1999

The Penguin Putnam Inc. World Wide Web site address is
http://www.penguinputnam.com

ISBN: 0-425-16780-1

Berkley Prime Crime Books are published
by The Berkley Publishing Group,
a division of Penguin Putnam Inc.,
375 Hudson Street, New York, New York 10014.
The name BERKLEY PRIME CRIME and the BERKLEY PRIME CRIME
design are trademarks belonging to Penguin Putnam Inc.

PRINTED IN THE UNITED STATES OF AMERICA

10 9 8 7 6 5 4 3

I thought I knew enough about needlework to write this novel. I didn't. Fortunately, people can be generous with their time and talents. Foremost are the owner, staff, and customers of Needle Nest of Minnetonka—particularly Pat Ingle, Sandy Mattson and the Wednesday Bunch. Denise Williams designed the T'ang horse pattern and told me about painting needlepoint canvases. Elizabeth Proudfit encouraged and advised me, and lent generously from her own library of needlework books. And the people of rec.crafts.textile.needlework (an Internet newsgroup) have cheered me on, answered my questions, and continue to be an excellent resource.

To all of you, humble and heartfelt thanks.

1

Nowadays, when she stopped for lunch, Margot sat with her back to her shop's big front window. That gray monstrosity they'd built across the street had taken away her view of the lake. She ate the last Frito and wadded the empty bag into the plastic wrap that had held her sandwich and dropped both into the little wastebasket under the table. She drank the last of the green tea in her pretty porcelain cup—brewed from a bag, but good nevertheless—and took the cup to the back room for a quick rinse.

There were no customers waiting to buy needlework patterns or embroidery floss or knitting yarn when she got back, so she made a quick tour of her shop, rearranging the heap of knitting yarns in a corner, adjusting a display of the new autumn colors of embroidery floss in a basket on a table, and moving a folding knitting stand an inch closer to the traffic lane. Her shop appeared aimlessly cluttered, but every display was calculated to draw customers ever deeper into the room, with items virtually leaping into their hands.

Satisfied, she sat down again and got out her own knitting. She was working on a bolero jacket she intended to wear to a meeting on Saturday. It was a simple pattern, just knit and purl, but she was doing it in quarter-inch ribbon instead of yarn, so the jacket had an interesting depth and texture. It helped that the ribbon blended every few inches from palest pink to soft mauve to gray lavender.

Margot started knitting, her hands moving with swift economy. The jacket was nearly finished—if it wasn't finished already. She was slender enough to look good in a bolero jacket, but short enough that she had to try on everything in clothing stores, even things labeled petite, and nearly always had to adjust knitting patterns. After all these years she should be accustomed to it, but every so often she'd miscalculate or just get carried away with the pleasure of the work, and end up with the voluminous kind of garment teenagers wore. Of all the silliness of the current age, the silliest was a young thug who had to hold up his pants with one hand while he held up a shopkeeper with the other.

Margot Berglund was fifty-three, blond, with kind blue eyes and a bustling but comfortable manner. She had always been happiest with something to keep her busy, and so, when simply doing needlework and teaching her friends to do needlework and organizing expeditions to needlework stores and gatherings wasn't enough, she had opened Crewel World. That was back when crewelwork was the rage; just because it was needlepoint nowadays, she saw no need to change an established name.

The front door went *bing* and a handsome woman whose dark hair was pulled into a fat bun hustled in.

"Sorry I'm late," she said breathlessly. "It's so beautiful out, I found myself walking slowly to enjoy it."

"I don't blame you, Shelly."

Shelly went to hide her purse in the checkout desk's bottom drawer, looked around with a settling-in sigh, and asked, "What's first?"

"The window, I'm afraid," said Margot. The shop was

deep but narrow; its front was mostly window, currently ornamented with canvases and patterns featuring brightly colored leaves and one-room schoolhouses.

"What, already? School hasn't even started yet."

Margot smiled. "Our customers are always working in advance of a holiday. Half of them are already making Christmas ornaments. So don't get too elaborate with the window; soon we'll have to advertise Christmas projects for the procrastinators."

Shelly picked up the stack of display items Margot had chosen and went to the front window.

"Ooooh, I think I'd like this one for myself," she said a minute later. Margot looked up to see her holding a counted cross-stitch pattern featuring an enormous pale moon with a silhouetted witch riding her broom across it. In the foreground was a heap of pumpkins out of which rose a windblown scarecrow.

"You'll have to do it on black," warned Margot.

"Yeah, well, I've been thinking of buying one of those Dazor lamps anyway," said Shelly. She traced the tatters of the scarecrow with a finger. "Isn't this just beautiful?"

"Shall I deduct it from your pay?"

"Let me think about it. Maybe I won't have time."

Margot laughed; Shelly sounded almost hopeful.

Shelly Donohue was a schoolteacher who'd taken this part-time job to earn a little spending money over the summer; she'd spent most of it on floss and counted cross-stitch patterns. "How many did you order?" she asked.

"Only three; not many people like working on black."

"Ask me again when there's only one left." Shelly turned to find a place in the window to hang the pattern.

The shop fell silent except for classical music coming from a radio tucked under a table near the back. Mozart's flute concerto, played on a flute for a change.

After a while Margot put down her needles to spread the jacket on the worktable. Was it done? She reached into a basket on the table and among the scissors, marking pencils, knitting needles, and all, found a fabric measuring tape.

"I thought I'd find your sister here when I came in," Shelly said.

"Yes, I've been thinking she might be here today." Margot stretched the tape down the back of the jacket.

"When did you last hear from her?"

"Day before yesterday. She was in Las Vegas." She adjusted the jacket to measure the front.

"Did she win?"

Perhaps just one more row, then she would bind off. "Hmm? Oh, I don't know; she didn't say anything about gambling."

"Is she the sort to gamble?"

"A year ago I would have said yes, definitely. But I'm not so sure now." Margot tucked the tape measure back into the basket and sat down to resume knitting.

Shelly made a concerned face and said, "Oh, Margot; is she coming because she's *broke*?" Shelly had a cousin who mooched.

Margot considered that. "No, I think she's at loose ends right now, and just doesn't know what she wants to do next."

Betsy was Margot's only sibling, her elder by two years. They had been close as children, despite having very different personalities. Margot had been the placid and obedient one; Betsy had been impulsive and adventurous. At eighteen, Betsy had run away to join the navy. A year later she married a sailor in one of those hasty justice-of-the-peace ceremonies, phoning home with the news only afterward. This completed the breach between Betsy and her parents, which was some years healing.

Margot had lived at home until she finished college, then married the boy she'd dated since junior high. The sisters had stayed in touch over the years, but had not seen much of one another. Betsy's first marriage hadn't lasted long.

She had moved around a lot, and then wrote of belated plans to get a degree. The Christmas after that she announced her marriage to a college professor. Letters were fewer after that, and less exciting. Margot had thought Betsy settled at last.

Then, just a few weeks ago, Betsy had written a long letter. Her college-professor husband had fallen in love with one of his students and was divorcing Betsy. Apparently there had been a pattern of affairs with students, so Betsy was letting him go. The tone of this letter was very unlike Betsy's normal cheery exuberance. She sounded sad and tired. Margot, worried, wrote back at once and, after an exchange of letters, invited her sister to come for an extended visit. Betsy's reply: *Keep a light on for me, I'll be there in a week or ten days.* That had been just over a week earlier.

"... funny that," Shelly was saying.

"Funny what?"

Shelly's voice thinned as she strained to put a clear suction cup with a hook on it way up near the top of the window. "It's usually the oldest child who's conservative, more grown-up, the one who helps parent the younger ones."

"You think so? But there was just the two of us, and I'm only twenty-seven months younger. . . ." Her needles slowed as she thought that over. Betsy had been the voice of enthusiasm, the "what if" and "wouldn't it be fun to" child; Margot had been the cautionary, worried "we could get hurt" or "Mama will be mad" child. Each had brought some balance to the tendencies of the other; perhaps that's why they had been so happy together growing up. Perhaps they could recapture some of that balance.

Her musings were interrupted again by the electric *bing* of the door opening. An older woman, tall and very slim, came in. She was wearing a beautiful linen suit in a warm gray a shade darker than her hair.

"Good afternoon, Mrs. Lundgren," said Margot, putting down her knitting.

Mrs. Lundgren loved needlework, but was too busy to do her own. She frequented craft fairs and often came to Margot for bonnets and booties for her granddaughters and needlepoint pictures and pillows for her several homes. Margot rose and went behind the big desk that served as a checkout counter.

"Margot, I've been thinking some more about that T'ang horse," said Mrs. Lundgren.

"It's not for sale, Mrs. Lundgren," said Margot, politely but firmly.

"So you keep telling me." Mrs. Lundgren got just the right light and rueful tone in her voice; Margot relaxed into a smile. "But as I said, I've been thinking. Would it be all right to ask you to make a copy of it for me? It won't be displayed here, but in our winter home."

Margot turned and looked at the wall behind her, where a framed needlepoint picture of a midnight-blue horse hung. The animal had his short tail closely braided, his feet well under him and his neck in a high arch, the head somewhat offset, as if he were looking backward, around his shoulder. He had a white saddle, white stockings, and a golden mane combed flat against his neck. The original was a pottery T'ang Dynasty horse in the Minneapolis art museum.

"Do you know, I should have thought of that," Margot said, surprised at herself. She frowned. "But I threw my old sketches away, so I'd have to start over, take a piece of graph paper, go to the museum and plot the horse on it, and then needlepoint over that."

"I understand. And then could the background be a different color?"

"Of course. Do you know what color?"

Mrs. Lundgren reached into her purse and produced a fabric swatch. "Can you match this?" The color was a faded, dusty red. A trip to the silks rack produced a sample nearly the same color.

"But not quite," said Margot with regret.

"Yes, and not quite won't do. How about this pale olive?" Mrs. Lundgren lifted a skein off its hook.

"Are you sure? I mean, it will look very good as a background color, but you don't want to offend your decor."

"There is a dark olive in the drapes," said Mrs. Lundgren.

"Very well." Margot took the silk from Mrs. Lundgren and the two walked back to her desk.

"How much for the entire project?" asked Mrs. Lundgren.

Margot went to the big desk that was her checkout counter and got out her calculator. "Do you want yours the same size?"

"What is that, fourteen by fourteen?"

"Yes, plus the mat and frame, of course."

"That's what I want, even the same narrow wood frame, please."

Margot began to punch numbers. "I'll have to charge you one hundred and fifty dollars to paint it," she began. That was a very fair price; painting a needlepoint canvas was harder than it looked; not only did the picture have to be artistically done, the curves and lines and color changes had to be worked in a pattern of tiny squares. "Then two dollars a square inch for the stitching, that comes to four hundred dollars; and another hundred and fifty for stretching and framing." Margot punched the total button. "That would be seven hundred dollars."

"How long will it take?"

"I could have it for you by Christmas."

"I'm sure that's a reasonable time allowance, but could it just possibly be sooner than that? We're spending Thanksgiving at our winter home in Honolulu, and I'd like to take it with me."

Margot closed her eyes and thought. As the Christmas season began to loom, her finishers wanted more and more lead time. On the other hand, the bolero jacket was all but done and she had nothing else urgent on her own horizon. If she started right away . . .

"I'll pay you a thousand," coaxed Mrs. Lundgren.

"Yes," Margot said. "Yes, I can do it that quickly for a thousand dollars."

"Oh, wonderful, I'm so pleased! Do you want something down on it?"

"No, but payment in full on delivery."

"Yes, of course. Thank you."

"You're welcome, Mrs. Lundgren."

When the door closed on Mrs. Lundgren, Shelly said, "You were waiting for her to up the offer."

"No, but I should use that tactic more often." Margot touched the frame of the horse, adjusting its position very slightly. It had come back from the framer only four months ago, and was Margot's finest effort at an original needlepoint to date. "Mrs. Lundgren knows a lot of women with time on their hands and money to pay for ways to fill it. She may not hang that picture in her Edina house, but she'll show it around before she takes it to Honolulu. A thousand-dollar price makes the artwork more attractive to some people, who may come in looking for something to hang on their own walls. But it might also bring customers wanting to save money by doing the needlework themselves." Margot smiled and Shelly laughed out loud. There were women, wealthy women, who shorted their families on groceries in order to buy more canvases, more silk floss, more gold thread, more real garnet beads for the endless stream of needlepoint and counted cross-stitch work that had become an obsession. Margot sometimes felt like a dope peddler.

When Shelly finished the window, she started dusting. She paused when she came to an old rocking chair with a cushion on it, the cushion almost hidden under an enormous, fluffy white cat with tan and gray patches along its spine, sleeping on the cushion.

"Is Sophie nice and comfy?" cooed Shelly, stroking the animal. Sophie lifted her head to yawn, displaying teeth absurdly small in a cat her size. Then she put her head back down as if to sleep again, but a loud purr could be heard.

Margot had found the cat bedraggled and hungry in her shop doorway one morning and took her in. She had meant for her to live in the apartment over the store, but Sophie had followed her down one morning and been so quietly ornamental—and friendly to anyone who stopped to stroke her—that Margot had allowed her to stay.

Margot picked up her knitting and made an exclamation. She'd done two rows instead of one.

Shelly said, "Do you think Betsy will like it here in Excelsior? This is kind of a quiet place."

"Excelsior has plenty of things going on." People who lived in the small town were gratefully aware of its charms and Margot was among those who worked hard to preserve them. "Anyway, I have a feeling that she was looking for a refuge. Though, of course, how she'll like actually living in one we'll have to see."

Margot began pulling out the extra row. She had carved a safe niche in this small Minnesota town and stayed there content even after her husband died three years earlier.

Now Betsy was seeking a place to be safe in for a while. Apparently she had lost that zest for adventure, perhaps even grown a little afraid. Margot hoped she could give her sister what she needed. She picked up her knitting and began binding off.

Betsy wasn't scared, not really, just . . . nervous. It was one thing to be twenty-five and newly divorced, and not own a home or have a job with medical insurance or a retirement account whose deposits are matched by your employer. It's quite another to be fifty-five and be once again in that same boat.

Betsy wasn't averse to adventure. Crossing the mountains alone in an old car had brought moments that sent the blood rushing along with its old verve.

On the other hand, she'd spent her one night in Las Vegas at the Fremont Street light-and-sound show and having a drink in a beautiful old bar, followed by a phone call to her sister and then turning in early.

When she saw an exit sign pointing to the Grand Canyon, she did give a moment's thought to giving the Japanese tourists a thrill by throwing herself off the rim. But she didn't. In her experience such low thoughts, if not yielded to, tended to be brief and followed by something more interesting.

Later, crossing Iowa, Betsy remembered reading somewhere that while men are scared of birthdays ending in zero, women are frightened by birthdays ending in five. Certainly Betsy was. Fifty-five is no longer young, even when considered while you were in good spirits. Fifty-five can see old age rushing toward it like a mighty tree axed at the root. All too soon it would be *crash*: sixty! And if she reached retirement age with no savings to speak of, she might live out the last years of her life in one small room, fighting off the roaches for her supper of canned cat food.

But Betsy had also read somewhere that there were good jobs going begging in the upper Midwest, and she had her sister who had kindly offered to put her up until she got her feet under her again. Okay, so her sister lived in a small town; that small town was near the Twin Cities. That meant two newspapers, two job markets, right next door to one another. Twice the number of chances to start over.

And a ferocious Minnesota winter might be interesting, another adventure. After all, Betsy had grown up in Milwaukee, where the winters could also be hard.

Betsy pushed the accelerator down a little, and the car

responded. Good little car, acting as if it didn't already have a hundred and fifty thousand miles on it. Ahead was the road sign saying WELCOME TO MINNESOTA. She hoped it didn't smell of pig, like Iowa.

Sometime later the freeway forked. Thirty-five-E went to St. Paul, 35W came into Minneapolis. Margot hadn't mentioned this; her directions said to take I-35 into the Cities, and Highway 7 to Excelsior. Betsy chose Minneapolis; she had a notion that Excelsior was west of the Twin Cities and Minneapolis was the western twin. Right? She was pretty sure she hadn't already missed an exit onto Highway 7; certainly she hadn't missed an exit sign saying EXCELSIOR. A pity she had left the road atlas behind in an Omaha motel. She would stop at the next exit and buy a map.

She saw a little strip mall just this side of an exit, featuring a store whose sign advertised GUNS LIQUOR PAWN. Despite this warning that the owner liked to live dangerously, she got off and made her way back to it on a frontage road. She didn't go in; a store next door to it added to the explosive mixture by selling used snowmobiles and those noisy adult tricycles with puffy tires. But people who bought vehicles might also want maps.

They did, and the store sold them. The man behind the counter helped her plan a route to Highway 7. "Thirty-five don't cross 7," he said. "So what you do, you stay on 35W till you get to 494, take 494 west to 100, which only goes north from there, and it'll give you an exit onto 7. Go west and look for a sign." He moved a grubby finger along the map as she watched. It seemed clear enough.

"Thanks," she said, taking the map and folding it on the first try—Betsy was a traveler.

"You bet."

Amazing, they really did say "you bet" in Minnesota, just like in that book on how to speak Minnesotan Margot had sent her one Christmas.

Back on the highway, Betsy drove ten miles over the

speed limit—she had to, if she didn't want to be rear ended—and was so excited at the approach of the end of her journey that she didn't really notice that though it was not yet September, the ivy climbing the wooden sound barriers on 35W was turning an autumnal red.

2

Margot was selecting colored silks for the T'ang horse. She had her original needlepoint of it on the table, still in the frame, which had no glass in it. "I remember it was ten-oh-seven," she murmured to herself.

"What?" asked Shelly.

"The blue color of the horse, I remember it was ten-oh-seven, ten-oh-five, and ten-oh-three." She tried a skein of 1007 Madeira silk, which was a midnight-blue shade, against the neck and shoulder of the horse. "Still is, it seems."

"You have the most amazing memory," remarked Shelly, coming to look.

Margot smiled and preened a little, but said nothing. She had cut a blank canvas to the right size; it was on the table beside the horse, the olive-green skein on it. She put the blue silks beside the green.

But the creamy gold of the mane was harder to match. It was an odd color, not cream, not yellow, not gold. Nothing on her racks came close enough. She closed her eyes, thinking, then said, "I'm going upstairs for a minute."

Shelly waved assent and noticed that Sophie raised her

head at the sound of the back door opening. Was it suppertime already? Shelly chuckled; Sophie was fat and cosseted now, but she had a long memory and was determined never to miss a meal again.

Margot was back in three minutes, holding one partly used and two whole skeins of pale gold silk aloft. "I knew I had some left over!" she cheered. She gave Sophie a brisk rub just to share the joy. Sophie raised her rump and her bushy, tan-and-gray tail and purred ecstatically.

Shelly laughed. "You and Sophie are so easy to make happy!" she said.

"If I had gone up there and not found this, we'd all be singing another song," said Margot, but pleasantly, because she had gone up and found it. She put the golden skeins beside the blue on the canvas. "Now we need chalk white for the legs and saddle." She went to the silk rack and began examining the whites.

Highway 7 was a divided highway, mostly under repair. Betsy wove her way among the white and orange pylons, concentrating fiercely in order not to switch lanes in the wrong direction and end up facing an oncoming truck. At the same time she was looking for a sign—and there it was: EXCELSIOR, with a warning that it was a left exit. Betsy followed the lane, which led up and over the highway and a railroad bridge. Then there was a thicket of high bushes, a red apartment building, and she pulled up to a stop sign marking an asterisk of intersections.

Ahead were a little post office and the tree-shaded clapboard houses of a small town. Atop a steep hill on her left was a multiroofed Victorian house. A sign said it was the Christopher Inn Bed-and-Breakfast.

On the right was a parking lot with a small carnival Ferris wheel in it, though no other rides were visible.

A block later, at Water Street, was another stop sign. She was supposed to turn here, but which way? To the left the street was lined with old-fashioned, false-front brick stores; to the right, a block away, was a big blue lake with sailboats on it. Toward the lake, that's what the directions said. She turned right.

Just short of the lake was Lake Street—yes, that checked. A bar and grill with a wharf theme marked the corner. HASKELL'S, said the sign, which also checked. Betsy turned right. Two blocks later the lake disappeared behind a sprawling apartment complex of gray and white clapboards. She pulled over across the street from it, in front of an old, two-story, dark redbrick building. The middle one of the three shops had a pastel-colored sign hanging over the door: CREWEL WORLD, the letters done as if cross-stitched in various colors. From the *D* came an outsized needle pulling yarn in a matching color. She had arrived.

Something made Margot glance up as a car pulled to the curb. It was an older white hatchback, thickly layered with road dust, a woman driving. Margot had a feeling the license plates on it would be Californian.

Shelly said, "Is that her? Is that her?"

But Margot was on her way to the door, and didn't answer, because what if it wasn't? She opened it and watched the woman climb tiredly out on the driver's side. She was about five-three, plumper than Margot remembered, her brown hair well streaked with gray. She was wearing jeans and an ancient green sweatshirt with the sleeves cut off above the elbow.

And no glasses.

"Betsy, how can you drive without your glasses?" she scolded before she could stop herself.

"Contact lenses, of course," replied Betsy, defense at hand, as usual. "Oh, Margot, I am so happy to see you!" She came blundering up onto the sidewalk, blinking away tears, to enter her sister's welcoming embrace.

An hour later Betsy was in Margot's apartment. It was a nice place, with proportions at once unfamiliar and cozy.

The rooms were small, with low ceilings. In an efficient space were two bedrooms and bath, living room, and kitchen. A dining area off the kitchen was too small to be considered a separate room, but it was lit by a window that overlooked a small parking lot behind the building. If Betsy cared to lean sideways, she could see her weary old car pulled up under a lilac bush. Betsy was weary herself, but at the same time wound up tight, her body still swaying to the remembered movements of her car on the highway, her ears a little stopped up.

Last night, in a cheap motel in Omaha, she had been thinking of the ancient fable of the grasshopper and the ant. The prudent ant worked all summer, storing up seeds and dried fruit against the coming winter, while the grasshopper played in the sun. Then winter arrived and the grasshopper came knocking on the ant's door, hoping for shelter. The ant had turned the grasshopper away.

Margot had invited Betsy to come, but in that motel Betsy had worried that her sister might think of her as a grasshopper. What if Margot was critical, or worse, condescending? Betsy wouldn't put up with that. Maybe she should just call tomorrow and say she'd changed her mind, she was going to Chicago.

But Betsy had finished her trip to Minnesota and Margot had indeed seemed very glad to see her. On the other hand, this apartment wasn't exactly the big fancy house Margot used to live in, back when she was married to Aaron Berglund. Betsy had thought Margot had been left a wealthy widow, but apparently not. Did the shop make enough for Betsy to have a lengthy free ride? Maybe she'd better look for a job pretty soon.

Still, "I hope you're planning on a nice, long stay," Margot had said down in the shop, right in front of a witness, a woman with long hair in a knot. Sally was her name, or was it Shelly? Whoever, she unashamedly eavesdropped on everything the sisters said to one another. Margot had finally noticed it was making Betsy uncomfortable,

and all three unloaded the car, carrying mismatched suitcases up the stairs.

Margot had given her a quick tour of the apartment, told
her to help herself to anything in the kitchen, and went
back to work. Betsy had tried lying down on the comfortable bed in the guest room to take a nap, but was too
wound up to sleep. She had wandered the apartment
awhile, then gone to the refrigerator—eating when she
couldn't think of anything else to do was her worst fault—
and poured herself a glass of milk, then took a couple of
peanut-butter cookies from a cookie jar shaped like a pig—
a hint, obviously, but it didn't stop her.

Now she sat at the little table in the dining alcove, trying
not to think too much about the suitcases waiting to be
unpacked.

The building was only two stories high, so there were
no apartments overhead. Margot's apartment took up one
end of the second floor, with a stairwell between it and the
other apartments. Between its location and the old-
fashioned solidness of the building, it was very quiet up
here. Of course, it was a quiet little town, too; no fire and
police sirens, no traffic's roar. Even the lake's little wave-
lets could hardly approach the sussurant crash of the Pa-
cific. Oh, dear, she thought as her eyes began to sting, was
she going to miss the ocean, too?

No, no, she'd be just fine. She was here, in Excelsior,
Minnesota, a nice little town, and welcome. She finished
the milk and put one uneaten cookie back in the jar, put
the glass into the sink, and as she did noticed the grubbi-
ness of her hands. She went into the bathroom to wash,
but when she looked at herself in the mirror, she changed
her mind. Just washing her hands and face wasn't going
to do.

The tub was a big old-fashioned porcelain one, with
claw feet. Real porcelain tubs held the heat much better
than fiberglass ones and were therefore great for long
soaks. A long soak suddenly seemed very desirable. And

here was a jug of bubble bath, herbal-scented, just waiting. So she filled the tub, peeled off her clothes, and sank gratefully into the bubbles. She'd forgotten to go get a paperback, but that was all right; she just closed her eyes and fell into a kind of doze. When she stirred herself half an hour later, and rinsed out her hair, and toweled off with one of the big, thirsty bath towels, she felt a whole lot better.

She had put on fresh clothes and was halfway unpacked when she heard someone come in. "I'm home!" came Margot's voice.

Betsy found Margot in the kitchen. "Early closing tonight," she said. She was measuring out a portion of Iams Less Active for Sophie as the cat watched anxiously.

"Can I help with supper?" asked Betsy.

"No, the kitchen's too small, especially with Sophie in it, too. You sit down and we'll talk."

So Betsy sat at the round table in the dining nook and said, "How's business?"

"Not bad. Would you like to help out in the shop? With school starting, I'll need to replace Shelly."

"Sure. But—um—I mean—" Because she needed a salary.

"I pay six-ten an hour for beginners. Plus room and board, special for you." Margot, gathering things from the refrigerator, chuckled.

"Can you afford to do that?"

"Of course I can. You don't have to worry about that at all." Margot looked around the door, face as surprised as her voice.

"I don't want to be a burden."

"You're not a burden, and even if you were a burden, you wouldn't be a burden, okay?"

"Thanks. When do I start?"

"How about Monday? That will give you tomorrow and the weekend to get settled in."

Supper was a tuna salad made with every kind of lettuce

but iceberg, a little sweet onion only on Betsy's salad—
"I remember you like onions," Margot said—a sprinkle
of herbs, four large croutons, and a dressing that was
mostly a flavored vinegar with just a smidge of olive oil.
It came with a hot loaf of crusty bread that would have
been even better with butter instead of a "lite" margarine
that was mostly air and water.

Afterward, over an herbal tea that was supposed to encourage the body to shed fat—Betsy was beginning to see
how Margot stayed so trim—Margot said, "Would you
like to take a walk and get a look at our city?"

Betsy grinned. "City?"

"It's a legalism. The county passed a law years back
that made all the little towns out here incorporate as cities
or fold up. Wait till you drive through Navarre, which you
must do without blinking or you'll miss it, but it's a city,
too. Anyway, come on, I'll show you our famous Lake
Minnetonka."

They went back to the corner of Lake and Water, where
the lakeshore was marked by small wooden wharves. The
sun was bright, but already the sun was well on its south-
ward path, and their shadows pointed north as well as east.
Large square-built excursion boats were tied up here, along
with one odd little boat whose shape reminded Betsy of
an old-fashioned streetcar.

"The *Minnehaha*." Margot nodded. "Built in 1906,
sunk in the lake back in 1926, then raised and restored a
few years ago. Used to be owned by the public transit
company, which explains its shape. It runs on weekends
between here and Wayzata."

"Minnetonka, Minnehaha? Do I see a pattern?"

"Indeed you do. The poem 'Hiawatha' was set in Minnesota and was very popular when things were getting
named around here."

"Ah."

Beyond the wharves, the lakeshore was marked by a
park, where some of the younger maple trees showed

traces of orange. Apparently autumn arrived in September here. On their left, away from the lake, the ground swooped up, and was topped by grand old houses with big porches. How pleasant it must be to sit up there and watch the lake in all its moods.

The lake drew away, the park enlarged and grew a hill of its own, marked with big trees, and Lake Street ended at a tennis court. The sisters turned left and Betsy found she was now on *West* Lake Street. Well, okay; the lake itself also turned the corner, she could see it through the trees.

Here the houses were smaller, but still prosperous. None were new but all were in excellent repair, with neatly kept lawns. Some even had picket fences, and from one big tree hung a tire swing.

It was all so charmingly sweet, Betsy remarked, "What is this place, Mayberry-of-the-North?"

Margot laughed. "I'll have to repeat that next time I'm trying to get the city council to understand why it's important we fight to preserve the amenities of Excelsior."

They turned left at the next corner, and there was a quaint little church across the street, with a new, large, and modern church hall attached by a covered walk. "Trinity Episcopal," said Margot. "That's where I go."

"Uh-huh," said Betsy, and pointed to a window on a house on her side of the street where a large brown tabby sat watching them suspiciously. "That cat looks almost as big as Sophie." She didn't want to start a discussion of churchgoing, because she almost never went anymore.

Safely past the church, Margot continued with her tour. "If you look across the parking lot," she said, pointing, "you can see the library, the fire department, and our little city hall on the other side."

Betsy, squinting, nodded. "I see the sign that says CITY HALL," she said, "but it seems to be pointing to the same building that says FIRE DEPARTMENT."

"It is," said Margot. "City Hall is in the basement of

the fire department building. I voted against them moving into a building of their own," she added. "Keeps them modest."

They walked to the corner, and found themselves in the heart of the miniature "downtown" of Excelsior. To the left was the movie theater, pet shop, and bookstore, with a gift shop on the corner. Margot turned right and Betsy went with her, past the hardware store, a toy shop, an antique store, and so on. The stores were small, in good repair, apparently prosperous. Delicious smells came from the pizza-by-the-slice shop and the bakery. The wallpaper-and-paint store was having a sale. An art-supply store up the way and across the street had its side painted with a mural of a small cottage and a pond covered with water lilies. In the mural, an artist had set up a large canvas and was painting the water lilies. Betsy saw it and started to laugh. "Monet, I love it!" she said.

They turned and started back, past a dress shop and a florist. "I guess you're farther from the Twin Cities than I thought," remarked Betsy.

"What makes you say that?"

"Well, this isn't a bedroom community, is it? I mean, there are real stores here, open for business."

"Actually, we're very close to Minneapolis. Even back at the turn of the century, people would commute from here to the Cities, using that streetcar boat to get to where the regular streetcars ran. But somewhere, somehow, when a lot of little communities gave up trying to be towns, Excelsior didn't. And the people who live here have decided they wanted to keep the town intact. So they patronize the stores and organize lots of festivals, like Apple Days, which is coming up soon. Excelsior is an old-fashioned word that means 'upward,' and I like to think the name inspires the people who live here."

Betsy said with artful carelessness, "I thought excelsior was wood shavings used to pack fragile items."

Margot looked at Betsy with just the beginning of indignation, then both sisters laughed. Margot said, "All right, I'm a shameless booster. Just you wait, in a few weeks you'll love it here, too. Here's my bank, and up ahead is Haskell's, where we turn to go home."

Back in her cozy living room, Margot sat down in the comfortable chair, opened a kind of wood-framed folding canvas bag at her feet, and took out a large roll of white fabric with needlework on it. She unrolled it to reveal a complex, stylized picture of a field of flowers and small animals, most of which was covered with small stitches. "Last week of the month we work on UFOs," she said.

Betsy, standing behind the chair, said, "That is obviously not a flying saucer, so what does UFO mean in needle talk?"

"Unfinished projects. Like a lot of needleworkers, I'm always buying something new and I get impatient to get started on it and sometimes abandon old projects in the excitement of starting something new. So the last week of every month I've promised to get out something unfinished and work on it. I started this over a year ago and stopped working on it back in February—but now it's going to get finished at last." She smiled up at her sister. "I hope you don't mind if I work while we talk. Is there something you want to work on, too?"

Betsy shook her head. She'd once done quite a bit of embroidery, which had kept her occupied while her husband stayed late on campus. Not, as he'd said, grading papers or attending staff meetings or conferring with colleagues, but making love to various female students. Betsy had not touched an embroidery needle since filing for the divorce, and she had no intention of ever picking one up again.

She went over to the heavily draped window and began lifting layers—drape, sheer, blind—"How big is the lake?" Of course, all she could see was the gray siding of the condominium across the street.

"I think the shoreline is something over four hundred miles."

Betsy dropped the drape's edge and said, surprised, "You must mean forty miles, and I'm surprised it's that big."

"Oh, what you saw today was just one bay. The lake is a collection of bays—a collection of lakes, more like. Very untidy and sprawling. It's hard to describe the shape, but I can show you a map in the store tomorrow. The only way you can see the whole thing is from the air. It's spring-fed and very clean. Big bass-fishing attraction, we have competitions going all summer long. Draws people from all over the country." As she was drawn into her needlework, Margot became telegraphic in her sentences. "You fish?"

"No."

"Sail?"

"Not lately."

"What do you do for fun?"

"Go out with friends to dances and plays and movies. Body-surf. Read a good mystery or something by Terry Pratchett. Margot, how do you stand it?"

"Stand what?"

"It's so quiet and peaceful here. Doesn't it drive you crazy?"

Margot laughed. "I don't think it's so peaceful. In fact, when things get too much for me, I take a week off up in the Boundary Waters. There's peace and quiet for you. Of course, I used to travel all the time, with Aaron. Miami, Cancún, even London and Paris one glorious spring. I've always been glad to get back here, though."

"I don't understand how you can feel a need for some-place even quieter than this."

"After a week or so you'll see how busy I am and you'll understand. There's plenty to do, committees to work on, church business, and of course Crewel World. They tried to get me to run for city council once, but I managed to slip by them that time." She paused to put a new strand of floss into her needle. Betsy noticed she could do it that tricky way involving the edge of her needle.

"That's needlepoint, isn't it, what you're working on."

"Yes, do you like it? I haven't decided if it's going to be a pillow or a wall hanging."

"The colors don't look as if they'd go very well in here."

"It's not for up here, it's going to be a display item in the shop. I have four canvases by this artist and want to encourage my customers to buy them."

"How much does one cost?"

"Three hundred and fifty dollars."

"No, I mean unfinished. Like if I wanted to try one."

"Three hundred and fifty dollars. Plus the yarn, plus finishing." Margot glanced sideways at Betsy, a tiny smile on her face.

"That's ridiculous!"

"No, it isn't. Each canvas is hand-painted, and has to be done in a way so that the stitches that cover the painting will fit. It's a difficult art, trust me. Tomorrow I'll show you some of the really great work done by my customers on these canvases. Fancy stitches, beads, special flosses. Or maybe you'd prefer to take up counted cross-stitch."

"I'm not as fond of needlework as I used to be." A little silence fell. "I have a friend back in San Diego who does counted cross-stitch, but I don't think my eyes could take the strain," amended Betsy. Margot's needle went down and through then up and through. "It's beautiful stuff," further amended Betsy after a while. "She did this angel all in blues and golds that just blew me away." The silence fell again. "But she showed me the pattern and I knew right away that wasn't something I could ever do, not with my eyes." More silence. "I think I'm too tired to keep up my end of this conversation. I'm going to turn in."

But just as Betsy was entering the little hall, Margot said, "Betsy?"

"Yes?"

"I can't tell you how pleased I am that you called on me when you needed someone to take care of you for a while."

"Thanks, Margot. Good night."

"Good night."

3

It was Saturday, late in the afternoon; the sun was going down, its reddening beams streaming through the open door of the back bedroom. Betsy had spent Friday resting, talking with Margot or her employees down in the shop, unpacking, and going for a brief swim (the water wasn't salty, the waves were nonexistent, and the beach could be walked end to end in about a minute).

Now she was secretly enjoying a cream-filled sweet roll from that very nice little bakery on Water Street in the privacy of the apartment while Margot, unaware, sold floss and evenweave fabric downstairs. She wished you could still see the lake from the living-room window—it really was a pretty lake. But lakeshore property had surged in value, Shelly had told her; new houses were being built that had kitchens bigger than the cottages they replaced. So the little wetland across the street had been filled in and a condominium built on the site.

The price of a condo must be very high if it never occurred to Margot to buy one.

Betsy sat at the small round table in the dining nook drinking a glass of orange juice with her sweet roll, and thinking.

She'd been here three days, if you counted her day of arrival as one, rather than the less-than-half it was. She wasn't sure what she had expected, but Excelsior wasn't a disappointment, yet. If this were still the fifties, Excelsior would be positively typical of a Midwestern country town, down to the lack of used-car lots and warehouse shopping outlets siphoning shoppers from the little downtown. They must have draconian zoning laws around here, she thought.

The people in Excelsior she had met so far were friendly, and the worst teenager she had seen had not been scary, only very oddly dressed. Thoroughly pierced, of course, with hair colored Kool-Aid red. But even he had offered a halfhearted wave.

Crewel World was a going concern, so far as Betsy could tell. Who would have guessed one could make a living selling embroidery floss, hand-spun wool, and bamboo knitting needles? But there had been a steady trickle of customers yesterday while Betsy watched. Two of them had spent lavishly, buying "canvases," stiff white fabric woven so loosely the holes showed, with paintings of dolls, Christmas stockings, cute animals, woodland scenes, or whatever on them. That the customers then also bought yarn and flosses so they could carefully cover every inch of the paintings with wool or cotton or silk only made Betsy sure that they were crazy, especially since the artists who painted the pictures charged so much for their work.

Of course, there was a trick to the store as well, Betsy had learned. Margot had somehow wrangled a lease at an extraordinary rent, even at upper Midwest prices. With the rent so low, it was easier to show a profit. Certainly the furniture in the apartment was of a quality to indicate the opposite of poverty.

There was, of course, a fly in the ointment, and it was, not surprisingly, the landlord. Shelly, who turned out to be friendly and kind, also loved to gossip. She had told Betsy all about him. He was the brother of the original landlord, who had died a year ago, she reported. This brother was by no means the saint the original had been. The new landlord wanted to take advantage of the soaring land values. He proposed tearing down the old brick building and putting up something bigger.

But Margot, bless her kind but stubborn heart, wanted to stay where she was, where people anxious to buy just the right shade of green silk to complete their counted cross-stitch pattern knew where to find her. And Margot had four years to go on that extraordinary lease.

Shelly had described with awe the one visit she had had from the new landlord, whose name was a very prosaic Joe. He had come into the shop last Monday, she had said, with fire in his eyes, looking for Margot. Fortunately, Margot had been at the post office and he'd gone away again breathing threats and tucking some kind of paper back into his pocket.

Earlier today, over an incredibly delicious fruit salad bought at the sandwich shop next door, Margot had chuckled at Betsy's alarmed query as to what Joe Mickels was up to.

"Oh, it was probably just another summons."

"Another *what*?"

"Summons. It's a tactic he's come up with. Unlawful detainer of rent, possibly, or some other clause of the lease he's trying to invoke against me. He figures a new one up every few weeks, he's been doing it for the last four or five months. But I have James Penberthy on my side, he's been wonderful." Margot had smiled at Betsy's inquiring face and explained, "He's my attorney. He just laughs and says he'll handle it. And he does. But it's annoying, especially when I have to make a court appearance. I'm so glad Aaron taught me to keep very careful records. The last time, Joe tried to say I hadn't paid my deposit when I first moved in here; but the canceled check was in my files, so I presented it in court and that took care of that. There's no way Joe can run me off with those tricks, so long as Mr. Penberthy represents my interests."

So not everyone who lived in Excelsior was friendly. And Betsy wasn't as sanguine as Margot about legal maneuvers. What if Joe Mickels succeeded in driving Margot out? Where would Margot move her shop? There didn't seem to be many empty stores in Excelsior—Betsy hadn't seen a single one on Water Street, in fact. If Margot had to move to another town, and pay a higher rent, she'd lose customers. Could she then afford to keep Betsy as a guest? When Betsy had tried to talk to Margot about this again, Margot had laughed and waved her hand.

"Oh, for heaven's sake, Betsy, don't worry, we're fine. Anyway, I've already told you: Joe can't possibly do anything, not really."

Sipping her juice, Betsy's frown deepened. Okay, with the low rent and the fact that her customers were faithful, Margot was doing all right here. But if Joe Mickels did succeed in making her move out, then she'd have to start all over again at an unfamiliar address and a much higher rent. If that happened, could she still afford to pay Betsy a salary and at the same time house and feed her?

Maybe Betsy should start right in looking for work somewhere else. Tomorrow was Sunday, she'd take a good look at the employment section of the *Minneapolis Star Tribune*, called by Margot (in that casual way that meant everyone else did, too) "the *Strib*."

There was a sound of a key in a lock. "Hello!" called a chipper voice.

"In here, Margot," called Betsy. "Is it time to close already?"

"Ten minutes past," came the voice, traveling rapidly through the short hall that passed the kitchen and into the living room. "But I had a good customer and I couldn't deny her the chance to spend an extra hundred, could I?"

Betsy got a brief glimpse of her sister as she hurried into the other short hall off which were the bathroom and the bedrooms. From the back one the voice continued, "Are you dressed for the meeting?"

Betsy looked down at herself. She was wearing an ivory knit dress with short, caped sleeves and a moderately low square-cut neck. Her shoes were a trifle clunky, with gold buckles. "Yes," she said.

Something big and furry moved in to block Betsy's view of her shoes: Sophie. When the cat saw she had attracted Betsy's attention, she walked into the kitchen to sit significantly beside her empty food dish.

"I'll feed Sophie," Betsy called, having learned almost as quickly as the cat that if she didn't tell Margot, Sophie would cadge an additional feeding. She took a half scoop of dry food from the big sack under the sink and poured it into Sophie's dish. Iams Less Active certainly described Sophie. *In*active might be even better, but Iams apparently didn't make that variety.

Betsy had gone through boot camp to learn to shower, brush, make up, and dress in an amazingly short time, but somewhere Margot had learned it, too. In just under forty minutes she came into the living room with her hair rearranged, her makeup redone, and wearing a dark sheath dress topped with a short-sleeved sweater that caught the light strangely. Betsy approached her for a closer look.

"Oooooh," she said, fingering the weaving. "Oh, it's that ribbon sweater you were making! It's beautiful!"

"Thank you. Is it too long?"

Betsy stepped back and tilted her head while Margot did a slow pirouette. "N-no," she said. "Actually, it seems just about right. Golly, I like the way it moves. Is there a trick to the way it's knitted?"

"No—Betsy, are you going like that?"

Betsy looked down at herself. "What, am I daringly short for Excelsior?"

"Heavens no; but it cools off quite a bit around here when the sun goes down. You'll want something over that."

Margot went into her closet and brought out a cream-colored shawl with extravagantly long fringe that had been tied into a complex pattern of knots for its first ten inches.

"McNamara lace!" Betsy exclaimed on seeing it, and explained, "In the navy, sailors unlay canvas and tie the fringe into patterns. It's used as trim, on the captain's gig for example."

"Well, the fringe is too long for me, so why don't you keep it?"

Betsy stroked the silky fringe, then looked at her sister, eyes stinging. "Oh, Margot, it's beautiful. Thank you."

"Well, it matches your dress, so you're welcome. Now drape it over your shoulders and let's go. Can you walk in those shoes? We're only a few blocks from the house, it's ridiculous to drive that short a distance."

The house was Christopher Inn, the Victorian bed-and-breakfast Betsy had seen on coming into Excelsior. On the way over, Margot said that the purpose of the gathering was to form a committee to plan a fund-raiser for a child who needed heart surgery. The family had no health insurance and the father was working three jobs to try to raise the money.

It was typical of Excelsior to rise to such an occasion, Margot had told Betsy proudly, noting that there were round plastic coin collectors at nearly every cash register in town supporting some cause or other. But this would be the most important fund-raiser of the year.

They climbed the steps to the house and crossed the big old porch and went inside—the door wasn't locked.

There were eight people attending the meeting, which was to begin with a light supper served by George Anderson, the proprietor of the Christopher Inn. He was a dark, quiet man with a tennis player's build.

Betsy was pleased to note that the house hadn't suffered much remodeling. The front parlor was intact, with two bay windows, and the dining room was large, with a fireplace. Only two of its eight round tables were set for this meal, marked with bouquets of roses and baby's breath—

leftovers from a wedding, noted Margot as they greeted Shelly.

Assigned to Betsy and Margot's table were a handsome man with sun-streaked auburn hair and a big young woman with ash-blond hair that looked natural. Betsy had already noticed more natural blonds in Excelsior than anywhere else she had lived.

The man was Hudson Earlie, the assistant curator of Asian art at the Minneapolis Museum of Art; the woman was Jill Cross, a police officer.

"But she comes of a very good family," added Margot while making the introduction.

"I'm sure being a cop is no disgrace," remarked Betsy, a trifle surprised at her sister, taking Jill's proffered hand, which was large and strong. There was an air of calm about Jill that inspired confidence, even while she gave you a look that seemed to read every peccadillo you had ever done. She was wearing a simple frost-blue dress that matched her eyes.

Jill said with patently feigned indifference, "It's okay, even my mother apologizes for me."

"What would she have preferred you to do for a living?" asked Earlie as Betsy and Margot seated themselves.

"Nurse," replied Jill thoughtfully. "Journalist. Business administrator. Stock-car driver. Checkout clerk at a 7-Eleven. Street sweeper. Street*walker*." Though her expression remained impassive, Margot had become helpless with giggles and was waving at her to stop.

Betsy smiled at Hudson Earlie. He was extraordinarily handsome, with an outdoorsman's permanently sunburned skin. "And how about you, Mr. Earlie? What would your mother have preferred you do?"

"Doctor," he said in a good imitation of Jill's smooth, expressionless voice. "Lawyer. Street sweeper. Used-car salesman." He leaned forward and concluded in an undertone aimed at both Betsy and Jill, "Cop." His eyes were a hot blue, his nose short but straight. His mouth, not large, hinted at arrogance, even stubbornness. Then he smiled, a wicked, lusty smile, with laugh lines cut deep. "Call me Hud."

"Sure—Hud," Betsy said, smiling back. As an excuse to tear her eyes away, she arranged her napkin over her lap. "When do we eat?" she asked.

"In a minute," said Margot dryly, and when Betsy looked at her and at Jill, she saw them grinning.

Fine, thought Betsy. "I think you would have made a wonderful policeman," she said to Hud, batting her eyelashes a trifle. "I bet every woman crook in the city would line up to be interrogated by you."

Hud's smile broadened, and he closed one eye in a not-so-surreptitious wink. "You have a right to remain silent," he said in his own voice, a pleasant baritone, "but I hope you continue."

Betsy made a mental note to find out if he was married.

For supper, Anderson served big, locally grown tomatoes stuffed with crab-and-celery salad, and sesame toast. Dessert was devil's-food cake with coconut-caramel icing, cut into generous slabs. Betsy, with the sweet roll still undigested, earned a smile from Margot by taking only two bites. The coffee that came with it was very strong and delicious. Betsy followed Margot's lead and turned down a refill.

But without it, she began to sink into that happy languor that generally follows a generous meal. A thin man with dark hair and eyes rose at the adjoining table and rapped gently on his water glass with his dessert fork. "Let's get started here," he said with a strong Midwest twang. He rapped again, and when he had their attention, he said, "I think first we need a chairman of this committee."

"Who's he?" Betsy murmured in Margot's ear.

"Odell Jamison. He's our mayor." She raised her voice. "How about you, Odell?"

"No, I haven't got time to do a good job," said Odell. "I'm already working with the historical society for their

Christmas pageant, playing at being mayor, and remodeling my house—if I don't stay on those painters, they'll never get it finished.''

Betsy smiled. Mayor Jamison had listed his profession both second and offhandedly; such a low-key politician couldn't get elected mayor anywhere but in a small town.

"How about you, Paul?" said Shelly, who was sitting next to the mayor.

A young man with a broad, black, closely clipped mustache lifted both hands in protest. "I've got enough on my plate right now," he said.

"How about you, Margot?" suggested Jill.

"No, no, I'm on three committees already, plus the shop. And now my sister is in town, so I'll be busy with her—everyone, this is my sister, Betsy Devonshire, here on an extended visit." She smiled at the mayor's table. "I'd like you to consider her an honorary member of this committee, as she'll be a big help to me on it."

There were polite words of greeting from the other table, and an all-around murmur of agreement that Betsy could be a sort-of member; when it ended, Mayor Jamison said, "How 'bout you, Joe?"

There was a sudden silence during which every head turned, oddly, toward Margot, who became interested in stirring her coffee.

A white-haired man seated across from Jamison said, "No time for that, thanks," in a gruff voice.

The tension eased and Paul said, "Then how about you, Jill?"

"Not till I retire." That brought chuckles; Jill was probably not yet thirty.

Betsy studied Joe curiously. His hair was thick and wavy, and looked as if it might once have been blond— his immense eyebrows were the color of sand, as were his old-fashioned bushy sideburns. He looked immensely strong, with a proud nose, wide mouth, and fierce eyes set well back under those eyebrows. Viking blood there, thought Betsy.

She glanced at Margot, who nodded once. So this was the evil landlord, Joe Mickels.

"How about you, Shelly?" This came from George Anderson, the inn's owner, and Betsy was suddenly aware that he was seated between the two tables in a way that made him one of the group. And on the committee, apparently.

"How about you?" she countered.

"Well . . ." he said, and everyone jumped happily on this sign of weakness.

"Oh, all right," he said, and there was applause mixed with laughter.

George proved as deft at running a meeting as he was at serving tables, and soon the committee had agreed to hold the event at the Lafayette Country Club in a month's time, offering a dance, buffet, cash bar, and silent auction.

"These silent auctions can be a big success," said George, "but you've got to deliver the goods." He pointed a finger at every member and asked him or her to pledge something of significant value to the auction and to badger friends and acquaintances to do the same. Margot offered a slash jacket. Shelly groaned with approbation, or acquisitiveness, as Betsy wondered what a "slash jacket" was. Hud offered a Dick Huss glass bowl, and this time the acquisitive sigh came from Margot. Jill offered sailing lessons next summer. The finger wavered, and Betsy, ashamed of being passed over, said she would contribute something, but would need time to think what it might be.

Joe Mickels offered a luxury weekend at a ski lodge; Shelly ten hours of private tutoring; George a getaway weekend at Christopher Inn, "including an afternoon of bass fishing."

When other ideas were solicited, Hud said in his pleasant voice that he had a friend who used to play with Lamont Cranston, and that he would send a request via the friend that they play for this fund-raiser. "I'm sure they'll at least come up with a good excuse for not doing it," he said, with an air of confidence that promised better than that. Betsy wondered who Lamont Cranston was—it was a band, of course, not the man who was the Shadow—but what kind of music did they play? She also wondered what she should do if Joe Mickels said anything to her. He looked easy to offend, but should she let him know that of course she supported her sister in their quarrel?

Betsy was impressed at how Margot gave ideas and recommendations to the committee. She would ask a question or go halfway with an idea so that someone else would answer or complete her thought and so at least share credit for it. At first, Betsy thought nothing of it, but the third time it happened, she realized it was a deliberate and clever ploy.

Later, reluctant to break up, or perhaps just so caffeinated that going home to bed was not an option, the committee stood in couples or trios on the porch, talking and looking at the houses peeping through the trees that lined the lake, or at the restaurant down on the lakeshore. The Ferris wheel in the parking lot, trimmed in moving red lights, spun gently.

For all the summertime appearance of the scene, Betsy was glad for the shawl. The breeze was definitely chilly.

"I don't understand the Ferris wheel," she said.

Margot replied, "There used to be a big amusement park down there, years ago. It sort of commemorates it."

Hud said, "I hear they found a buyer for the restaurant and the new owners are going to sell the Ferris wheel."

Margot smiled at Betsy. "So things do change, even here in Excelsior."

After a little silence, Betsy asked, "How did Joe Mickels get on this committee?"

Margot only shrugged, so Hud replied, "He's turning into a big-time developer; he's got pieces of land working for him all over the state. That ski lodge is his, for example. We can use his money, and his influence.''

''If he's what Margot says he is, I'm surprised he's interested in raising money for causes like this.''

''Oh, he's a proactive vulture, all right,'' said Hud, displaying that wicked grin. ''But this is a relatively small community, and you have to play along to get ahead. People who don't take part in things like this may find doors closed to them when they want to do business. But I'm surprised he got asked to be part of this fund-raising effort. How about it, Margot; will you be able to work with him?''

Again Margot shrugged. ''At this distance, yes. But you could mention to George that he shouldn't assign us to the same subcommittee.''

''You're nicer than I'd be about him,'' said Hud. ''But who knows? Maybe this will soften him up. And even if it doesn't, we might find his hardheadedness useful. He's got a good business sense, even if he keeps his heart in cold storage.''

Shivering under her shawl, Betsy smiled. ''I should think in Minnesota, you don't need cold storage; just put things out on your back porch.''

Hud laughed. ''Wait till next July, you'll change your tune.'' He turned to Margot. ''That's when we had summer this year, right, Margot? July seventh and eighth, as I recall.''

Margot chuckled. ''I think you're right; that was the weekend you took your Rolls off its blocks, right? Hud, I'm coming to the art museum on Wednesday to take a new look at the T'ang horse. It's for another needlepoint project. So long as I'm in the city, I'd like to stop by your office and talk about some board business. How's your schedule?''

''Pretty tight, but I can make a hole Wednesday morning, I think. About eleven, say?''

"Thanks. It won't take long."

Mayor Jamison came over then to ask Margot what she had done with the Founders' Day parade sashes, and from there the talk wandered to other things.

4

Shelly Donohue sat at the white plastic table on a white plastic chair outside the Excelo Bakery shop on Water Street. She was eating a "wicked" sandwich—so designated on a hand-lettered placard—consisting of sprouts, tomato, avocado, two kinds of cheese, and green-goddess dressing on herb-flavored foccacio bread baked on the premises. Her own designation of it was "messy but interesting," as in, "Will you make me one of those messy but interesting veggie sandwiches?" Shelly would not describe anything as wicked except murder and child abuse.

She also had a cup of cranberry juice, not further designated.

She was feeling frazzled, and looking a trifle frazzled as well; her hair was coming out of its bun and tendrils of it were lifted up here and there by a cool, vagrant breeze. An all-day preschool session was under way, and there were new laws and regulations to master, new textbooks (one with several egregious errors of fact) to study, and a new principal full of new ideas. And retirement was twenty years away.

But the morning's harsh edge was being smoothed away

by a bit of friendly gossip. She was sharing her table with Irene Potter, a fellow needleworker, who was not drinking her coffee and was pulling fragments off a poppy-seed muffin with her lean, nimble fingers in lieu of eating it.

Irene's shining dark eyes encouraged Shelly to go on with what she was saying.

"You know, you'd hardly think they were sisters at all," Shelly continued. "Margot's such a dainty little thing, so sweet and . . . and . . . oh, I know the word's not considered nice anymore, but she's a _lady_. A real lady. Betsy's nice, too, don't get me wrong. But it's not just that they don't look very much alike; I mean, that sort of thing happens in any family that doesn't marry one another's cousins. But Betsy's . . ." She paused to think of the right words. "She's . . . more so," she said with an air of having at last put her finger on it. "You should have seen her putting the moves on Hudson Earlie Saturday night. And Hud was moving right back—you know Hud—but Margot couldn't say anything right there in front of him."

"Yes, we all know Hud," said Irene, waggling her eyebrows.

"But did you know Margot hired Betsy to work in the store?"

"She did?" Irene had worked a few hours in Crewel World, and wanted to work more.

"And Betsy doesn't know anything about running a store, or all that much about needlework, for that matter. She asked the dumbest questions."

"No!" said Irene.

"Yes. But she's trying really hard to pick up on things. And she's fun to have around, she really seems to like talking with the customers. She sold a whole lot of yarn to this woman by asking her questions about knitting. It was so funny to watch."

By her face, Irene didn't get the joke. "I hear she used to live in _San Francisco_." Her expressive voice turned the name into a synonym for depravity.

Shelly shrugged eloquently. "Yes, she mentioned that. *And* London, *and* New York. As if none of us ever go anywhere. She's been married a few times, too. But no children." Her face was disapproving of both those facts, though she herself was divorced—once—and had no children.

Irene said, "Of course, Margot never had children, either. Though I always *understood* it was Aaron's fault." They shared a slightly different expression this time, then smiled to show it was all just in fun. Each considered herself very close to Margot.

Shelly glanced at her watch then quickly stood and began gathering the remnants of her meal. "Lunch break's about over. I have to get back."

"Yes, you only get forty-five minutes, don't you?" said Irene, also rising. Her job as a supervisor in the shipping department of a local manufacturer wasn't as prestigious as Shelly's, but they gave her an hour for lunch. "So," she went on, walking Shelly to the trash barrel, her voice hopeful, "if Betsy doesn't know much, it seems Margot will still be in the market for a part-timer to help out in the shop?" Irene Potter's ultimate goal in life was to own a needlework shop, and meanwhile to gain full-time employment in Margot's. When she'd heard Margot's sister was coming to stay, she had trembled for the few hours of work Margot would give her.

Shelly, secure in her summer hours in Crewel World, smiled. "Probably not, but why don't you go talk to her? Meet Betsy, too. Maybe you two would get along. Got to run. Bye-bye."

Irene stood on the sidewalk in the bright sunshine, staring after her. Irene had a tendency to see everyone as a rival or potential rival, so Shelly's parting remarks gave her an idea that was positively *brilliant*. Know thine enemy, that was biblical, wasn't it? Or was it Shakespearean? Never mind, if she went over there and made friends, then she might see how to sabotage this Betsy person. Who, after all, knew next to nothing about clerking in a needle-work store, while Irene knew everything; that alone might nullify the blood connection.

She hurried to scoop up the remains of her muffin and the paper coffee cup and toss them into the trash container. She dusted crumbs off herself with her napkin, then inspected herself in the window of the bakery. Dark slacks, white blouse, gray vest hand-crocheted herself with cotton thread in a pineapple pattern, and her favorite earrings, shaped like tiny scissors. She patted her dark curly hair, cropped close to her narrow head. She looked neat and competent. She smiled at the reflection, admiring the whiteness of her teeth. Perfect!

She rose onto her toes before stepping off in the direction of Crewel World, a mannerism she had seen in a musical once and copied whenever she was feeling ebullient. She had twenty minutes left of her lunch hour, time enough to get there and start *making friends* with her new rival. What fun!

Betsy sat behind the big old desk that Margot used as a checkout counter. She was biting on her lower lip. In her hands were two metal knitting needles and a ball of cheap purple yarn. Open on the desk was a thin booklet that promised to teach her how to knit in one day.

The reason her lower lip was being held in place was that doing so prevented her from sticking her tongue out.

Betsy considered herself very well coordinated. She could ride, she could shoot, she could thread a needle on the first try. Back when her hair was long, she'd taught herself to French-braid it down the back of her head without looking. But knitting was different.

"Casting on" she could do. She'd cast on twenty-five stitches, as instructed, and on the second try done it loosely enough so that knitting was something she now could also do, after a fashion. She'd proved that by doing about an inch of knitting.

But purling was not possible. The needle went through the knitted stitch, apparently as illustrated, and allowed itself to have a bit of yarn wrapped over it, but it wouldn't capture and bring through the purl stitch. Not without the aid of a third hand, which she didn't have.

Not that she could see why anyone wanted to purl anyhow. It looked like the same thing as knitting, according to the illustration, except up and down instead of across. Which is why it was impossible. One knitted from one side to the other, not upward.

Could it be some kind of secret knitters' thing? They let outsiders try and try to purl while they, the cognoscenti, the in-crowd, the clique, rolled on the floor snorting and giggling? And after a week or two allowed as how there was no such thing as purling? Sure, it was just a hazing thing they did to people who wanted to join the knitting fraternity—er, sorority. Though Betsy knew there were men who knitted. Sorternity?

Wait a second. If she tucked the end of the empty needle under her arm . . . Rats, for a second there she'd thought she'd got it.

She gave up and went back to knitting another row, slowly easing the needle through, wrapping the yarn, lift-twist-tipping it back, slipping the old stitch off.

She remembered how her mother would sit and watch television or her children play in the park, while her hands, as if with an intelligence of their own, moved in a swift, compact pattern and produced sweaters and scarves and mittens by the yard.

And she'd watched Margot do the same on Sunday evening up in the apartment.

While here she struggled slowly, stitch by stitch. Still, she was actually knitting. If she kept this up, in a year she'd have a potholder.

Margot hadn't watched television while she knitted, but talked with Betsy. Of course, there had been the odd pause while Margot counted stitches—knitters were forever losing track, it seemed—but on the whole, Margot had been able to keep up her end of the conversation.

It had been very comfortable up in that apartment, the puddles of yellow light making everything warm and intimate. They'd done some catching up—though now that she thought about it, Betsy had been allowed to do most of the talking, about Professor Hal (the pig), and the cost of living in beautiful San Diego (the sunlight in April on the white buildings and the endless sussurant crashing of the ocean, the dry, harsh, beautiful desert), and the big El Niño of '97 spoiling things.

Margot had said El Niño had even reached as far as Minnesota that year, giving them a very mild winter. Betsy, recalling the news footage of snow up to the eaves of Minnesota houses, decided that mild temperatures were a relative thing. Was she up to a Minnesota winter, she who could not knit well enough to produce a pair of mittens? Maybe she should cut this visit short and be on her way before the hard freeze set in.

She had asked, "Is living in a small town like it is in books, everyone knowing everyone else's business?"

"It is harder to be anonymous, because there is only the one main street where everyone shops, so even if you don't know someone's name, you recognize the face. It's like when you take the bus to and from work; you don't know the people who ride with you, not really, but you recognize their faces. And if someone's been absent for a few days and then gets on with his leg in a cast, you might express concern, even ask him what happened, as if he were a friend."

Betsy had nodded. Okay, living in a small town was like sharing a commute. She could do that.

"And if you get really sick of small-town living there's Minneapolis and St. Paul down the road—and hey, there's the Mall of America, right? Is it as big as they say? How often do you go there?"

"About as often as you visited the Statue of Liberty when you lived in New York City."

"But that was different! You go, you climb, you look out, you go home. At the Mall of America you can . . . *shop*."

"That's true. I went when it first opened, and I've been back, I think, twice. No, three times, twice to take visitors and once because they have a specialty shoe shop. You wouldn't believe it, but I'm hard to fit." Margot had stuck out a small foot complacently. She counted stitches for a bit, then continued, "But you know, there's so much *stuff* there, a great deal of it things you don't really need, like dried flower arrangements and personalized scents for your bath. To be so rich that you can shop as a form of recreation is . . . sinful. Yet people come from all over the world to entertain themselves by buying things they don't really need." She moved her shoulders. "It makes me ashamed somehow." She stopped to count stitches again, and then twinkled over at Betsy. "I know, you want to go glut yourself in all that shopping anyhow, be sinful for a day. Okay, maybe a week from Wednesday?"

And while they had continued talking, about movies and books, Margot's hands performed the same compact dance as Mother's had, and before they stopped to get ready for bed, the sweater she was knitting had become longer and developed a braid pattern.

So if Margot and Mother could do it while talking, by gum Betsy could do it while concentrating. She bit down harder on her captured lip and sped up to three stitches a minute.

She was concentrating so hard that when the door made its electronic sound, she jumped and, dammit, the needle slipped and pulled out of about seven stitches. Before she could figure out what to do, a bony, ice-cold hand covered hers.

She glanced up and saw a stick-thin woman with short dark hair that stuck up in odd-looking curls all over her little head. Like Betty Boop, thought Betsy. Except the face wasn't Boop's merry square, it was long and narrow, with deep lines from nostril to mouth. The eyes were dark and intent. The woman suddenly showed bright, patently false teeth, and Betsy wanted to back away, but was held by the icy grip.

"M-may I help you?" she asked.

"No, my dear, may I help *you*?" said the woman in a chirpy voice that rang as false as the teeth.

"Help me what?" asked Betsy.

"With what you are doing," said the woman, the smile slipping a trifle, looking pointedly at the knitting and back at Betsy.

"Oh, this. Why, do you know how to knit?"

The woman laughed a genuine laugh. "Of course I do! I know how to do every kind of needlework there is, except sewing canvas into sails. What seems to be the problem with your knitting?"

With a small effort, Betsy managed to free her hands. "It's not the knitting, exactly. It's the purling. I just don't get how to do it. And anyhow, now I've spoiled what I was doing, pulling the needle out."

"Oh, that's easy to fix." The woman took the knitting from Betsy's hands and deftly rethreaded the stitches onto the needle. "See? Now, to purl, you hold the needles like this," she said, putting them together in what Betsy was sure was the same way she herself had held them while trying to purl. "See, you go through like this, come around like this and off, and through and around and off, and-through-around-and-off." If she'd continued as slowly as she'd begun, Betsy might have learned something. But she repeated "through and around and off" faster and faster while her hands worked more and more vigorously, until she'd done the row. Then she handed the needles back to Betsy. "Now you try it," she said briskly.

Betsy took the needles, turned the work around to begin the next row and tried to remember where to poke the empty needle through the first stitch. It went in front, she remembered that, but was it through the same direction as the filled needle was pointing, or the other way?

"Here, dear, let me show you again," said the woman impatiently, starting to grab at the needles. Betsy lifted her hands, trying to keep possession.

Bing went the electronic note as the door to the shop opened.

The woman turned toward the door, and Betsy pushed back from the desk, rising.

It was Jill Cross, the police officer, this time in uniform, looking even taller and broader, probably because of that odd hat police officers wear and the thick belt around her hips, laden with gun and flashlight and handcuffs. She looked very authoritarian, and Betsy, who had been growing uneasy about the mad knitter, was glad to see her. But the other woman was already out into the aisle, one hand lifted in greeting.

"Good afternoon, Officer Jill!" she gushed, touching Jill familiarly on the upper arm. "What are we buying today?"

"Good afternoon, Irene." Jill nodded, swinging her elbow forward to free it. "Hi, Betsy," she added. "Did that ultrasuede I ordered come in?" Jill took off her hat, exposing her ash-blond hair, pulled back into a firm knot.

"Let me just check," Irene said, fawning.

"Wait a second, Irene," said Jill. "Margot's trying to bring Betsy up to speed on running the shop, so let's let her find the order for me."

Irene obediently halted and turned toward Betsy, a malicious gleam in her eyes.

Betsy began trying to think where Margot kept incoming orders.

"Shall I show you?" asked Irene.

"No, I remember now," said Betsy, and looked in a cardboard box on the floor under the desk. When she came up with the small package, Irene Potter's superior smile turned into something scary. It may have been a desperate attempt at a broad smile, but there was menace in it. Then she whirled and fled from the shop.

"Is . . . is she all right?" asked Betsy.

"Irene? Sure. Well, maybe she's a hair off center. She's so desperate to buy her own needlework shop that it colors everything she does. It's possible she's been hoping Margot would die of something so she could start her own needlework shop. The town isn't big enough for two of them."

"So why doesn't she move?"

"Because her ancestors were among the first settlers out here, and she would never think of moving away. But now you're here, and it would be too much to hope that both of you die." Jill grinned.

"Both . . ." Betsy hardly knew where to begin her response to that. "She thinks *I'm* going to take over the shop?"

"She probably suspects you and Margot are going to run it together. At the very least, you have put her out of her part-time work here. She just doesn't realize she hasn't a prayer of succeeding on her own, even if this place closes. I mean, would you go into a store a second time to buy something from her?"

Betsy grimaced. "She isn't dangerous, is she?"

Jill said sharply, "Now don't go getting weird ideas! The only thing she's crazy about is needlework. She's actually tremendously talented at it. Most of it is museum quality. She routinely takes first prize in any contest she enters. Her problem is, she was never properly socialized. A few years ago Irene begged and nagged until Margot hired her to teach a class, but Irene has no patience with people not as talented as she is, and every one of her students quit by the fourth lesson."

Betsy nodded. "Yes, she was trying to show me how to purl when you came in, but wouldn't slow down enough for me to catch on. Now let's see if I remember how to open the cash register.''

A few minutes later Betsy was handing over the correct change. "Where's Margot?" Jill asked, pocketing her money. "I've got a question for her."

"Upstairs having a bowl of soup. She'll be back any second. Do you want to wait?"

"I can't, I'm on patrol. Tell her I've got a pair of tickets to the Guthrie, and my boyfriend went and switched shifts with someone, so now he can't go. Ask her if she wants to come with me."

A new voice asked, "What's the show?"

They turned; it was Margot, coming in from the back. *"The Taming of the Shrew."*

"Oooooh," sighed Margot. "When are the tickets for?"

"Tomorrow. I know Wednesdays are your day off, so I was hoping you could make it."

"The Guthrie!" said Betsy, remembering. "I've heard about the Guthrie. It's been written up in national magazines, hasn't it? It's supposed to be a great place to see good plays. I'd forgotten it was way up here in Minneapolis—or is it in St. Paul?"

"Minneapolis," said Jill, and for some reason there was disapproval again in her voice.

Margot explained, "Minneapolis and St. Paul don't like being mistaken for one another. Jill, I'm sorry, I can't go. I promised to make a presentation at our city-council meeting about next year's art fair tomorrow evening. Debbie Hart's going to be out of town and I promised her I'd do it. I'm really sorry."

"Yeah, well, maybe another time. Though I hate to see this ticket go to waste."

"Why don't you take Betsy?"

"Me?" They looked at her and Betsy tried to explain the tone of voice that had come out in. "I mean, I like Shakespeare very much, but if this is a grand production, you don't want to waste that invitation on someone you hardly know. Surely another friend . . ."

But some signal must have run between Margot and Jill because the latter said, "Betsy, you'll have to take a look at what passes for the big city in this part of the world sooner or later. Might as well be tomorrow. So let's make a night of it; we can have dinner at Buca's, and you can tell me how awful Italian food is in the upper Midwest. Then we'll go see how badly our legitimate theater compares to the stuff on the Great White Way."

Betsy took a breath to say no, but Margot had that look that meant she was hoping Betsy would not be rude, so Betsy turned to Jill and said only a little stiffly, "Well, I've only seen one Broadway production, so I hardly think I'm qualified to compare the Guthrie to the Great White Way. But on the other hand, I lived just two blocks away from the best Italian restaurant in Brooklyn, so I'll be glad to come sneer at what the upper Midwest dares to call Italian food."

Margot laughed, but Betsy wasn't sure Jill was amused. After she left, Betsy asked, "Margot, do you really have to go to a city-council meeting?"

"Yes, why?"

"I'm grateful for the ticket, but I'm not sure Jill and I will get along."

"Oh, nonsense. I'm sure once you get to know her, you'll like her very much."

"Well, there's no need to go out of your way just to be nice to me, when I'm guessing you'd really like to go."

"You're right, I would like to go, but I really do have to attend that meeting. The art show is one of our biggest annual events, thousands of people come here for it, and advance planning is very important. Anyway, I enjoy being nice to you."

"Then I thank you very much."

Margot went behind her desk to check Betsy's entry of

the sale to Jill. Betsy followed, asking, "Margot, what are your plans for me?"

"What do you mean?"

"I hope you aren't planning on my being here forever."

"I haven't, but all right, I won't. Why?"

"Irene Potter was in here a little while ago. Don't you find her a little scary? She has the falsest smile I've ever seen. Then Jill came in, and when Irene tried to wait on her, Jill said to let me do it, and when I did it right Irene gave me a look that nearly froze my earlobes off."

"Oh, Irene just has this problem about being nice. She tries, but she doesn't know how."

"No, listen. Jill says that Irene knows you are going to teach me how to run the shop. It seems Irene has her eye on this place, and she's scared you've cut her out entirely by giving me her job."

Margot grimaced. "Hardly. I only hire Irene when all my other part-time help has flu, broken legs, and brain concussions."

Betsy insisted, "Margot, I think Irene Potter seriously hates me."

"How can she hate you? She doesn't know anything about you."

"She thinks I'm taking something that should be hers. And if she hates me for taking her job, I bet she hates you for giving it to me."

But Margot wasn't listening; she was examining Betsy's knitting. "This is very good, Betsy. The knitting is a trifle tight, but this row of purling is really well done!"

5

Margot woke early the next morning. Her usual first thought presented itself: What day is it?

Ah, Wednesday, her day off. What was on the agenda? Well, there was that art-fair presentation this evening, at seven sharp. Her notes were still on the computer. She'd read them over one more time, then print them out.

Betsy's here, came a sudden memory, almost an interruption. That was something new in her normally predictable life. But not a disruption, came the reassurance, Betsy was all right, Betsy was fitting in fine, Betsy was enjoyable company.

But it did make a difference to have someone else living in the apartment, if only because she had to remember to wear a robe and to check the refrigerator rather than think that just because she had not used the last of the milk that there would be some for the morning coffee.

The question was, was Betsy enjoying herself? Margot hoped so. Because despite what she had said yesterday, this was someone who was not just a weekend guest but a long-term arrangement. All Margot's immediate plans had to be changed, and some of her long-term ones, now that there was another person who had to be considered. It was almost like being married again.

So while it was okay, even enjoyable, to have Betsy here, it was also different.

She must decide when she would formally talk to Betsy about her future. Betsy made a nice salesperson, she was interested and friendly; she would make an excellent one once she got up to speed on the terminology and practices of needlework. Yesterday she had sold a beginning inquirer an impressive amount of silks and evenweave fabric and counted cross-stitch patterns, though she knew almost nothing about counted cross-stitch.

But was Betsy really interested in the shop, or was she only "helping out," as any polite guest would? Perhaps it was still too early to get an honest answer. Betsy had always been interested in something new.

But today was not the day to start inquiring. Margot was going to be out all day today. First, to the Minneapolis art museum, to make a detailed drawing of the T'ang horse for the canvas.

And about time, too, if she wanted that project finished by Thanksgiving. She wished she hadn't thrown away the original drawings; then she wouldn't have to make this trip. No, wait, she was also going to meet with Hudson Earlie at the museum, so she had to go anyway.

She found herself smiling at the memory of Betsy meeting Hud at Christopher Inn. Betsy was attractive and witty and she enjoyed flirting. But twice burned by bad marriages, what would she do when she found out Hud was himself a three-time loser? Run? Or make another bad choice?

Probably neither. Betsy wasn't a youngster anymore; she knew better than to get mixed up with someone like Hud. And she was in the process of sorting herself out, which was not the time to be starting a courtship, or even an affair. But what if she was her usual reckless self and got involved, and it turned out badly? Where would she run to this time? She'd confessed she was here because she had nowhere else to go, no one else to turn to. Perhaps Margot had better say something to Hud, though if he got on his high horse about it, she'd warn Betsy, too.

Margot eased herself out of bed, remembered her robe, and used the bathroom as quietly as she could. Once Betsy had been a morning person, but confessed she had gotten over that. The sunrise over Excelsior still had two hours of travel before it reached the West Coast; morning would come early until her internal clock adjusted.

Margot went back into her bedroom and booted up her computer, checked her E-mail, and started to download a couple of newsgroups. RCTN took forever; its thousands of members were incorrigible chatterers. While it was working, she went into the kitchen and started the coffee-maker, then went back to the computer to scan the messages, reply to a few, and send them. Then she finalized and printed the presentation she was going to make this evening. By the time that was done, she could hear Betsy in the bathroom.

Betsy sighed and rolled over. Margot hadn't used to be such an early bird! It was barely light out, and already Margot was putzing around in the bathroom. Betsy pried an eye open and checked her watch. Six o'clock. God, these Midwesterners; you'd think they all were farmers. Didn't they know that early to bed and early to rise means you miss all the parties?

Betsy rolled back onto her side, seeking more sleep. After all, it was only four A.M. in San Diego; some of last night's parties were just breaking up.

It was awkward living in someone else's home. You had to adjust your sleeping patterns, your TV-watching habits, your eating habits. No more cereal for supper, no more cold pizza for breakfast. And in this place, *lots* more salads.

Which Betsy could use a little of. So okay, bring on the salads.

Very faintly, Betsy heard a series of beeps, and then a chord of music—just the one chord. Ah, Margot was surfing the net. Interesting how her sister, who, back in high school, had difficulty mastering the electric typewriter, was now so proficient on the computer.

Betsy herself was computer literate. A shame she hadn't known Margot had an E-mail address; she could have saved herself this trip. A few weeks of E-mail exchanges and—no, that wouldn't have done it. She had needed to get away, start over.

She had sold her own computer along with most of her other household items when she'd decided to come to Minnesota. Too much trouble hauling a trailer over those mountains, too expensive to put things into storage. And wiping the slate clean was part of the process of starting over.

Should she talk to Margot about her computer? Margot kept it in her bedroom, and had yet to invite Betsy into that sanctum. Margot might think she wanted to pry, though she didn't. Certainly Margot hadn't come into the guest room once she'd turned it over to Betsy. Not that she wasn't welcome.

Margot was a much more private person than Betsy. That could be because Betsy had been such a snoop when they were kids. Margot had had to fight for privacy, and gotten into the habit.

But Betsy was willing to respect that. There were things she didn't want to share with Margot, either. Such as how uncomfortable she felt taking her sister's charity. She wasn't sure whether her sister's offer of a paying job in the shop was a sop to Betsy's pride or because she could really use the help.

But did any of that matter right now? Betsy felt herself sinking into the pillows, a very pleasant sensation. She dozed until the smell of coffee brought her awake again, and had a good breakfast with Margot—mushroom-and-

green-pepper omelette with toast—then Margot left for the
city and Betsy went down with Sophie to open the shop.

Shelly was somewhat distracted; school was going to start
in five days, and she'd just found out that there would be
thirty-five children in her fourth-grade class. That was far
too many, and with the list of children's names came a
little memo saying there would be no teacher's aide until
halfway through the semester.

So Betsy's constant stream of questions about Crewel
World, its history and profitability, were a nuisance. Shelly
made her answers as brief as possible, though she sensed
Betsy's growing frustration.

Officer Jill came in around ten-thirty for a cup of coffee
and to place an order for more ultrasuede floss. On her
way out she said, "Don't forget this evening," and closed
the door.

"What about this evening?" Shelly asked Betsy.

"We're going to dinner and the Guthrie."

"Well, isn't that nice! I'm glad you two are going to
be friends."

"Us, friends?" said Betsy with a little laugh. "I'm only
going because Margot can't go. It was her idea that I take
her place."

"What, you don't like Shakespeare?"

"Sure, but I'm not so sure about Jill. Is she always like
this?"

"Like what?"

"Frosty."

"She's not frosty, she's just Norwegian. They're not big
on showing their feelings. She likes you."

"How can you tell?"

"She came in for coffee, and Wednesday is Margot's
day off, everyone knows that. I don't think she knows my
schedule, so it wasn't me she came in to see. I think she
likes you, or wants to."

"Do you like her?"

Shelly laughed. "Sure, but I've known her since kin-
dergarten."

Betsy wanted to ask more, but a customer came in with
a lot of her own questions, and Shelly took her to the back
of the store, where a pair of upholstered chairs made answering the questions so comfortable the customer tended
to stay a little longer and buy more than she might have
otherwise.

Betsy drove to Jill's house about five-thirty. It was time
she learned her way around, so she was driving into the
city. Jill got in and directed her back down Highway 7,
then onto Highway 100 north to 394, then east to Minneapolis. They got off on the Twelfth Street North exit.
"When we cross Hennepin it will become South Twelfth,"
Jill said.

And so it did. Almost immediately, Jill said, "There's
Buca's." It was on a corner, marked with an old-fashioned
vertical neon sign, showing a wine bottle filling a glass.

The restaurant was in the basement of an apartment building, a series of small rooms. The walls were covered with
old photographs of thickly dressed children—presumably
the owner's ancestors—and photos of Joe DiMaggio, Yogi
Berra, Pope Pius XII, Al Capone, Frank Sinatra, and other
notable Italians.

There were the correct checkered tablecloths, and a
shabby-friendly atmosphere that felt authentic, down to
last Christmas's tinsel still wrapped around the overhead
pipes. The plates didn't quite all match, nor did the sil-
verware. The wineglasses were simple tumblers.

Betsy, remembering the shabby little restaurant in
Brooklyn, smiled. This was a very authentic look.

And the smell was both authentic and heavenly.

The menu was on the wall, on a big rectangle of white-
board. Betsy felt alarmed at the prices, which were anything but shabby. A small dinner salad for $6.95? She
began to wish she hadn't insisted dinner be dutch treat.

Jill must have read her face, for she said, "We'll get one salad and share—the portions are large."

That was an understatement; the "small" salad came on a platter, a great heap of mixed greens and purple onions, glistening with oil. Dark olives clung precariously to what showed of the rim. The garlic bread they ordered with it was the size and shape of a large pizza, crusted with Parmesan, greening with basil, thickly flecked with slices of roasted garlic.

Betsy had thought it was only New York cops who loved Italian food, but perhaps it was a universal trait; certainly Jill seemed familiar with the menu.

"How long have you known Margot?" asked Betsy as they waited for the entrée.

Jill considered. "Fifteen years, or thereabouts," she replied, and added, "She taught me how to embroider and do crewel. And, more recently, needlepoint."

"Do you knit?"

"No. And neither do you, I guess."

Betsy thought for an instant that this was a witticism, but when she looked up from her second slice of garlic bread, all she saw was that implacable calm and a penetrating pair of eyes.

Jill had the full face the Victorians so admired; not a bone sticking out anywhere. And her eyebrows were so pale they were almost invisible. So there was no quirky eyebrow or quiver of jaw tendon to read in that face.

A little defensively, Betsy said, "Knitting's a dull business, don't you think? It seems so mechanical, knit, purl, knit, purl, on and on—but you have to pay attention, or you end up with a mess."

"You did learn how to purl, then?"

"Yes, Margot showed me. I thought I had taught myself, but Margot looked at it and said she thought I had invented a new stitch."

Was that a glint of amusement in those cool eyes?

Encouraged, Betsy continued, "And while I thought I

was dropping stitches, it turned out I had added six. Did you ever notice how knitters have to keep stopping and counting? Always dropping or picking up stitches. Give me the kind of needlework where all I have to do is look and I know where I am.''

"Me, too.''

The chicken Marsala was to die for. A single serving came as three large chicken breasts in a caramel-brown sauce, covered with big hunks of fresh mushrooms. They shared that, too.

"Well?'' said Jill coolly as the meal drew toward its end.

"Well what?'' replied Betsy, feeling overfed, and a little fuddled with Chianti. It was too easy to be generous when pouring it into a tumbler.

"Is it as good as that little restaurant in Brooklyn?''

Betsy tried to think. "Frankly, it's been too many years since I was in Brooklyn to remember. But I think so. In any case, it was delicious.''

"I'm glad you liked it,'' said Jill. She looked at her watch. "We don't have time for dessert.''

Betsy began to laugh, she couldn't help it.

Jill's inquiring glance had the wintry look in it again, even though she, too, watched as the waitress packed up half a slab of garlic bread and most of the garlic mashed potatoes and one of the chicken breasts. Was it a local custom always to order dessert, even when all you could manage was a polite bite of it? Did Jill think there was an empty refrigerator at home?

But Betsy didn't feel like explaining why she thought Jill had made a joke. She was glad they were going to a play; soon she wouldn't have to try to keep up a conversation with this unreadable ice maiden.

They were well into the first act of the Guthrie production of *The Taming of the Shrew* before enough of the wine wore off that Betsy could look around with appreciation.

The theater was not small enough to be called intimate,

but it wasn't a huge cavern by any means. The stage was a thrust, so the audience sat on three sides, but it went well back behind a proscenium as well. The seats were very comfortable. The actors were of the caliber that makes Shakespearean English sound natural, the special effects, while not Broadway spectacular, were well done, and the costuming was beautiful.

It had started raining sometime during the play, and was still raining when they came out of the theater. But the farther west they drove, the lighter the rain became, until out in Excelsior it ceased altogether, leaving platinum puddles as markers of its passing, and tree branches hanging lower, their leaves heavy with water.

They didn't say much on the way home. Betsy dropped Jill off at her house, then drove up Water Street toward the lake. The small downtown was quiet, already mostly asleep. Of course, it was eleven o'clock at night. But there were not the boarded-up windows so sadly evident in many small towns. There was the bakery; Shelly had said they had nice sandwiches. Certainly their sweet rolls were good. And here was Haskell's, where she turned toward home. Interesting, she already thought of it as home. Maybe she would stay and see if she was up to a Minnesota blizzard.

As she pulled up to the curb in front of the dark brick building, her headlights caught the door of Crewel World. It seemed ajar. Probably just the way the lights hit it, thought Betsy.

But when she got out, she went to take a closer look. The door was open a couple of inches. Betsy, sure she had locked it firmly earlier, reached to pull it shut, and saw, dimly, things all over the floor. The drawers of the white dresser were open and canvases were sticking stiffly up and out of them.

She nearly went in, then remembered what she'd been told by a policeman during a National Night Out lecture about coming home to a burglary: *Don't go in; he might still be in there.* A chill ran right down her spine.

She let go the door latch as if it were red-hot and scurried into the little alcove that held the door to the upstairs. It seemed to take forever to locate her key, and it was horribly reluctant to go into the lock. Then it turned and she was inside. She dashed up the thinly carpeted stairs.

She reached the top all out of breath, her hands trembling so that she had to use both of them to unlock the apartment door.

"Margot!" she called, falling into the little entranceway and slamming the door shut behind her. "Margot! There's been a burglary in the shop!"

No answer. Was it possible the meeting at City Hall was still going on?

"Margot?" No reply.

Betsy hastened into the kitchen, flicked on the light. The phone was on the wall. She lifted the receiver and dialed 911.

"This is 911, what is your emergency?" asked a woman's voice.

"A burglar! I'm afraid he might still be in there!"

"Is this burglar in your home?"

"No, in the shop downstairs!"

"Is it your shop?"

"No, my sister's. It's called Crewel World." Betsy gave the address and promised to stay where she was until the police arrived.

Betsy stood by the window, arms folded tightly until, through the closed blinds, she could see the erratic pattern of flashing red and blue lights.

She ran down the stairs and waved to the two husky young men who climbed out of a patrol car, then pointed to the door of Crewel World. They nodded and, with drawn pistols, went inside.

A little later Betsy gave a little shriek and jumped aside, and was surprised to find she had squeezed her eyes shut and stuffed her fingers in her ears against the possible sound of gunfire. The person touching her shoulder was one of the officers.

She sighed with relief. "He's gone, then?"

"Who?"

"The burglar. I was afraid you'd have to shoot him."

"Are you the owner of this store?"

"No, my sister is. I mean, Mr. Joseph Mickels is the owner of the building, and my sister rents from him. I'm just visiting. From California."

They were looking at her in some kind of expectant way, but she'd told them everything she could think of.

"Do you know where your sister is?"

"No. That is, she was here earlier this evening, up in the apartment. That was at about five-thirty, when I left to pick up Jill and we went into Minneapolis for dinner and then to a play. Margot was supposed to go to City Hall for a meeting about the art fair. I can't believe it's still going on. It's after eleven."

"Who's Jill?"

Betsy said, surprised, "She's one of you. A police officer, Jill Cross."

"What's your name?"

"Betsy Devonshire."

"What's your sister's name?"

"Margot Berglund."

"What does she look like?"

"She's about five-feet-one, slim, blond hair—why? Is she—"

A sound that had been growing louder got loud enough to impinge on Betsy's concentration. It was another siren, and it belonged to one of those boxy ambulances that come to the scene of accidents. The officer turned to start toward it.

Betsy called, "Wait, what's going on? Is someone in the store? Is it—is she all right?" She turned toward the shop's entrance, but the officer was in front of her and he put both hands on her shoulders.

"Just take it easy, Ms. Devonshire."

Two people ran from the ambulance into the shop, one carrying a large, square suitcase. Betsy felt her knees growing weak. "What's going on? Is someone in there?"

"Yes, ma'am."

"Who? Is it Margot?"

"We don't know right now who it is."

The door to the upstairs opened and three people came out, a young couple and a middle-aged man, tenants from the other two apartments. Their faces were alarmed, and they stood close together, clutching bathrobes. The older man was wearing unlaced dress shoes. He stared at Betsy.

"Why don't you come with me and sit in the squad car?" said the policeman, taking Betsy by the elbow. "Let's get you out of all this." His voice was kind but firm. In a kind of dream, Betsy allowed herself to be ushered into the backseat of the squad car, whose engine was running, and lights still flashing. The policeman went away.

Except for the radio, it was darkly silent in the car. Everything in it was black—the upholstery, the seats, the shotgun clamped vertically to the black dashboard. Betsy could almost smell the testosterone and suddenly wondered how Jill could stand it.

The radio muttered again, the words too mixed with static to understand. She didn't like being put in the squad car, it indicated her place in this affair was worse than those spectators standing on the sidewalk, merely alarmed.

After a while she noticed raindrops on the windshield; it had started to rain again. The people on the sidewalk went back inside.

After a long while the ambulance people came out. The policeman followed behind them to open the squad car's back door. "Come with me, please," he said, and held out a hand.

"Where are we going?" she asked.

"We want you to look at something," he said, and led her into the store.

Someone had turned on the lights. Betsy could not believe the disarray. The floor was covered with yarn and floss. The spin racks were on their sides, magazines had been crumpled and ripped, baskets that had held knitting yarn had not only been emptied, but stepped on.

The policeman led her past Margot's desk, which was pulled out of place, toward the back of the store. Here shelves came out from the wall on either side. Behind them, on the side where the pretty little upholstered chairs had sat around a little round table, was even wilder disarray. The chairs were overturned. The shelves had been divided vertically into cubes, which had once held yarn and evenweave fabrics; books, magazines, and canvas needlework bags had been emptied onto the floor. Behind the chairs was a big heap of wool and books, and beyond them, as if they had been moved aside to uncover her, was a woman.

She was on her back, her head turned to one side. Her eyes were partly open, as was her mouth. She looked as if she were crying out in pain. Her skin was an odd, pale color. She was wearing a black wool skirt hiked up over one knee and a dark wine sweater, the sleeves pushed up. One of her sensible black shoes was off the heel of her foot and her arms were bent at the elbows, hands clenched. Her blond hair was mussed.

"Do you recognize her?" asked the policeman.

"Margot," whispered Betsy. "It's my sister Margot."

6

As Jill prepared for bed, she began to smile—though it hardly showed on her face. Betsy Devonshire was an interesting person. And funny; it had been hard to keep from laughing out loud at some of the things she said. On the other hand, Betsy was kind of slow to pick up on a joke. She probably didn't get Jill's crack about knitting, and Jill thought it had been pretty obvious. But never mind; Betsy liked Italian food, complimented Buca's, stayed awake all through the play, and made some intelligent comments on it afterward. And above all, she was the sister of her best friend, Margot Berglund.

She wondered how long it would take Margot to understand the prank of insisting Betsy take home all that garlic-laden food. Margot disliked garlic almost as much as she did onions. Jill snorted softly and climbed between the crisp sheets. She loved jokes whose punch lines went off sometime later.

She was fast asleep when the phone rang, and it took her a minute to understand what the caller was asking her—and why.

"Wait a second, Mike!" she demanded. "Take a

breath!'' She took one of her own. ''Now, what's this about a burglar?''

Betsy sat in the dining nook of the apartment. Jill was in the kitchen and there was the smell of coffee.

''Here, drink this,'' said Jill, and a mug of coffee appeared in front of Betsy. She put her cold hands around it, burning them. But she left them there; it was an honest, understandable hurt.

''What happens now?'' Betsy asked.

''An autopsy. Then the ME—medical examiner—will release the body, and you'll have to make funeral arrangements.''

''I don't know how to do that.'' And she didn't want to learn. She felt sick and weary, all her senses dulled, as if she were coming down with flu. She didn't even have the strength to lift the mug to her mouth. Margot couldn't be dead, Margot had just stayed late at her meeting and would be home any minute, asking what all the fuss was about.

''I assume you want her buried beside her husband?'' asked Jill.

''At Aaron's funeral she said something to me about being buried in the same plot. Can you do that?''

''Yes, people do it all the time. Especially if they're cremated. Aaron was cremated. Call Paul Huber, he's good.''

''Who's Huber?'' asked Betsy wearily.

''The local funeral home. And you should call Reverend John at Trinity.''

''Okay. Sure.''

''Not this minute, of course.''

Betsy, hearing criticism in Jill's voice, looked up. And saw that implacable stare looking back. Suddenly she wanted to punch that smooth face. She wanted to rail, scream, and tear her hair, dress herself in sackcloth and pour ashes on her head, and weep for days, weeks, forever. Margot was dead.

But she didn't scream, or say anything, or do anything, only stared at Jill.

Who looked at her watch, a small, delicate thing, clinging to that sturdy white wrist. "It's very late. You should go to bed."

"I'm tired, but I'm not at all sleepy," said Betsy, looking into the dark liquid in her mug.

"Then just go lie down for an hour."

"I don't want to lie down! Why don't you just go? Go bother someone else!" said Betsy, surprised at the venom escaping through her voice. "You don't understand!"

"Sure I do. Here, let me get you something else." Jill slid the mug out of Betsy's still-clasped hands and went into the kitchen.

Betsy slid back into her felt-lined stupor. She shouldn't shout at Jill, who had gotten out of bed to come and be with her. And there were things that must be done, she knew that. She just wished there could be a period of doing nothing until she could summon some energy.

Margot had been the coping one. She wouldn't be sitting here as if wrapped in thick flannel, her brain turned to oatmeal. Betsy remembered when she herself had seen trouble as a challenge, but that seemed a very long time ago. Why couldn't she be that way now? What was the matter with her? She should be paying attention to Jill, and feeling grateful for her advice. Buck up, she told herself. But her mind replied sullenly that it wanted to be left alone.

"I don't understand why Margot went into the store when you knew enough not to," said Jill from the kitchen, where the refrigerator door was being closed, a pot was being put on the stove.

Betsy pictured Margot walking home—Margot alive and walking!—and seeing the open door. But Margot went in—no, no; don't go in!—but she went in, she went in.

While clever Betsy had seen the door open and come running upstairs to call the police. Why had it happened that way?

"Possession," said Betsy. "Territory. You ever read Ardrey's *Territorial Imperative*? Popular sociology, from back in the sixties; forgotten now, probably. He said most animals, including primates, select and defend a territory, whether as an individual or a tribe. That's what we do, and that's why humans fear strangers and fight wars."

Jill said doubtfully, "You think she saw the burglar and went in to run him off?"

"No, of course not! Margot's not an idiot. But she's been having trouble with Joe Mickels trying to throw her out of the shop, so I guess her territorial instincts were all inflamed anyhow. So when she saw the door open she just went in without thinking. I nearly did—" Something like a sob choked Betsy but the relief of tears would not come. "God, I can't bear this."

"Yes, you can," said Jill firmly, coming to put a hand on her shoulder. "You've got to, you're the sole surviving member of your family. But you're not alone. Margot had lots of friends. When they hear about this, you'll have all the help you need." She went back into the kitchen and there was the sound of cabinet doors being opened and closed. "Where's the cocoa?"

"I don't know." The flannel wrapped her again. She didn't care where anything was in a world inexplicably emptied of Margot.

Jill looked everywhere for the cocoa, even, apparently, the bathroom. But she must have found it, because soon a mug of hot cocoa was thrust into Betsy's hands.

"Drink this." It was an order.

Betsy drank. And to her surprise, in a few minutes she was helplessly sleepy. Jill walked her into her bedroom, helped her undress and get into pajamas, tucked her in. Betsy tried to ask a question but instead fell into a black pit.

• • •

"She okay alone up there?" asked Mike.

"I put a couple of sleeping pills into her cocoa," said Jill. "She's good for a while. What's the situation?" She shivered against the chill and damp night air—she'd come out only in jeans and a white T-shirt—and glanced into the brightly lit store, where people moved in the routine of a crime-scene investigation.

"It looks like she interrupted a burglar, all right. Cash drawer broken into. And since there's no calculator, I assume it was taken. Did she use a computer?"

"Yes, but it's upstairs," said Jill. "In her bedroom. And she emptied that cash drawer every night."

"Maybe that's why he trashed the place. Pissed because there was nothing of any value to steal."

"Little he knew. Those hand-painted canvases over there cost a lot of money."

The curiosity that'd gotten Mike Malloy promoted from patrol to investigation stirred. He glanced toward where Jill was looking, at the white dresser near the front door. "No kidding?"

"Of course, I don't think there's much call for hot needlepoint canvases; eighty percent of the women who buy them wouldn't know where to find a fence, and the rest don't know what a fence is."

The interest faded. "I wonder why our burglar picked this shop in the first place," grumbled Mike. "It's not like it's a jewelry store, watches in the window, diamonds in the safe. And even more, I wonder why Mrs. Berglund decided to confront him."

"Territorial imperative, maybe."

Mike squinted at Jill, who didn't crack a smile. He gave a dismissive shrug and said, "Well, I better get back to it. You gonna stay?"

"No, I'm back on first watch. Gotta be up pushing my squad first thing in the morning. Mind if I call you about this later?"

"If you got anything of value to tell me, be my guest."

• • •

The phone started ringing early Thursday, first a reporter wanting details, then Irene Potter offering to open the shop—which offer Betsy curtly refused—then another reporter, then someone named Alice who went on and on about how everyone who did needlework would miss her, each word scalding Betsy's heart. When the woman slowed enough that Betsy could get a word in, Betsy thanked her through clenched teeth and hung up. Before it could ring again, she took the receiver off the hook. And she discovered that no one buzzed at the door more than three times before going away. She spent the entire day watching television, stupid show after stupid show. She didn't turn the lights on at nightfall, but sat up for hours in the darkness. But she did not cry. At three A.M. she put the phone back on the hook and went to bed.

The Hennepin County Medical Examiner's call woke her early Friday. A woman said they had released Margot's body and someone needed to make arrangements for it to be taken away.

Betsy said she would do so, and wandered the apartment in a mild panic for five minutes. Then she recalled Jill saying there was one funeral home she could trust—but what was its name? She picked up the slim phone directory for Excelsior, Shorewood, Deephaven, and Tonka Bay, and saw there was exactly one funeral home in Excelsior, Huber's. That was it. She phoned and got an answering service, and left an urgent message.

She had just finished brushing her teeth when the phone rang. It was Irene Potter, asking if there was anything Betsy wanted done.

"You want to do me a favor?" said Betsy. "Stay off the phone. I'm waiting for an important call and I don't want the phone tied up."

She was still trying to decipher the coffeemaker's methods when the phone rang again, and it was Paul Huber.

Instead of the oily voice she expected, Huber sounded

perfectly ordinary, except he was also brisk, knowledgeable, and efficient. He said he would bring Margot's body to the funeral home; yes, he knew the procedure, it was all routine and she needn't worry. He then made an appointment with her for first thing that afternoon, to discuss the rest of the arrangements.

Betsy sat curled in Margot's chair, sipping coffee and worrying. Didn't funerals cost a great deal of money? Betsy had some money, not much, and most of it was in an IRA, inaccessible.

How was she going to pay for this?

What did other people do?

Betsy knew there were special life-insurance policies people took out to cover final expenses. But Betsy remembered when her father had died; it took weeks for insurance companies to pay off. Betsy needed money by this afternoon.

Maybe funeral homes allowed people to charge funerals.

Betsy had a charge card. She used it sparingly, having learned to fear debt during her first marriage. So it was nowhere near its limit, which on the other hand was a modest five thousand dollars. She had hoped to save it for an emergency—but surely this was an emergency. She couldn't store Margot in the refrigerator until she saved enough money to bury her. Was it bad manners to ask a funeral director if he took Visa?

And was the three thousand seven hundred dollars left in credit enough?

Maybe Margot had cash somewhere. Jill had told her that Margot emptied the cash drawer every night. Where did she put the money? Betsy remembered walking to the bank's night deposit with Margot on Monday evening. But not all the money went into the bank—she needed some to prime the drawer every morning.

Betsy looked toward the little hall that led to Margot's bedroom. Betsy had to go see, go pry. Feeling guilty as a child about to steal a quarter from her mother's purse, she slipped down the short hall to the bedroom door.

Margot's bedroom was beautiful, with designer elements Betsy had not expected. The bed had slim iron pillars and a translucent lace canopy. There was a comforter, all ruffles of ivory lace, a shade lighter than the walls. A thin scent of Margot's perfume lingered on the still air.

The rug on the floor was thick and lush, iron gray with a gold and green fringe. The window had layers of ivory lace curtains pinched and pulled into a complicated pattern. The small, low dresser was wood, stained gray, the low chair in front of it had an iron frame and a plush seat. The mirror over the dresser was round. A pair of badly snagged panty hose draped half out of the otherwise empty wastebasket. The desk in the corner had a modern-looking computer on it, with an ergonomically correct office chair and a two-drawer wooden file cabinet beside it, the bottom drawer not quite shut.

Betsy searched the desk drawers first. She found three checkbooks. One belonged to Crewel World and showed a balance of $2,523.50. The other was a personal checkbook and showed a balance of $372.80. The third was a Piper Jaffray money market account with a balance of close to four thousand dollars. And there was also a savings-account passbook showing a total balance of $3,253.74.

Betsy rubbed her nose, her sign of befuddlement. This was more money than she had expected to find. Why would Margot keep all her money where she could get at it? Didn't she believe in IRAs or certificates of deposit, for heaven's sake? Or was there even more hidden away somewhere? Probably not much—Margot wasn't really wealthy, or she wouldn't be living in a rented apartment.

Not that it mattered in the present emergency. Betsy could not sign Margot's name to anything. What she needed was cash.

The next drawer held sixty dollars in paper and silver, neatly lined up. Is that all it took to prime a cash register?

She could find no more cash, so apparently that was all that was needed. The dresser held perfumes in one drawer, cosmetics in another, and hair curlers, bobby pins, and an electric curling iron in the middle.

Betsy found Margot's plain black purse in the closet and opened it. Inside the wallet were forty-six dollars and ninety-six cents.

That was more than Betsy's wallet, but hardly enough to pay for a funeral.

Now wait, now wait, surely these Huber people were used to this. Unexpected deaths happened all the time; not everyone had access to the cash to pay for a funeral. Doubtless the people at Huber's would know what to do.

Which is exactly the attitude funeral directors enjoy encountering, thought Betsy in a sudden flash: customers coming in all confused and scared. That's how some of those really expensive funerals happen. You go in and hold out all your assets and hope they won't hurt you too badly. But they do, they do.

So it was with her chin firmly set and both hands on the closed top of her purse that Betsy walked up past the post office in the cool morning sunshine, rounded the corner, and crossed Second Street to Huber's, a whited sepulchre with bloodred geraniums in a planter by the entrance.

The lights were dim inside, the carpet soft underfoot. A dark young man with a thick mustache and a Mona Lisa smile stood waiting. Betsy had a vague feeling she'd seen him before.

"Mr. Huber?" said Betsy.

"Ms. Devonshire," said Mr. Huber. "Come with me."

He led her to a small office with dark wood paneling, soft lighting, and samples of ground-level grave markers in the corner. He seated her and went behind the desk.

"I am very saddened by Margot's death," he said.

"You knew her personally?"

"Yes, of course," he replied, by his voice a little puzzled at her tone. "We're both members of Lafayette Country Club, and we worked together on a Habitat for Humanity house in Minneapolis this summer."

That hadn't occurred to Betsy, though it should have. Margot had said that in Excelsior everyone knew everyone else. But Betsy hadn't known her sister was a member of a country club. Of course, that probably didn't mean out here in the wilderness what it did in, say, Rancho Santa Fe.

Still, better tell the bad news up front. "I haven't much money," she said. "What I do have is tied up in an IRA, and of course I don't have any way to access what assets Margot had, so this is going to have to be a . . . an inexpensive funeral. I hope you understand."

Mr. Huber was frowning now, though more in puzzlement than anger. "You haven't spoken with Margot's attorney yet?"

"I haven't talked to anyone, much less Margot's attorney, whose name I don't know. I'm practically a stranger here in town. But there's no time now for that. I know this has to be taken care of promptly, so I want to tell you right now that it can't cost a whole lot."

"What do you consider 'a whole lot'?"

"Why don't you tell me what the very least is I can spend, and we'll see if I can meet even that amount?"

Mr. Huber lifted his hands in a gesture of surrender. "Very well." He helped Betsy fill out a death certificate and write an obituary. He said he'd take care of sending it to the local papers. He was kind and patient through all of this, but then they were back to the big question of the funeral.

"I want her cremated," said Betsy, "so we don't have to do all that chemical stuff, do we? Can you do that right here in your place?"

"No, we don't the facilities. There are two choices in the area. There's Fairview Cemetery in Minneapolis. They can make it part of a service—"

"No, I want a funeral service in a church."

"Margot was a member of Trinity Episcopal."

Betsy nodded. "Yes. I'm going to call the rector to-day."

"You'll find Reverend John a pleasure to work with."

He led Betsy upstairs to look at the urns. And here she weakened. She picked a very nice Chinese-vase style in a pearl color with cranberry-colored lotus blossoms on it. Three hundred and forty-nine dollars was the price, which she thought outrageous, but what could she do? The polished wooden box wasn't much less, and it looked like something you keep recipes in.

They went back downstairs to the little office and Mr. Huber got out his calculator. "Two thousand four hundred dollars," he announced with a little sigh.

By now Betsy had a fierce headache. She'd cut every corner she could think of, and it still seemed an enormous sum. She wanted to weep and change her mind about the lotus urn, but she hadn't the strength.

"Do you take Visa?" she asked.

They did.

7

Paul Huber sat at his desk for a while after Betsy Devonshire left. It was not uncommon for survivors dealing with unexpected death to look for someone to be angry at. Often they settled on the funeral director. After all, he was doing unknowable . . . *things* to the body, and charging for it besides, which put him right out of the category of friend.

While Betsy Devonshire was not the worst example of this phenomenon, she was one of the saddest he had seen in a very long time.

He wondered if he should have been more persistent in telling her that there really should be a wake of some sort, where all her friends and the many people Margot had touched in her life could get together informally and talk, and pay their last respects.

And that there was no need to be parsimonious about the funeral service.

But Ms. Devonshire was in no mood whatsoever to listen to advice from a funeral director, who, so far as she was concerned, was interested only in lining his pockets.

He shook his head and blew his nose and went to deal with the body of a friend he had long admired.

•   •   •

"Oh, my dear, I tried to call you yesterday, but couldn't get through," said the pleasant voice on the phone. It was Reverend John Rettger. "I'm so sorry about Margot."

"Thank you, Reverend. I'm calling about the funeral."

"Yes, of course. Do you want to come here, or shall I come over there? As it happens, I'm free right now."

"I'll come to you."

Betsy was startled to find that what she had thought was the church hall was, in fact, the church.

"We still use the little church, as a chapel," said Reverend Rettger. He was short, with a broad face, low-set ears that stuck out, and fluffy white hair around a bald spot. He had the kindest blue eyes Betsy had seen in a long while. "It was the first church built in Excelsior, so we want to preserve it," he said in his mild voice. "We use it for early-Sunday services and small weddings and funerals. But of course you'll want to use the big church for Margot." He started to lead her back to his office.

Betsy frowned. "I will?"

"Of course. And the church hall after, for coffee. Half the town will come, and people from all over the area."

"They will?"

The blue eyes twinkled. "You haven't been keeping up with your sister's activities for a while, have you?" He opened the door to an outer office. "Hold my calls, Tracy."

"Yes, Reverend."

He gestured Betsy through the door to his office. "She was a driving force in this town," he continued, following her in and closing the door. "She worked to improve the Common, to run the art fair, to aid the schools, to build this new church and repair the chapel, to get better fireworks for our Fourth of July celebration, to raise money for various fund drives."

Betsy allowed him to seat her in a very comfortable leather chair, one of a pair. His office, while not large, was light and airy. She said, "I went with her to a committee meeting to hold a fund-raiser for a child in need of heart surgery. I didn't realize she did a lot of this sort of thing."

"She wouldn't have thought it a lot, she was always pushing herself to do more. Yet she was very patient with the rest of us, who couldn't keep up."

"Sounds like her eulogy should be given by you."

Rettger gave a little bow from his seat facing her—he hadn't gone behind his desk. "I'd be honored. I have known her a long while, and her husband even longer. Have you spoken with a funeral director?"

"Yes, Mr. Huber. He's taking Margot to be cremated right now. When can you find time in your schedule for the funeral?"

Rettger's white eyebrows lifted. "No visitation?"

"I can't afford it. I want a no-frills funeral service here, and then burial in the same plot as her husband."

Rettger appeared to be about to say something, then visibly repressed whatever it had been and said, "Let me show you the two burial services of the Episcopal church. You have some decisions to make."

It was not unlike selecting a wedding service. There was a framework of ceremony, with options in the hymns and readings. Rettger said, "I want to assure you that there are people in this congregation who are going to insist on having a part in the service. They would be insulted at the notion that you might offer to pay for their efforts." His mild voice and kind eyes took the sting out of his words.

"All right, that's fine," replied Betsy. "Now, I know 'Amazing Grace' is a cliché, but we both loved that hymn." A huge lump suddenly formed in her chest and sought to climb up her throat. But she swallowed it and went on.

Rettger took notes as Betsy made her choices, but had a suggestion of his own for the Old Testament reading, not one of the options. Betsy agreed to it—why not? His intentions seemed at least benign, and surely he knew what he was doing. The funeral was set for Sunday afternoon. "We'll have to form a committee to let people know," he said. "It will be my great honor to take care of that for you."

"Thank you."

Even forewarned by Reverend Rettger, Betsy was astonished at the turnout. She recognized the mayor and decided the people with him must be others from the city government. Shelly was there, with a contingent of women who might be fellow stitchers, or perhaps some of the part-time crew. The crazy lady—what was her name? Potter, Irene Potter—sat behind Betsy, dressed in a shapeless navy-blue dress, dabbing a handkerchief edged in black crochet lace to her eyes and sighing audibly.

There were children and adults and elderly, people dressed beautifully and people dressed very casually, and even some dressed rather shabbily.

Betsy had a black dress, but it was for cocktails, not funerals. So she wore an old purple suit that was too hot.

The music stopped and Reverend Rettger came out. To her astonishment, he was wearing white vestments. Then she noticed he had covered the beautiful funeral urn with a white cloth heavily embroidered in gold. What does he think this is? thought Betsy angrily. We're here to bury Margot, not confirm her.

A small, good choir did a lovely arrangement of "Amazing Grace," which was not spoiled by everyone joining in. Except Betsy, whose breathing had gone all strange, so that she couldn't sing. I'm going to cry at last, she thought. But she didn't.

The first reading, from Proverbs, was done by Mayor Jamison. It was the one suggested by Rettger.

A wife of noble character who can find?
She is worth far more than rubies.

Her husband has full confidence in her. . . .
She selects wool and flax
and works with eager hands. . . .

Some in the congregation began reacting with sounds
suspiciously like snickers.

She gets up while it is still dark;
she provides food for her family
and portions for her servant girls. . . .
She sees that her trading is profitable,
and her lamp does not go out at night.
In her hand she holds the distaff
and grasps the spindle with her fingers.

Now Betsy was sure she heard a giggle.

She opens her arms to the poor
and extends her hands to the needy.
When it snows, she has no fear for her household;
for all of them are clothed in scarlet.
She makes coverings for her bed;
she is clothed in fine linen and purple.
Her husband is respected at the city gate,
Where he takes his seat among the elders of the land.
She makes linen garments and sells them.
And supplies the merchants with sashes—

That last line sent everyone over the border and there
was audible laughter. The mayor himself was grinning.
Betsy felt her cheeks flame. How dare they! And how dare
Rettger persuade her to allow this reading! She wanted to
crawl under the pew—no, she wanted to stand up on it
and shout at them to shut up, shut up! But she sat in
shamed silence as the reading went on and on.

She is clothed with strength and dignity;
she can laugh at the days to come.
She speaks with wisdom,
and faithful instruction is on her tongue.

Betsy heard a sound and looked over. She saw Jill and Shelly and some other women. Tears were streaming down their smiling faces. Those tears gave her the courage to sit through the rest of the service.

The urn was carried out in Mayor Jamison's arms like a stiffly wrapped baby, the priest leading the way, the choir singing, "All we go down to the dust; yet even at the grave we make our song: Alleluia, alleluia, alleluia." No, no, no, thought Betsy, her heart a stone in her breast, not alleluia, how can they sing alleluia!

After the ugly work at the cemetery, Betsy sat on a metal folding chair and looked at the raw earth covering the gorgeous urn she'd paid so much money for, that contained all that was left of her beloved sister. Everyone else had gone now, gone to eat and drink and be glad it wasn't they who were reduced to ashes and buried deep underground.

She couldn't stay here, not in a town that turned a funeral into a joke followed by a party.

But what was she going to do? Where was she going to go?

She sat so long that her joints stiffened. It was hard to rise from the chair, and her knees were so stiff she nearly fell making her way to the narrow dirt lane that wound around the hill and down to the street, down which she stumbled, back to the empty apartment, there to fall across her bed and descend immediately into sleep.

Hudson Earlie stood beside the coffee urn, cup and saucer in hand, watching the crowd. Big turnout, which was to be expected, of course. And it had gotten cheerful, as these things tended to do. He hadn't seen the grieving sister, though. Not a bad-looking woman, if you liked them with a little meat on their bones, which he did when no one was looking. She had some intelligence and sophistication to her, too, which he also liked occasionally.

But she was too old, only five or six years younger than he was. He had a strict rule that the women in his string not be older than thirty-five.

Which was too bad in this case, as this one might be the sole heir of her sister's estate, which he knew was considerable.

"Hud, whatever are you thinking about?" said a voice beside him.

"Me? Thinking? You know me better than that," he jested quickly, grinning at Shelly Donohue.

"Seriously," she said.

"I was thinking how the museum would miss Margot. She was on the board, you know, and she brought some good, businesslike attitudes with her to meetings. And I liked her myself—" He had to stop and swallow. That surprised him, and he took a sip of his coffee to clear his throat. "She was a hardworking, capable woman," he concluded.

Shelly nodded. "Yes, she was a terrific friend as well as a good boss. I loved working in her shop. That reading at the funeral had me bawling like a little kid, the one about wool and flax and dressing her servants in scarlet when winter comes. That's from Proverbs, did you know that?"

"No, I didn't."

"I thought Proverbs was all one-liners of advice, like fortune cookies. But that was a long one. And it described Margot so well! Even about the sashes—did you get that?"

"Yes, it came up at Christopher Inn the other night."

They'd held a Founders' Day parade last year, and Margot had helped with costumes. One thing she had done was make sashes for the people who were playing founder

George Bertram, and the Reverend Charles Gilpin, and schoolmistress Jane Wolcott, so people would know who they were.

"I don't think her sister is going to be the one to replace her," said Shelly.

"It would take four people to do what she was doing," said Hud.

"Too bad, what happened to her." This was a new voice, and they turned to see Irene Potter in her dark dress and alert face, a cookie stuffed with M&Ms in her slim fingers.

"Terrible," said Shelly.

"What do you suppose he hit her with?" asked Irene.

"Irene!" scolded Shelly.

"Does it matter?" asked Hud.

"Whatever it was, he took it away with him. I was just talking to the detective in the case. He's here, you know. Says it's true murderers always come to the funeral of their victims."

Hud opened his mouth, but Irene talked right over anything he might have said. "I was wondering if maybe Margot didn't bring it down with her, to scare him off with, and he grabbed it away and hit her with it."

"Stop it, Irene!" Shelly turned and walked away and Hud quickly made an excuse to leave her as well. When Irene got into one of her "speculating" moods, there was no talking to her about anything else. You just had to let her get over it.

Reverend Rettger watched this exchange as he sipped the coffee. He was unhappy that Ms. Devonshire had insisted on being left at the cemetery. The manner in which she refused almost made him think she was angry with him, which he knew was impossible. He had thought that when she saw how the congregation reacted to the Proverbs reading, she would understand that everyone present stood eager to give her comfort and aid of any sort. But she seemed to be in a mood to resist any help. He'd seen grief in many forms, but the sort that resisted comfort was the saddest kind.

Of course, she had reason to be angry, her sister being taken from her in such a sudden, dreadful way. Perhaps if the police were to find and arrest her murderer quickly—it was probably one of those teenagers who would be unable to explain himself, unfortunately so common nowadays. It was small satisfaction to a bereaved family, to learn that the captured murderer could only shrug when asked why.

Irene watched Shelly join another group. What was the matter with her? Just a few days ago she'd joined eagerly in speculating about Betsy and Margot. Speculation—Irene didn't call it gossip—was so interesting, and it was great to have found someone who liked it even more than she did. Why did people do what they did? Whatever were they thinking? Irene, perhaps because people were such a mystery to her, never tired of speculating about them.

Why on earth had Margot gone charging into her shop? She hadn't brought a knife, or she would have been stabbed. Irene thought about that, the blood spattering all over the walls—she'd seen a photo once of a crime scene and been quite shocked.

But Margot hadn't been stabbed; she'd been mashed in the head. They'd done an autopsy. But she couldn't speculate on the autopsy, she didn't know how they were done.

So instead she pictured the darkened, ransacked shop, and Margot striding in, hand up, holding a golf club. Margot didn't golf, but her husband had been an avid golfer, which made it kind of strange that he had joined the Lafayette Country Club, with its piddly nine-hole course. Of course, the Lafayette was a very prestigious club, and with such a pretty building. And the setting was quite beautiful, the lake on three sides. Irene had been out there once, as a guest.

But that wasn't relevant. It was the golf club that was relevant. Widows, Irene (who was a spinster) speculated, were inclined to hang on to some of their late husbands' favorite things. So at the back of a closet in that apartment was Aaron's golf bag. What was it Margot had grabbed? A mashie? A nine iron? Irene had heard those were the names of golf clubs. Too bad Shelly—whose former husband was a golfer—didn't want to speculate on this; it would have been very enjoyable.

Joe Mickels drank his coffee and thought. Awful the way Margot had died, he'd agreed six or seven times with people about that. And murder was an ugly thing, to be sure.

But she was gone, really, truly, wholly gone. Forever; and he no longer had to scheme to find ways to make her move out.

How long should he wait before he served notice on the sister to vacate? Not too soon, or the whole town would come down on his neck, and he didn't need any more ill will. But there was a lot to be done, arrangements to be made. Clear the building, remove anything salvageable; find a contractor who wouldn't charge an arm and a leg to tear that old place down. It could be done by Christmas, surely. And maybe by spring the architect's drawings would start coming to life. He meant to put up a high-rise with stores on the ground floor, offices on the second and third, condos above that. First high-rise in Excelsior, a historic building from the git-go. And cut deep in the stone above the entrance: THE MICKELS BUILDING.

And it would make money, more money than he'd made to date, which was already more money than anyone but his accountant knew, more than most people saw in their lifetimes. What a kick it was, making money. The first two million were the hardest, that was what old Aaron Berglund used to say. But he was wrong; what was hardest was parting with hunks of it trying to make more of it. Mickels hated parting with money, even more than he hated pretending he was basically doing good, improving the community, helping his fellowman, and that the money was just sort of a side effect.

As a local radio host liked to say, *B* as in *B*, *S* as in *S*.

He was making money, first and foremost. If others rode his coattails, or got good out of what he was doing, that was fine, sometimes it was even necessary, but that wasn't what he was doing.

And now the pigheaded impediment to his biggest project was at last out of the way, and he was going to make great heaps of money from that property.

He found himself breathing a little too audibly and buried his nose in the coffee cup. He'd waited for over a year for a way to open and now it had. How long, O Lord, how long did he still have to wait?

8

It was just starting to get light when Betsy woke, stiff and grubby from sleeping in her clothes. She'd slept nearly fourteen hours. She rose, got undressed, put on a nightgown, and tried to go back to bed. But though she felt exhausted, she was awake, at least for now.

She went into the kitchen and had another fight with the coffeemaker. This fight was shorter than the first, and more in the nature of a quarrel—after all, the manufacturer hoped people would like its product and recommend it to friends, and so it had to make its features accessible even to people whose sisters had thrown away the manual. Soon a rumble and wakening fragrance filled the kitchen. While it worked, Betsy took a shower. She put on her oldest jeans and sweatshirt, combed her wet hair straight back, and went toward the warm smell of coffee barefoot.

She filled a mug, doctored it shamelessly with milk and sugar, and went into the living room. She went to the front windows and lifted the layers of coverings to peer out. It was raining again, and the sky was that dreary dark color that indicated serious intent to rain all day. She turned away and curled up on the love seat. Time to begin planning.

Mr. Huber at the funeral home had wondered if Betsy
had talked yet with Margot's lawyer. And Margot had
mentioned him, too, as her ally against Joe Mickels, the
evil landlord. What was his name? One of those old-
fashioned English names. Penwiper? Wellworthy? Never
mind, his name would be around here somewhere. She'd
call him today. He could tell her how to access Margot's
accounts, close them out. How to get the shop put out of
business. How to do a legal going-out-of-business sale.

There were no heirs, except herself. She and Margot had
remarked on that one time, how there were no other de-
scendants of this branch of the family. She looked around.
All this furniture was hers, and if Margot had paid the
September rent, then perhaps Betsy could stay through the
month.

But she wouldn't stay here in Excelsior longer than that.
And she would probably have to sell the furniture, which
was sad, because there were some nice pieces, but they'd
bring a good price, and she needed the money.

She tried to think of where she wanted to go. New York
City? Like California, it cost the earth to live there. Besides, she was pretty sure she'd outgrown both New York
and California.

She needed someplace cheap. She wasn't used to winters anymore, so someplace south. Not Phoenix, too hot.
Ditto Florida. Besides, Florida had hurricanes and the people were a little too handy with firearms. Ditto Texas. Arkansas, someone once had said, was very inexpensive. And
the Ozarks were both beautiful and relatively cool in the
summer. "Not everyone in Arkansas lives in trailer
parks," he'd said. "There's a long waiting list." They'd
laughed and laughed at that.

But that was where she was going to end up, probably.
On that waiting list.

The doorbell rang. Betsy frowned and went to the door
of the apartment. There was only a button, not an intercom.
Still frowning, she pressed it.

In a minute someone knocked on the door and she opened it a fraction, keeping one set of toes pressed firmly against it.

"Hi, Betsy, it's me, Jill."

"What do you want?"

"To talk to you. Please, it's important."

Reluctantly, Betsy released the door. "Come in," she mumbled, and returned to the love seat.

After shedding a raincoat, Jill detoured into the kitchen and poured herself a cup of coffee, then brought it with her to the comfortable chair. She hesitated very briefly before sitting down in it, and with an almost ceremonial gesture shifted the needlework holder farther out of her way. She was wearing slacks and a soft gray flannel shirt, which made her fair hair look almost silver. "How are you doing?" she asked quietly.

"I don't know. Okay, I guess."

"When are you going to reopen the store?"

"I'm not. I have to get in touch with Margot's lawyer to find out how to get everything shut down and sold off."

"Why?"

"There's a silly question! Because I don't know how to run a business—especially a needlework store!"

"You've done fine the times I've come in and found you behind the counter. Besides, we can help you."

"Who's 'we'?"

"First and foremost, the people Margot hired to work in the shop. Some of them have worked in that place for years and know all about running it. And there's the Monday Bunch."

" 'Monday Bunch'?"

"Today's Monday, so you'll meet them today. They'll turn up around two. They meet to talk and do needlework. Give advice. Help out. Buy supplies. When it's my day off, I join them. Like today. But I decided to come over early to warn you they'll be here, and see if there's anything that needs doing. Have you been into the shop?"

Betsy felt her shoulders tighten. "I don't want to go down there."

"What, you think the police are going to clean up?"

Betsy thought to reply sharply, and instead asked with genuine curiosity, "Who cleans up after a murder?"

"Unfortunately, that's left to the survivors. There are companies you can hire to clean up horrible messes, like after an ax murder or deaths that don't get discovered for weeks and weeks."

"Please!"

"You asked. You don't want to hire someone in this case, unless you can find someone who also knows floss and silk and wool and canvases, so they don't just dump it all in bags and toss it. And, of course, you'd have to supervise them if they do know about it so they don't walk off with the good stuff."

"Sure. Okay."

"You don't have to do it right this minute, of course."

Jill's tone seemed familiar, and Betsy glanced up. Was there the merest hint of a twinkle in those ice-blue eyes?

Still. "I just can't go down there, Jill."

"Sure you can. I'll come with you. Come on, let's go right now and see how bad it is. Up, up, on your feet. Whoops, shoes first, want me to fetch them?"

Jill in this mode was like a bulldozer, and Betsy was too exhausted to resist.

The shop was even worse than Betsy remembered. The damp air seemed to have gotten into all the fibers, dimming their colors and making them sink down on themselves in hopeless tangles. Even turning on all the lights didn't help; it only made the ruin clearer.

The long triple row of wooden stems on the wall that had held skeins of needlepoint wool was nearly empty, and some of the stems were broken. Most of the wool was in a crooked, broken drift along the floor, as if someone had scuffed his feet through it.

Pyramids of knitting yarn had been kicked apart, baskets

crushed and broken, magazines torn. The burglar didn't seem to have missed any opportunity to wreak havoc.

"What, was he angry at something?" wondered Betsy aloud.

"Some burglars get upset when there's nothing of value to steal," said Jill, squatting beside a heap of knitting wool and starting to untangle skeins from a webbing of loose yarn.

"Then why did he break in in the first place?" demanded Betsy. Goaded by Jill's labors, she went to the wall where the drift of wool was and stooped to begin sorting by color. The skeins were not actually skeins, but working lengths gently knotted by color. Betsy remembered a customer who had bought a single strand of orange, all she needed to finish a project. The wool was soft in her fingers.

"Because he's a burglar; that's what they do."

They worked in silence for perhaps ten minutes, then Betsy said, "Could it be he was looking for something?"

"For what?"

"I don't know. But the way things are all pulled off the shelves and walls—it's just odd, somehow. It would have to be something small, I guess."

Jill said impatiently, "What could he have been looking for, small *or* big? Nothing in the store is hidden; all the stock is on display." She had found a usable basket, dented on one side, and was putting intact balls of knitting yarn into it.

"Yeah, well, I wonder if anything's missing."

"You'll have to take an inventory."

"I suppose so."

"We'll help," said Jill, apparently sensing her dauntedness.

"Who, you and the Monday ladies? I thought you said not to trust people who knew silk from wool."

Jill did not reply to this, and after a moment's reflection

Betsy realized how insulting that sounded, but she did not take it back or say anything more.

They had made barely a dent in the mess by lunchtime, when, prodded by her conscience, Betsy took Jill upstairs and made a tuna salad to share with her.

While putting the plates in the sink, Betsy heard Jill say something and turned off the water to ask, ''What was that?''

''I said, where's Sophie?''

Betsy felt a sudden chill. The cat!

''Did she follow us down to the shop?'' inquired Jill.

Betsy shook her head. ''I haven't seen her for a long time. Days. Since . . . since that night. Since Margot.''

''What?'' Jill was staring at her.

''I forgot all about her. I'm sorry, but it's true, I haven't seen her since I left that evening to pick you up.'' She felt stricken.

Jill seemed about to say something, changed her mind, and said instead, ''This is very . . . odd. You know how she is when it gets to be suppertime and there's nothing in her dish.''

''Indeed, yes. But maybe—does she go off by herself?''

''No, never. I wonder if—no, if she had somehow gotten locked in the shop, she would have come out as soon as we came down there, crying over being left so long.'' Jill, frowning, began opening floor-level cabinets and looking inside. ''Maybe she's scared and hiding because Margot hasn't come home. Have you heard a cat crying?''

''No. I would have been reminded if I heard her, and gone looking.''

''Yes, of course you would. Well, this is really strange.'' Jill closed the last cabinet door, and puffed her cheeks then released the air slowly. ''It's darned odd, in fact.''

''Maybe she is down there, in the store,'' Betsy said. ''Maybe she got kicked or stepped on or—something.''

They hurried down the stairs and through the back hall into the shop. A thorough search proved fruitless.

"Well, I'll be dipped," said Jill.

"Whatever could have happened to her?" Betsy, shying away from worry over Sophie's fate, began instead to consider this as a piece of the greater puzzle. "She was here Wednesday. Margot was out all day, she went to the museum and then somewhere else, she didn't get home until after we closed up, and then she was in a hurry to get changed to go do her presentation at City Hall. So that day I fed Sophie both her breakfast and her supper. I remember Sophie followed me downstairs to the shop in the morning, and came back up with me at lunchtime, hoping for a snack. Which I was told I shouldn't give her, so I didn't. And she came up with me again when the shop closed at five, and I fed her supper."

"And she was in the apartment when you left?"

"Yes, she followed me to the door as I was leaving for your place. Margot was still there." Betsy stooped to pick up the sorted clusters of wool and put them on the table. "Jill, do you know if Margot actually went to City Hall?"

"Yes, that was checked. The council meeting started around seven-fifteen and broke up a little after nine-fifteen. Some members stood around talking with her for half an hour or so, and then Mayor Jamison offered her a ride home; but it had stopped raining and she said she wanted to walk." Jill went to the white dresser and began carefully lifting out painted canvases, shaking her head over the ones badly bent by being caught in a drawer.

"Where else did she go that day? Do you know?"

"She went to the Minneapolis art museum."

"Yes, but would that take all day? How long does it take to make one of those needlepoint canvas paintings?"

Jill shrugged. "I don't think she was going to paint it, just do some sketches, take notes. I don't know how long that takes."

"Not all day. I wonder where else she went? Who else she saw?"

"You can ask around, I guess. Probably Mike has already."

Betsy said, "Well, we know she didn't see someone in the shop on her way home and go in to confront him."

"We do?"

"Yes, because now we know Sophie was with her. She had to go upstairs and then hear something and come down with the cat. Probably she heard the noise he made breaking in."

Jill said, "The lock wasn't forced, or the door broken. The assumption is, he tried the front door and it wasn't locked."

"It was locked, I locked it when I closed up."

Jill didn't say that maybe Betsy only thought she locked it, but her face showed it.

"I did lock it," repeated Betsy stubbornly.

"Okay, you locked it," said Jill. "He picked the lock. But about Sophie: I think you must be right, she came down with Margot. And was frightened by what followed, and ran out the open front door. You said you found it partly open."

"Yes, that's true. But, Jill, if I was going to sneak downstairs to see if there was a burglar, I sure wouldn't bring a cat with me."

Jill shrugged. "Maybe Margot opened the door, and Sophie sort of darted out. And maybe Margot didn't see her."

Betsy snorted. "Not see her? Twenty pounds of white longhair who insists on leading the way? Anyhow, Sophie doesn't dart, she ambles."

Jill shrugged again and returned to lifting out canvases.

"No, listen to me," said Betsy. "I'm trying to picture how this happened. Margot's just gotten home—"

"How do you know that?" interrupted Jill. "Maybe she'd been home an hour."

"Maybe, she got home at ten and I got home at eleven. But she was the kind who takes off her good clothes right away. She would put on something casual to lounge around in, or her pajamas if it was close to bedtime. But she was wearing her good clothes—'' Betsy paused to swallow, then shook her head determinedly and continued, ''So she hadn't been home more than a couple of minutes. Now, suppose she heard someone breaking in downstairs and decided to go down and get a description for the police. Apart from that being one of the dumber things you can do, it's beyond belief that she'd bring a cat along. Even if she did open the door and Sophie walked out, you'd think she'd have got in front of her and herded her back inside. Sophie's a good cat, she lets herself be herded. Anyone with brains would have done that; you don't want a big white cat going ahead and letting the burglar know someone's coming, *or* hanging around your ankles and tripping you, *or* getting in the way in case you have to hurry back to the apartment and call the cops. *Which* is what she would have done in the first place, so I don't understand why she ended up down here to begin with!'' Betsy had been getting more heated in her argument as she became more convinced of its soundness.

She turned away from Jill's doubting look and walked toward the back. She paused by the big heap of yarn, floss, packets of thread wax, yarn organizers, scissors, magnets, and bead nabbers, leavened with counted cross-stitch graphs, needlework books and magazines, then turned to reach for the nearest upholstered chair and put it back on its feet facing the mess. She sat down and reached for a fistful.

''This is just terrible!'' she continued in the same angry voice, lifting her arm high and wriggling it to shake a packet of soft thimbles off. Soft thimbles belonged on the other side of the back area, with the counted cross-stitch stuff. So things weren't just tumbled off shelves, they were kicked or even carried around and dropped. ''It must have taken the burglar hours to get things this tangled up!'' she grumbled.

She looked again at the heap, dropped everything, and

said in an entirely different voice, "Now, that's *really* crazy."

"What is?" Jill had come to turn the other chair over.

"All this stuff piled up here." Betsy gestured at the mess in front of her. "If he was doing this for hours before Margot came in and stopped him, why didn't she notice it when she came home? Because there would have been a light on. He couldn't do this thorough a job in the dark."

"Flashlight," said Jill.

Betsy thought, then nodded. "Okay, flashlight. He sees her shape as she passes the window and turns it off. But how about this? When they brought me in to identify Margot, she was there." Betsy pointed toward the back wall, where there was a dark stain on the carpet, which until now she had almost succeeded in not noticing. "And see the edge to the way this stuff is heaped up? It looked that night as if she'd been buried in it, and they had to uncover her."

Jill nodded. "They did, Mike told me that. And?"

"So that would mean he kept on trashing the place *after* he killed her, dumping stuff on top of her. If he was angry there was nothing to steal, wouldn't killing the owner be enough? I mean, doesn't hitting someone over the head sort of take away anger and make you start to worry about going far away really fast?"

For the first time Jill really looked interested.

"No," Betsy continued, "he was looking for something, that's why he tore the place up. I think he came in here specifically looking for something. And he killed Margot and then kept on looking."

"But what?" said Jill. "There isn't anything secret or hidden in the store. Margot kept her valuables upstairs. Are you telling me she had some kind of secret?"

"If it was a secret, why would she tell me?"

Jill said, mildly exasperated, "If she did have a secret, she wouldn't go hiding an important clue to it in her shop, where people come and go all the time."

"Maybe she didn't know it was a clue."

Now Jill was totally back to disbelief. "Yeah, right; Margot had a secret, and she had a clue to it she didn't know was a clue; nevertheless she hid this clue she didn't know she had in her store. But someone knew she had it and that it was hidden in here. That sounds like a plot for the worst mystery novel ever written."

But Jill's sarcastic tone only fed Betsy's stubborn certainty that there was something wrong with the burglar theory.

On the other hand, she didn't know what else to offer as proof. She said nothing, and got serious about picking up and sorting.

Jill apparently didn't know what else to say, either, and went back out front to work. The two continued sorting wool and cotton yarn, thread, and floss by color, picking up canvases and fabric and smoothing them on the table, finding magazines that were only rumpled instead of torn, putting crushed baskets into a pile, sorting thimbles (soft and metal), knitting needles and crochet hooks on the desk, and wrapping loose yarn around their hands. At two, they heard someone knock at the front door.

Jill went to unlock and open the door, and stand back to let three women and their umbrellas come in. They were middle-aged ladies in slacks, complicated sweaters, and bright head scarves, each carrying a bulging canvas tote bag. They stood inside the shop, staring with dismayed faces at the wreckage.

Jill introduced them as "Patty, Alice, Kate," and said they were from the Monday Bunch.

Betsy came to say an uncomfortable hello. She was in no mood to host a gathering, and in any case didn't know what was expected of her with this group.

"We are so dreadfully sorry about Margot," said one of them, starting them all off on expressions of sympathy.

Betsy didn't know what to say to that, either. "Thank you," was all she could think of, said over and over.

"Well," said the stoutest of them at last, putting her bag and purse on the table. "Where do you want us to start?"

"How about you go up in front, Pat," said Jill immediately, "and pick up all those buttons and the bead packets. Put the whole packets into this basket, and the loose beads into this jar. And you, Kate, sit down here and I'll bring you the loose yarn as I gather it, and you can start making balls. If it's dirty, set it aside—here's a wastebasket. And Alice, come over here, we've got all this perle cotton on the floor, see what you can salvage." Jill went back to rescuing canvases and Betsy to sorting and smoothing graphs. With five people working, in half an hour there was a noticeable difference in the shop.

Betsy was glad she was in the back of the shop so her inability to contribute to the conversation going on up front wasn't as noticeable. The women discussed the best catalog source for patterns, how old the grandchildren had to be before teaching them to stitch, whether or not aida came in twenty-five count, what to do when your knitting yarn starts to kink, needleworkers who had shamefully messy backs on their projects, overdyed versus watercolors, small laying tools—until Jill (apparently hearing the silence from the back of the room) said, "Can't we talk about something besides needlework?" which surprised them as much as it gratified Betsy.

Obediently, one said, "I saw they caught that man who stole that painting."

"What painting?" asked another.

"A famous one. It was being delivered to Sotheby's New York for an auction, and he took it right off the truck. A Monet?"

"It was a Manet," said Betsy, glad at last to be able to contribute. "And they found the painting first, which led them to the thief. Apparently the buyer reneged."

There was a silence. Betsy looked around the shelves to find them all looking at her inquiringly. "Margot wrote to me about it,'' said Betsy. ''She said that when a valuable painting like that disappears, it very often is stolen to order. When someone with more money than morals wants a Rembrandt or a Monet or a Rubens, he mentions it to the right person, who will arrange to steal it. In this case, the buyer got scared for some reason and backed off. So the thief had to try to get rid of it through a dealer, and the dealer turned him in.''

One of the ladies said, ''How interesting,'' but not as if she meant it.

They worked in an uncomfortable silence until Betsy announced she was going to start the coffee urn perking and, for good measure, go upstairs for cookies. When she got back, the women were comfortably deep into a discussion of which was the best evenweave: luguna, jobelan, or jubilee.

Jill saw her coming and gave her an ''I tried'' shrug, to which Betsy replied with an ''I understand'' shrug back.

The women broke off their work and came gratefully to the table to drink and eat. ''Nice coffee,'' said one.

''Good cookies,'' said another—kindly, because they had been bought at the bakery four days ago and there is only so much a cookie jar can do.

''I don't know who was responsible for that funeral, but it was quite, quite wonderful,'' said one of the women.

''I don't think I ever—'' started another.

''Sophie's gone missing,'' interrupted Jill firmly, her eye caught by a pleading look from Betsy.

''What?''

''Yes, we've looked everywhere and we can't find her,'' said Betsy.

The ladies stared at Betsy.

''I'm sorry,'' apologized Betsy, not sure for what.

''Did you call the humane society?'' asked one of the ladies, the one who had been rolling yarn. ''That's where they take found animals.''

"N-no," stammered Betsy, now aware of what she should be ashamed of.

"Of course she didn't, poor thing," said Jill. "She's had far bigger things on her mind."

The lady who had been rolling yarn put it down, went to the checkout desk, found the phone, and dialed a number. "I volunteer over there," she said while waiting for someone to answer. "Hi," she said into the phone. "We're looking for a lost cat—yes, it's me; hi, Merle. A lost cat. Last Wednesday, in Excelsior. A white Persian cross, pastel tortie on top of the head, along the back, and all of the tail. *Big* cat, close to twenty pounds, female spay, no front claws. Very friendly. No collar. Answers to Sophie and any sound that means food. Yes, I'll hold." She smiled at the others, and they all waited in silence. After a while she said, "Thanks," and hung up. "No cat matching that description found."

There was a collective sad sigh from the Monday Bunch.

"We can still get an ad in the weekly paper," said the woman who had been picking up buttons and beads. "And maybe if we put up posters—is there a photo of her?"

Betsy shrugged. "I don't know. I could look, I guess."

"I'm sure there is," said Jill; and to the bunch: "Remember those pictures Margot took at the Christmas party?"

That brought smiles and comments.

The humane-society volunteer said, "Give me the best one. I finally figured out how to use that scanner on my computer, and my son gave me a really nice publishing program for my birthday, so I can make up some attention-getting posters. We'll put them up right away. Why, it wouldn't be the same store without Sophie in it." She looked around, saw the faces looking back, and a little silence fell. It wasn't going to be the same no matter what, they all were thinking.

And Betsy didn't have the heart right then to say there wasn't going to be a shop at all.

9

The shop looked almost normal, if you didn't look too close. Jill shut off the vacuum and one of the Monday Bunch pulled the plug. It was close to five o'clock. They had turned away six people; one, a part-time employee, was coming tomorrow to help with inventory.

"Count up what you have left, how much is ruined, and all that," said Jill, with a look in her eye that warned Betsy it still wasn't time to tell anyone she planned to close the shop.

"I think—" Betsy started to say anyway, but was interrupted by another knock at the door.

This time it was a handsome man of about thirty with fine dark eyes. He was standing under a big black umbrella, though it had stopped raining. He was wearing a good gray suit and carrying a large briefcase that looked older than he was.

"Hello, Mr. Penberthy," said Jill.

That was the name, this was Margot's attorney. Betsy had meant to call him today but hadn't gotten around to it.

"Ms. Devonshire?" he said, looking at Betsy.

"Yes?" she said.

"I was out of town, closing our cabin at the lake, and so missed this entire sad business of your sister's death. I was shocked to hear the news, and I hope you will accept my belated condolences." He spoke with a formality that somehow made him seem even younger.

"Thank you," said Betsy.

He made his umbrella collapse. "I hope you don't mind my just stopping by. I've been calling your apartment today without an answer, then someone told me you were in the shop." He put down his briefcase while he fastened the umbrella shut. "I live right across the street from you, so I decided to stop on my way home. Perhaps you know, I was Margot's attorney."

"Yes, I'd heard your name; how do you do, Mr. Penberthy?" Betsy extended her hand.

Penberthy had a nice, warm handclasp. The Monday Bunch began to make hasty excuses for leaving. Pat—was it Pat?—went out waving the photo of Sophie and promising, "All over town by nightfall!" which made Penberthy blink after her.

"Sophie's missing. Margot's cat," explained Betsy. "They're going to put up posters."

"I hope you get her back," said Mr. Penberthy politely, and followed her through the shop and up the back stairs to the apartment.

The lawyer declined the offer of a cup of coffee or a cookie, saying his supper was waiting.

He took a chair at the little round table in the dining nook and opened his briefcase.

"How much do you know about your's sister's financial condition?" he asked.

"Almost nothing," replied Betsy, and when she saw him notice how her fists were clenched on the table, she dropped them into her lap.

"Do you know the names of any heirs besides yourself?" he asked.

"I don't think there are any."

Penberthy nodded. "Yes, Margot once told me there was only her sister. That's the reason I could not persuade her to make a will, because everything was going to come to you in any case." He pulled a thick file folder with the name Margot Berglund on it from his briefcase. Betsy stared at it, then at Mr. Penberthy, who was smiling.

"This won't take long," he reassured her. "Most of the papers in here have to do with her ongoing quarrel with Mr. Mickels, the owner of this building."

"Yes, Margot told me about him, about how he's trying to get her to move out and suing her for things. She said you were taking care of all that." She added bitterly, "But I suppose he's won, now."

"That is not the case at all," he said.

Betsy hastily suppressed a triumphant smile. "I don't see how," she said.

"Well, first of all, there is this rather strange lease," said Penberthy, picking quickly through the documents and finding it. It had been typed as an original on ordinary typing paper, rather than filled in as a form or properly done on legal-size paper. "This lease was, I believe, drawn up rather carelessly, probably by the original owner himself. It is my opinion that the lessor at that time felt the lessee would not stay the full term of the lease." A glance showed she did not understand, and he started again. "That is, I don't think the original Mr. Mickels thought your sister would stay in business very long. That's why the rent was set so low, and that's why there are some curious omissions in the terms of the lease. For example, he failed to include a restriction on the assignment of the lease. That's where the current situation arises." Again he noticed she didn't understand.

"Normally a lease will state that the lessee—the renter—can't turn the lease over to someone else without the prior, written consent of the lessor—the landlord. This lease does not have that restriction. When your sister incorporated, she assigned the lease to the corporation, so it remains in force.''

"What corporation?"

"Crewel World. Your sister incorporated herself, and named two officers, herself as president and you as vice-president."

"She did?"

"She didn't tell you about this?"

"No. When did all this happen?"

"She began the process some weeks ago, and only signed the final papers last Wednesday."

"She came to see you the day she died?"

He raised an eyebrow. "Why, yes, she did die on that Wednesday evening, didn't she? How . . . dreadful."

"I thought you were out of town that day."

"I left right after I finished with her, and didn't get back until late Sunday evening. Long Lake is three hours from here, and my cabin has no phone or electricity. My grand-parents bought it in the twenties and added two rooms on to it, but preferred to get right away from modern conve-niences. I spent many summers up there as a boy. When I inherited it, I kept it just as they had left it. It's a dozen yards from the lake, and there have been loons nesting near the dock for as long as anyone can remember—'' Penber-thy brought himself back from his vacation with a little start. "Sorry."

"Margot never mentioned incorporating to me," said Betsy.

"Perhaps she meant to tell you once it was all done, and . . . and never got a chance."

"Yes, that might be. What time did she come to see you?"

Penberthy took a few seconds to think about it. "Her appointment was for two o'clock, but she was about five minutes late, which isn't like her. She apologized, I re-member."

"How long was she there?"

"Not very long. Perhaps half an hour. I had closed up and was on the road before three."

"Did she say where she was going next?"

"No, I assumed it was home." Penberthy looked around. "Are you going to keep the apartment, too? It hasn't got the same kind of lease the store has, you know."

"I don't know, yet."

"You are going to keep the shop open, aren't you?"

Betsy started to say no, but instead said, "I haven't finalized my plans. Does Mr. Mickels know about this incorporation?"

"I don't know how he could."

Her voice sharpened. "You mean she didn't tell him?"

"It is not required by law that she inform him ahead of time, if that's what you're asking. And again, I don't think there was time between the signing of the documents and . . . her demise."

"Then I know," she whispered. "I know. Thank you very much for coming by, Mr. Penberthy," she said, rising. "This has been very enlightening."

"But—" he began.

"Good-bye, Mr. Penberthy," she repeated, more firmly, and walked to the door.

He followed unwillingly. "I'll call you tomorrow," he promised. "There are still a great many details you need to be advised of."

"Okay. Or how about I call you later this week?" She all but pushed him out the door, closing it in his face as he turned to say something more.

Betsy slammed the door shut and ran to the phone. Margot had a list of phone numbers taped to the wall beside it, and Jill's number was first under the Cs.

Jill answered on the second ring, and Betsy said, "I got it, I knew there was something, and I've got it!"

"Got what?"

"The proof! Motive! Everything! Margot was murdered, I knew there was something funny about the whole burglary thing, and now I know who did it!''

"What are you talking about?"

"Mr. Penberthy was just here, and he told me about that legal business between Margot and Joe Mickels, over the lease. He wanted her out, she wouldn't go, there's a thick file of all the legal tricks he's been playing trying to get her out. So at last he just killed her!" Betsy made a huge gesture of triumph at the ceiling. "And now there's this incorporation thing! It's clear as daylight!"

"What are you talking about? How could Mr. Penberthy give you proof that Joe Mickels is a *murderer*?"

"Mickels tried every way he could think of to get Margot to give up and move out, but she wouldn't budge. And his threats turned ugly, so she decided to protect herself by incorporating—see, you can't murder a corporation! But she was waiting to sign the final papers before she told him—and he murdered her before she got a chance! Or maybe he somehow found out what she intended to do and tried to kill her before the deal could go through. Penberthy says Joe didn't know, don't you see? I told you that burglar idea was all wrong! And now we know he did it! Who do I tell, how do I get him arrested?"

"Betsy, Betsy, calm down. Take a breath, for heaven's sake. Tell me, exactly what did Mr. Penberthy say?"

"He doesn't know Joe Mickels did it, of course. But he showed me this thick file of legal stuff, the record of the fight Mickels and Margot have been having over the shop. Mickels wanted Margot to move out so he could tear down this building and put up a bigger one."

"Yes, I know. And?"

"Well, don't you see? Murdering Margot didn't do him any good. Margot finished incorporating, you see, and there was something wrong with the lease, some kind of assignment thing, which she did, so I get the shop. So it doesn't mean a thing, not a thing, that he murdered her!"

Jill, trying to understand, said, "So because it doesn't mean a thing, that's proof he murdered her?"

Betsy nearly shouted yes, then swallowed the word whole. Because that wasn't what she meant. What had she meant? Her "proof" that Mickels had murdered her sister was gone as suddenly as a hatful of smoke.

"Betsy?"

"Huh?"

"Are you all right?"

"I guess not." Betsy dropped the receiver back into its cradle and went to sit on the couch in the living room. What was the matter with her?

She remembered back when menopause had started, how she'd suddenly be overcome with some notion: to devote all her spare time to gardening or the study of medieval history, or becoming a vegetarian. She'd start with great determination and energy, only to wake from the vision in a week or a month and wonder what on earth she had been thinking of.

This seemed an echo of that curious time. Where on earth—she suddenly remembered that she was out of estrogen, had been for over two weeks. She'd meant to get here, find a doctor, get a new prescription, but of course all that had flown out of her head because of Margot's death.

So menopause was back. And where some people get hot flashes, Betsy got hot ideas.

She ran the conversation with Mr. Penberthy over in her head, looking for something that might actually point to Joe Mickels as a murderer.

What the attorney had given her was confirmation of the legal battle between her sister and her sister's landlord, and the incorporation trick Margot had pulled on him. Margot hadn't realized it might be important to tell Mickels right away. Well, maybe it wasn't important, maybe he wasn't the murderer. But there was the place Betsy had jumped off, assuming Margot was murdered because she failed to tell Joe Mickels. What had their mother called notions with no substance to them? Snow on your boots. Nothing but snow on her boots, sliding off as soon as you took two steps, melting as soon as you came inside.

No wonder Penberthy had stared at her so strangely. What he must have thought!

She suddenly realized that he had come to tell her about her sister's estate—and that they hadn't gotten to that. She was sure her sister wasn't rich, but maybe there was an IRA or life-insurance policy or something somewhere. And Betsy had wanted to ask what she needed to do to close the shop and turn whatever there was into cash so she could get out of this place.

She would definitely call Penberthy tomorrow. She went to the refrigerator and wrote on Margot's sheet of lined paper under Margot's magnet shaped like a sheep, *Call Penberthy*, and underlined it and put three exclamation marks after it. Then she started looking for something to fix for supper.

She hoped there was enough money to keep her in sandwiches until the closing sale was over. Funny she hadn't told Penberthy she wasn't staying.

Soon she'd have to figure out how to use Margot's computer. Margot had access to the Internet, and surely a search engine could find a Web site that would tell her how to get on that trailer-park waiting list.

Jill tried to lose herself in her current needlepoint project, but her concern about Betsy kept getting in the way of her concentration. The ultrasuede she was using for the horse's hide, not sturdy to begin with, kept getting frailer and frailer because she kept having to unstitch the section she was working on.

When she had first met Margot's sister, she had thought she was a live one, full of wit and good humor, just the kind of person she liked.

Now she was concerned for the woman's sanity. Betsy was shut down tight except for these nutso eruptions—Joe Mickels a murderer, for Pete's sake!

And wanting to close Crewel World. Well, that was more understandable. Betsy wasn't Margot and didn't have Margot's investment in Excelsior, and she didn't know how the store was a warm center of activity for the action-minded. Probably she wasn't a do-gooder like Margot had been in any case. And now the murder had taken away her chance to learn what Margot meant to the town and its people.

Jill put down the needlework. Whenever she was alone and any thought of Margot happened by, she had to stop whatever she was doing because her eyes filled. God, how she missed Margot! All her friends loved Margot's warmth and borrowed from her bottomless store of ideas and energy. But Margot and Jill had become closer than that. Jill was a good little Norwegian. She didn't show her emotions in public, or even to many close friends, but with Margot it had been different. With Margot she could let down all the barriers, talk about how tough it was being a cop, how her boyfriend was pressuring her to quit and start a family with him. And how tempted she was to do just that. Margot had listened, allowed Jill to talk until Jill herself understood that, for now, her sense of duty would not allow her to quit and be happy about it. But she had also nourished Jill's sense of humor until if Jill chose to laugh right out loud, laugh till her sides ached, that was okay, too. With Margot it was all right, with Margot—Jill sobbed once aloud, startling herself. Get a grip, she told herself. Get a grip.

It really wasn't fair that Margot should have died at the hands of someone who could have asked for her help and gotten it, gladly. Margot was always helping—kids with heart problems, people down on their luck, even Prisoner's Aid.

That did it; Jill broke down and wept bitterly. When the storm ended, she went to the bathroom and washed her face.

Back in the living room she picked up her project, found

her place, and resolutely stuck the needle in. If she could get into the rhythm of the needlework, she would find peace. That's why she loved needlepoint—it worked like meditation. It was better than meditation, actually, because after a while you found you had both peace of mind and a work of art.

In another minute she was calm and could think some more about what Betsy had asserted. The woman had been right about one thing: Margot had no business sneaking down those stairs to see who was burgling her store. It was a stupid thing to do, and Margot was nobody's fool.

So maybe there was something to Betsy's insistence that there was more to this than Detective Mike Malloy was saying.

But if it wasn't a burglar, then—who? To think Joe Mickels had turned into a murderer in order to break a lease—that was ridiculous!

Yes, yes, Joe wanted Margot out of his building. Jill recalled when Joe had made one of his early moves, thinking that if he got everyone else out, Margot would surrender. So he had sent out eviction notices and soon, except for Margot, the place was empty. Little good it did him. Margot was one of those short, thin women who looked like dandelion fluff, but who was actually made of steel. She wasn't proud or needlessly stubborn, but she knew the real value of Crewel World: what it meant to the stitchers in the area, to the women of Excelsior—to all of Excelsior, really. She had come to her full strength and purpose after her husband died, and Joe had been a fool not to see that. He'd ended up getting new tenants for the other two stores, and new renters for the apartments. None of them seemed very worried about the month-to-month conditions under which they rented, probably because they were locals and knew something about Margot.

But greedy and impatient as Joe Mickels was, Jill couldn't believe he'd resort to murder.

No, this was just Betsy wild to find closure, to get someone arrested. Jill was sure this was some peculiar form of mourning, that what she needed to do was cry her eyes out—Jill had a feeling Betsy hadn't shed any tears over this yet—and then she'd straighten up.

But meanwhile, what if she called Mike?

Or contacted some reporter?

Lord, what a stink that would make!

Jill leaned sideways and lifted the receiver of the phone off its base on the end table. Dialing swiftly, she was rewarded with a busy signal. She disconnected, waited, and tried again. Still busy. She'd better get over there.

10

Irene Potter struggled with her harried nerves until finally a good and necessary calm came over her. This was her great opportunity, and she must not, must not, must not mess it up.

She began quite coolly to reason this out, to be sure she was right in her plan of action.

Margot was dead, dead and buried, any quarrel between them gone, forgotten.

Excelsior had had a needlework shop for a very long time, and it was not right to discontinue that tradition.

Betsy Devonshire might be Margot's sister, but she didn't even know how to knit, and Shelly had said she didn't know anything at all about running a needlework shop.

Whereas Irene Potter knew everything about needlework, and almost everything about running a small business.

And she had over sixty thousand dollars in savings.

Therefore it was right, good, and proper that Irene should take over that shop.

Sixty thousand wasn't really enough, of course. Though

if Ms. Devonshire was as ignorant as she seemed to be, it might do. If not, then it would serve as a down payment.

With her energy and knowledge, Irene knew she could make a much bigger success of a needlework shop than Margot. After all, Margot hadn't needed to make a living out of it, as Irene did. So it was clear that she, Irene Potter, should take over the needlework shop.

And when she did, then everyone would see that she was good at this! She'd show those people who said she wasn't any good with people! When they had to come to her, then they'd see; the shop would be wonderful, better than before, and everyone would love her for ensuring that the tradition continued.

That thought set off an almost painful excitement, and she had to stop and take several calming breaths. That made her smile. Jill was always saying that: take a breath. Amusement calmed her nerves to steadiness.

Then she got into her raincoat, took up her umbrella, made sure her savings book was in her purse, and left her room. Outside, on the sidewalk, she raised herself onto her toes, pivoted in the direction of the lake, and began walking.

Jill's sharp questioning had brought Betsy to her senses, but she still had felt restless, needing to do something. So she went down to the shop and found the list of employees and their phone numbers, brought it up, and started calling. Before long she found two more of them available to help with inventory tomorrow during the day. Also, Shelly could come after twelve, and another would come by after five to help Shelly take up where the day workers left off.

One of the part-timers who had done inventory before said it would take at least two days, maybe three if it was as bad as Betsy said. This person—a male, oddly enough—recommended she call the insurance agent, which she did (TWENTY-FOUR-HOUR SERVICE his calendar on the kitchen wall advertised). Betsy wasn't up to seeing him tonight, so he would also come by tomorrow.

The phone rang. It seemed as if every time she hung up, it rang again. It was, as before, someone with a cat they thought might be Sophie. This one, by the description, was a kitten.

"No, Sophie's big, really big. Huge," Betsy said. "But thank you for calling, and I hope you find the owner of the kitten."

She had no more than taken her hand off the phone when the doorbell rang. She went to push the button that released the lock. She should go down and unlock it and stick up a note: *Bring Alleged Sophies Up to Apartment One*.

So far two people had come by with cats. The first time, seeing the large heap of white fluff in the woman's arms, her heart had leaped with joy—but it hadn't been Sophie.

The second one, brought in a carrier, hadn't any white on it at all.

It was sad and disturbing to realize how many homeless cats there were in just this small town.

So she was really surprised when she opened the door this time and it was Joe Mickels standing there.

Betsy nearly slammed the door in his face, but restrained herself. Still, she managed a good degree of frost in her voice as she asked, "What do you want?"

"We've got some business to discuss, Ms. Devonshire," he said. His voice was calm, so decided a contrast to his fierce expression that it occurred to her his face looked that way naturally. "May I come in? This won't take long."

"Very well." She stepped back and led him into the living room. Because she did not want him to sit in her sister's chair, she took it, and when she did, he sat on the love seat.

"I understand you are taking inventory in the store."

"We haven't begun yet, we're still cleaning up after—"

The words choked her, she could not finish the sentence. "Anyhow how did you find that out?"

He showed a fierce grin. "This is a small town."

"Then perhaps you also know I have spoken with Mr. Penberthy," she said, allowing the ice to show once more, "and he tells me we need to complete an inventory to close the estate."

"Any idea how long that will take?"

"At least three days."

"I can find some helpers if you need them to hurry things along, and to help you set up for the going-out-of-business sale. How about I let you stay in the apartment until everything's finished?"

Something about this offer of a favor got her back up. "What if I decide to keep the shop open?"

"Of course you won't decide that," he said, his certainty now reaching the insufferable stage. "You can't, since the lease ended when your sister died."

"You're wrong. I have the option of continuing the operation of Crewel World."

It was wonderful to see his color change, to watch his eyes widen, then narrow, to see the way the nostrils in that beak of a nose widened. "What idiot told you that?"

"Mr. Penberthy told me that Margot incorporated herself and 'assigned' the lease to the corporation. I was made vice-president of the corporation, and I can keep Crewel World open if I want to."

If she wanted proof that Mickels had not been told about the incorporation, she got it. He jumped to his feet and flung his hands over his head. His raincoat spread itself wide, making him appear enormous in the low-ceilinged room. "That's not true!" he shouted. "I don't believe Penberthy told you that! This building is mine, this property is mine, and the lease died with your sister! You're out, d'you hear? Out! I'll get an eviction notice on you. You'll be out of that shop in thirty days, and this building will be gone before the ground freezes! I've waited too long for this, and I won't have you start in on me like Margot did!''

Betsy was on her feet now, too. Some little alarm was ringing, but she was beyond hearing it, and was about to make the big accusation when the alarm became a real sound, the sound of the doorbell pealing. It rang in one long noise that continued until she ran to push the door release.

She opened the apartment door to look out and see who had such an urgent need to see her.

In just seconds Irene Potter's excited face appeared in the stairwell, and when she saw Betsy waiting, she raised a thin arm to shake a wet umbrella at her. "I'm so glad to find you at home, Betsy!" she said, rushing up the stairs. "I have something exciting to tell you; I just could not wait!"

Betsy had to step aside or be sluiced down by Irene's wet raincoat as she brushed by.

Irene trotted into the living room, shedding water all the way and exclaiming about the weather and her breathless state. "I hurried over because I was afraid someone else might be talking to you, and I wanted to be the first if I could—" She stopped in mid-sentence to stare. "Why, Mr. Mickels, what are you doing here?"

"This is my building, I can come here if I like," he growled.

"Do you mean to tell me that you often call on your tenants?" Irene demanded, her tone suggesting she had a personal interest in his answer.

"I have business to discuss with Ms. Devonshire," he said, a little more mildly.

"Why, I'm here on business, too." Irene turned to Betsy. "No doubt you have heard that I am quite an expert needleworker," she began in a reasonable tone, but excitement got the better of her and she continued all in a rush, "and I want you to know that I have some private financial resources, and a great deal of experience in running a small business as both an employee of Crewel World and as former manager of Debbie's Gifts, so when you are ready to sell Margot's shop, I know you will give me right of first refusal.''

"I'm tearing down the building," announced Mickels.

"What? What? But that would spoil everything!"

"If it spoils some nutty plan you've concocted, then I'm twice as glad I can do what I like with my own property."

Irene approached Mickels like a cat approaching a dog, but the man stood his ground. She came so close her forehead was nearly touching his nose. Then she lifted her face to his—for an instant Betsy was horrified to think she was going to lay a big wet one right on his lips—but she only said with quiet certainty, "I am going to be the new owner of the best needlework shop in this part of the state, maybe in the whole state, and if you get in my way, I'll hurt you!"

This statement was in such marked contrast to Betsy's first thought that she giggled. Both of them turned on her.

"What's so funny?" they asked in near unison.

"The both of you," said Betsy. "You're both hilariously wrong. I don't know what I'm going to do about the shop, but I doubt I will sell it to you, Ms. Potter; and until I decide, and so long as the lease is in effect, you can't evict me, Mr. Mickels."

She walked over to Margot's chair and sat down. "What's more, I am so greatly offended by the two of you squabbling over the shop like vultures that I think I'll do whatever I can to keep either of you from profiting from Margot's death. In fact—"

Again Betsy was interrupted by the doorbell. She rose to answer it.

"Can't you just ignore it?" implored Irene. "I have a great deal to say to you. I'm sure if you'll just listen a minute—"

"It's like goddamn Grand Central Station around here," Mickels growled.

"It may be someone bringing Sophie home," said Betsy, and she pushed the release button.

"Who's Sophie?" she heard Mickels ask.

Irene explained, "It's that nasty cat Margot allowed in her store. I won't have animals in my store."

Betsy opened the door and saw Shelly coming up the stairs. She was carrying something about the size of a large cat wrapped in newspapers.

"What do you have there?" Betsy asked apprehensively.

"A hot dish. I wanted to bring you one last Thursday, but someone said you weren't receiving visitors, so I brought you one tonight. It's diced chicken with onion and celery, mixed with cream of mushroom soup and green beans, and crispy onions on top. I hope you like it. I'll just put it in the kitchen. It's still hot, that's why I wrapped it in newspapers, to keep it hot." Her voice had become less and less certain of her welcome as she approached. "Have I come at a bad time?"

"Uh, well, I do have some people here."

"Then I'll just leave this on the counter."

"Shelly? Is that you?" Irene called.

"Hi, Irene. I brought a hot dish."

"I've already eaten. But come in for a minute, will you?"

Betsy wondered where on earth Irene got the notion the hot dish was for her. She must think Betsy was going to invite her to dinner. As if!

Shelly obeyed. "What's up?"

"I want you to tell Betsy what a good business head I have, and how good my needlework is."

"Her needlework wins blue ribbons all the time," Shelly said obediently, raising her eyebrows at Betsy.

"She wants to buy Crewel World," said Betsy.

"She'll have to find a new place for it," warned Mickels.

"Yes, I was afraid of that," said Shelly to Mickels,

coming out of the kitchen. "Are you going to be okay, Betsy?"

"I think so, thanks."

"But I can make the store the talk of the county," Irene insisted, now arguing with all of them. "I've wanted to open my own store for years and years. You know that, Shelly, but Margot got hers started first, so there wasn't anything I could do till she got out of the way."

"That's a strange way of putting it, Irene," Shelly commented. "She didn't exactly decide on her own to step out of anyone's way. She was murdered." Her face was suddenly sad.

Irene shrugged. "Well, it's how I think of it. She wouldn't let me become her partner, so what could I do?"

"What do you mean?" asked Betsy sharply.

"What makes you think Betsy's going to sell Crewel World?" asked Shelly.

Irene turned to Betsy. "Of course you are, everyone knows that. You don't know how to run a store, and you don't know byzantine from basketweave."

Shelly said, "And you don't know how to be nice, Irene."

"I don't have to know how to do needlepoint to sell silk or cotton or metallic thread to people who do," said Betsy, who had been quick to pick up some terminology from her few days in the shop. She turned to include all three of them in her next words. "I think you should know there are some unanswered questions about my sister's death," she began, but before she could continue, the doorbell started ringing again. This time it rang in an urgent series of pulses that continued until she hurried to press the release button by the door.

"What the hell does that mean, there's 'unanswered questions'?" said Mickels from behind her.

"Who knows?" said Shelly. "This whole business is so horrible, we're all acting a little strange."

"I'm not," said Irene.

Betsy heard footsteps coming heavily up the stairs and opened the door.

Jill finished the last steps and hurried toward her. Her light-colored raincoat was rain-spattered and all bundled up in front, as if in her haste she had buttoned it wrong; and she held her arms across her breasts as if she were huddled against the wind or rain. "I found her," she said.

"Who?"

"Let me in, she's hurt."

"Who's hurt? What are you talking about?"

"It's Sophie." Jill brushed by her. "Find something I can put her down on," she ordered. "Quick!"

Betsy ran to the bathroom and brought back a large bath towel. She flipped it open and let it drape across the table in the dining nook. "Here," she said.

Jill ducked and maneuvered something out of her raincoat onto the towel. It was wet, filthy, and made a thin cry of protest.

"Oh, my God," Betsy whispered.

"Take it outside, quick!" cried Irene. "It's sick, it'll give all of us its germs!"

"She was by the Dumpster in back," said Jill. "I had to park back there, and when I got out, I thought I saw something move. I think she's hurt pretty bad."

Betsy bent over the animal. She took up a corner of the towel to wipe its forehead. The backs of her fingers brushed against a small ear. "Hot," she murmured.

"Fever," agreed Jill.

"I'll call her vet," Shelly offered.

The cat hardly looked like Sophie at all, except that it was large and had once, perhaps, been mostly white. The coat was a dirty gray, streaked with mud and dirt, the eyes wide and staring, and one back leg was misshapen in a strange way.

Mickels came to peer over Betsy's shoulder. "It's dying," he pronounced. "All a vet can do is put it to sleep, and he'll charge you money for that. Best just take it back outside and let nature take its course."

But Betsy continued wiping, down her back, on her side, down her front paws. "Oh, Sophie, Sophie," she crooned, wiping gently under the animal's chin. "Poor baby, poor suffering baby." She let the dirty edge of towel slip out of her hand and just used her fingers to stroke. The staring eyes began to close, the head to sink. Tears began gathering in Betsy's eyes; the cat was dying right here in front of her. She could hear Shelly speaking urgently on the phone. Should she stop her?

Her fingers paused.

"Awww, is she dead?" asked Jill.

"No," said Betsy, and burst into tears.

"She's dead, she's dead!" Irene cawed from the living room. "I'm going home, she's dead!" An instant later the door to the apartment slammed.

"I'm so sorry," said Jill, stooping to put a hand on Betsy's knee.

"No, no," said Betsy, through her sobs. "She's not dead, she's purring!"

Jill rose and put two fingers against Sophie's throat. "I'll be dipped," she said. "She *is* purring."

"It's just a damn cat," said Mickels. "It'll cost you plenty no matter what happens."

"Shut up, Joe!" said Jill. "Shelly, what's taking so long in there?"

"Hang on, hang on!" said Shelly. "Yes, I know where you are. About five minutes, I guess. Thanks, doctor." She came over to the table. "He'll meet us at his clinic out on Oak."

Jill carefully picked up Sophie, towel and all, and put her into Betsy's arms. "You're the miracle worker, she didn't purr for me. Let me get my car."

"Mine's out front," said Shelly, "and I know the way."

"Fine."

Shelly drove a big Dodge Caravan with doors that

opened when she pushed a device in her pocket. "Slick," approved Jill. "Let's go."

Sophie purred faintly all the way to the vet's office, and continued purring on the examination table. The vet complained, half-amused, that he could not hear her lung sounds very well. She even purred through the pitiful cry she emitted when he tried to work her knee joint. He opened her mouth and said she seemed shocky. But, he also said, she did not seem in imminent danger of dying. She stopped purring only when he administered the anesthetic in order to set her broken hind leg.

Out in the waiting room, Betsy said, "What do you think, she was back there all that while? Why didn't she cry when we were out looking for her?"

"Hurt animals often hole up," said Shelly. "It's instinct for a hurt animal to hide from predators."

"Like we were going to eat her for dinner," snorted Jill. She added, "I wonder how she got hurt. Hit by a car, maybe?"

"Running out the open front door of the shop," Betsy agreed. "This is so wonderful, finding her alive, I was so worried. . . ." She began to cry again.

"Here now, that's enough of that." Jill put an arm around Betsy and rubbed her shoulders briskly. "She's going to be fine. Tell me, who were you on the phone with a while ago?"

"Who not? I've been getting calls all evening from people who thought they'd found Sophie. And people have been coming by with likely candidates." She hiccuped and smiled. "Unlikely ones, too. But now we have her, thanks to you. We'll have to go around tomorrow and take down the posters. And cancel that ad."

Jill said incredulously, "Joe Mickels and Irene Potter brought over some cats for you to look at?"

"No, Joe came to evict me."

Jill leaned in and asked quietly, "You didn't accuse him of murder, did you?"

"I tried to, several times, but kept getting interrupted."

"Good. Say, you didn't tell anyone else about this weird notion you've got, did you? Mike, for instance?"

"Who's Mike?"

Jill sighed in relief. "Never mind." She continued, "But don't go spreading that suspicion about Mr. Mickels around, okay?"

"Irene Potter is just as good a suspect, you know."

"Oh, for heaven's sake, now you're pointing at *two* innocent people! Listen to me, Betsy: it was a burglary that went really wrong. It's a tragedy, an ugly, senseless tragedy, but that's what happened. Please, please, stop making wild accusations. You can get your butt sued, and those two are just the ones to do it."

"You're probably right." Betsy sniffled.

Shelly rummaged in her purse and produced a clean if wrinkled piece of tissue. "Here, kid."

"Thanks." Betsy blew, wiped. "I know I've been acting crazy the last few days. And I want to thank you both for caring about me anyhow."

"That's what friends are for, right?" said Jill.

"That's right," said Shelly, rubbing Betsy on the back. "We're with you, we'll see you through all of this. There are a whole lot of us who want to be your friends, who want to do anything they can, because you're Margot's sister, and we loved her."

"Oh, Margot," Betsy whispered, and this time when she wept, it was for that terrible loss.

11

Betsy had been afraid she'd wake with a sick headache from all the weeping, or emotionally exhausted from all the talking and sharing, of the night before. She also anticipated a state of anxiety over Sophie, who had a badly fractured leg and remained in the care of the vet.

But instead she woke refreshed and lay a minute, stretching slowly, lengthily, enjoying the energy that tickled along her nerves. And also enjoying a new and welcome clarity of thought.

Once upon a time, years ago, Betsy had been a morning person. She had, as she told her sister, "gotten over that." But now she felt almost as if she were back in her twenties, when merely waking up meant a clear mind and high hopes for the new day.

And it was not cockeyed optimism here and now. Terrible as things were, they were not as bad as she had thought. There was hope, there was even a chance for future joy.

What a sad, blind mess she'd been! It was as if Margot's death had plunged her into deep, murky water, where she'd paddled unseeing, unable to find the bottom with her feet, afraid all those around her wished her ill—when all the while the bottom was solid beneath her feet, and she'd been surrounded by people who wanted to be her friends, if only for Margot's sake.

Margot was dead. Her kind and talented sister had been cruelly murdered, reduced to gray ashes, put into a beautiful jar, and buried in the same grave that held her beloved Aaron. Someday the jar would break, and her ashes would wash down through the soil to mingle with Aaron's.

Maybe she could think of an epitaph to put on the stone that would evoke that thought.

Probably she could afford to do that. Shelly and Jill had been emphatically sure of it.

She sat up and fumbled on the floor with her toes for her slippers. According to Jill and Shelly, those few thousand dollars Betsy had found in Margot's checking accounts were small indicators of a sizable money source. Jill said Margot's late husband had left her very well-off. Shelly said she'd chosen to live in this modest apartment because it was convenient to the shop, that she had sold a fine big house because it was too big and too much trouble for just her.

So Penberthy had better be first on the agenda today. He could confirm the size of the estate—and more importantly, how to get hold of some of it, to pay bills and rent and Sophie's medical bills, and buy food. Betsy couldn't live on Shelly's no-longer-hot dish forever.

There was a little bread left, and coffee; she would make toast for breakfast. Then she would call Mr. Penberthy, and apologize for her behavior the other night. And ask how soon she could see him.

And after that, she would go visit Sophie, who was going to be fine. Maybe even bring her home.

Hud Earlie leaned back in the comfortably padded executive chair in his office and thought for a while.

He'd had to resort to a far less reliable source this time.

However, she was certain in her assertions that Betsy was a mess. Some things he already knew: Betsy had shut out people trying to help her and had arranged the cheapest funeral she could for her sister. Now she was hysterical over a sick cat. That wasn't all: she had told her landlord he couldn't reclaim his property and at the same time she refused to listen to an offer that would get her out from under a business she didn't know how to run. And, possibly weirdest of all, Betsy had hinted that her sister's death was not just a burglary gone wrong.

He remembered the witty woman with the happy eyes at Christopher Inn. This sure didn't sound like her.

Though it did kind of sound like the wounded person he had seen at the funeral. Poor broken thing, obviously in need of comfort.

Maybe he should give her a call. They could discuss . . . the fund-raiser, sure.

To hell with Margot's warning him off—she was dead. And to hell with his rules. What were rules for, if not to be broken?

And maybe he could be of some help to her.

Mickels sat at his desk in his office. He could have afforded a bigger desk in a large, well-lit corner office in a downtown Minneapolis tower. But why spend the money when he was just as comfortable in this little second-floor suite in Excelsior? Here he had three rooms, one with a window that overlooked Water Street. Years ago, at the bankruptcy auction of a business rival, he had bought an old, solid oak desk and matching armchair (on casters, not upholstered) and they had served him ever since. His personal assistant (as she styled herself, though he called her his secretary) had her own small windowless office. The third room, whose only entrance was through his office, was a reinforced and alarmed walk-in closet in which he kept his records. There were other employees, of course, who ran some of his other properties. Many people thought these employees were the owners, which suited Mickels just fine. They never came to this office, and Mickels himself rarely spent an entire day at this desk.

He was there this morning because he needed to think.

He pulled a yellow legal pad from the middle desk drawer and a cheap ballpoint from his pocket. He clicked the point out and drew a dollar sign on the notepad, then a circle around it and a diagonal line through it. If this incorporation business was true, his plans might be in trouble. That Devonshire woman had had that tone of voice people use when they'd won one, but some people were pretty good at faking it. Was she pleased because she was right, or pleased because he'd lost his temper believing her lie? He drew another dollar sign, this one sprouting wings. Was she crazy? She'd acted nuts when Officer Cross brought that hurt cat into the place—but that lady cop and the schoolteacher had been all excited as well. What was that all about?

Okay, okay, he remembered seeing a cat belonging to Margot in the store, a big fat thing, sleeping in a chair. (He was drawing a cat's head, with crosses for eyes, as he thought this.) He didn't remember its name, but it had been white, like the hurt cat might have been under the dirt. So maybe it was Margot's cat. So what? Betsy Devonshire hadn't been in town long enough to get attached to it, had she? All three of those women went hustling it off to the animal doctor like it was a human emergency.

Check cat, he wrote on the pad, because he was a detail person, and it might be useful to know if it still lived.

But that wasn't the real problem here. The real problem was, what if Betsy hadn't been just making idle threats about the corporation? He unlocked his desk and got out a photocopy of the lease, almost illegible with scrawled notes. The original must have been drawn up by his brother from memory, to judge by the semilegal language of the thing. That was what the notes were about: they marked the chinks he'd found in it, hoping one would be the crowbar to pry Margot out of her place. None of them so far had proved strong enough, and now this sister claimed she had a chink of her own that meant she could stay if she wanted to.

"Assigned the lease," that was the term she used, a legalism he was familiar with, being a landlord. It meant that the tenant turned the lease over to a new tenant. In every lease Mickels had ever signed, when assignment wasn't flat forbidden, the landlord's permission was needed for assignment. He glanced over the document, more to refresh his memory than to glean information, because he was already pretty sure the clause forbidding assignment was not in Margot's lease. And it wasn't.

What a jerk his brother had been! On the other hand, as Joe understood it, his brother had been doing a favor for Aaron Berglund, Margot's husband, giving her that lease. He had thought Margot just wanted to play at owning a business, that she would get bored or do something terminally stupid and fold up in six months or a year. Ha! That had been nearly thirteen years ago. He shoved the photocopy back in the drawer and locked it.

Interesting that Betsy Devonshire not only used the right terminology, she was right about the lease not forbidding assignment. Was she brighter than she looked? Or did someone tell her about it?

Wait a second, he hadn't noticed that Margot was arranging to be incorporated! And he kept close check on all his tenants, especially Margot, the fly in his ointment, the bug on his birthday cake.

Margot had been a "d/b/a"—doing business as—back when she started Crewel World, but she'd never incorporated. Never needed to. Never hinted she was thinking about it. He began doodling again, drawing a big threaded needle and then putting a circle with a slash around it. But he added a question mark. Margot was smart enough not to talk about her business to people who didn't need to know. If she had incorporated, it was very recently. And wherever she was, she was laughing up a storm, because he was screwed once again. Dammit, he needed to know!

He reached for his phone, dialed. But Penberthy was still tied up with a client, said his secretary, and could not be interrupted. Mickels left an urgent message and slammed the phone down. Stupid secretary, wouldn't listen when he said he had one question that wouldn't take more than ten seconds!

He settled back to wait, but in a minute he was up and pacing the perimeter of his office, which after four trips put him in mind of a hamster in a cage. He started to reach for the phone to call Penberthy's secretary back and shout at her—but instead did the one thing guaranteed to cool his temper.

He told his own secretary he didn't want to be interrupted for half an hour (she wouldn't let anyone through even for ten seconds, either), locked the door to his office, and went into his strong room. He opened his safe and took out a chipped green metal chest about eighteen inches square, heavy by the way he handled it. He brought it to a small table in the strong room and unlocked its padlock with a key on a ring that was never out of his reach.

The box was nearly full of silver dollars and half-dollars minted in the era when they were all silver, not a base-metal sandwich. The coins were bright and worn from handling, and Mickels plunged his hands into the hoard, rubbing them between his thick fingers, lifting his hands and letting them pour back into the box, then plunging his hands in again. At first energetic in these motions, over the next ten minutes or so he gradually slowed, his actions becoming more playful, then almost sensual; at last holding just one in his palm, and rubbing it over his hands as if it were a sliver of soap. Then he dropped it back in the box with the rest, locked the chest, and put it back in his safe, smiling and calm.

•   •   •

Ms. Devonshire sat very straight and attentive in the big leather chair in Penberthy's office. He was relieved to see her looking far less scattered and unhappy than she had only yesterday. And much more prepared to listen. Poor Huber, he'd had to deal with her when she was truly distraught.

"You know your sister died intestate?" he began.

"Without a will," she replied.

"Yes." He nodded, pleased at this sign of intelligence. "I talked with her on more than one occasion, but she said there was only you and she wanted you to inherit, so there was no need. I believe she was wrong—she had many interests and charities, some of which would have been very glad to be remembered. But it is too late now to know what she might have wished done about that." He gave a subtle shrug. "Of course, she was so active and helpful during her life that perhaps she felt that was enough, and did in fact intend to leave everything to you."

Ms. Devonshire said carefully, "I have been told by two of Margot's friends that there is a rather large estate."

Penberthy replied, "That depends on what you mean by large. I think, when everything has been accounted for, and all debts paid, there should be in the neighborhood of two and a half million."

Ms. Devonshire froze and then her face began to flush. "Two—" she began, but her voice tripped over itself and she fell silent again.

"Two and a half million is only an approximation. And that's before taxes, of course."

"Wow. I mean, Shelly thought five hundred thousand, and Jill said maybe a million; but two and a half million—" She tried a smile, but failed. "That's a lot of money. I had no idea. When I saw how Margot was living, I mean, in that little apartment and running that little shop, and her car is a Volvo—what nationality is a Volvo anyhow?—I thought she wasn't doing as well as it seemed from her letters. What was it, the stock market? Is that where the money was, I mean? That there's so much of it?'' She touched her lips with her fingertips to stem the flow of words.

"You, as the personal representative, will conduct a search to discover where and in what form the money presently is held,'' replied Penberthy. "I know Margot kept good records, so there should be no trouble."

"We're already doing an inventory of the shop." Ms. Devonshire nodded. "But I don't know where to begin looking for anything more."

"I can explain how, if you like. I understand Margot put everything onto her computer. Have you, er, 'logged on' to it as yet?" Penberthy was glad to let his secretary run his computer.

"No. But I guess that has to happen soon."

"Do you know how to operate a computer?"

"Well, I used to own one, when I was living in San Diego, and I kept some records on it, and did my correspondence. I could even surf the net, and send E-mail. But I sold it before I came here." She shivered and rubbed her upper arms with her hands. "This isn't what I wanted to be doing right now," she said. "I came to stay with my sister because I've been having a midlife crisis. I wanted to figure out what to do with the rest of my life, because I didn't like where I was or what I was doing. Margot always had her life together and she seemed so content with herself that when she invited me to come I said yes, gladly. I gave up everything, threw my old life over, left San Diego shaking even the dust of the streets off the soles of my sandals.

"And then when I got here, I worried that Margot couldn't afford to keep me very long, because her shop is just that little place, and her apartment was kind of small. And then she was murdered and I was scared I couldn't even afford to bury her—oh!''

"Something wrong?''

"I was really rude to Mr. Huber at the funeral home. I

think he tried to tell me that I didn't have to pinch pennies but I wasn't in a state to listen to him. I'm not sure what I can do about that.''

"I don't think it would be a good idea to do the funeral over again."

After a startled moment, this seemed to strike Ms. Devonshire as funny, and when she smiled this time, it worked and she was suddenly very attractive. ''No, I suppose that isn't the correct thing to do. But I will have to apologize to him next time I see him. Now, what is the process of transferring Margot's accounts into my name? I will need some money—I'm about broke, and I don't have a job, and I probably won't have a place to stay real soon.''

"Then we will begin at once to get the process started—you will need to select a lawyer . . . ?'' He paused, hesitating.

And she replied on cue, ''I hope you will represent me. If Margot trusted you, then I know I can do the same.''

"Thank you. You will need to go through Hennepin County Probate Court. We'll draw up a petition to have you appointed as personal representative. I'll start that at once, and will help you write the announcement you will have to publish in the newspaper, telling people who are owed money to contact you. There will be a brief hearing in court. It will take about a month between the filing of the petition and the hearing." He consulted a leather-bound appointment book. "If I contact them today, we can probably get a hearing around October fifteenth. You must be there to ask the judge to appoint you, and anyone who has any opposition to that will have a chance to be heard. I doubt there will be any trouble of that sort.

"You will gather together all the assets, pay all debts, distribute what's left to heirs—that is, yourself—and close the estate. We'll ask for unsupervised administration, which should be no problem. Then you file a personal-representative statement to close the estate. It will take at least four months before you can do that, to give creditors time to file claims. So six or seven months overall.''

Betsy said, "It sounds very complicated."

"It's not, trust me. The procedure is well established and easy to follow. The most complicated part will be computing the taxes, because Congress is reworking the tax codes again. With the old six-hundred-thousand exemption, you can figure a little over two million subject to tax. They are reworking the exemption now, but you'll probably be paying thirty-two percent or more. Minnesota estate tax starts at nine percent."

"So the checks to the state and fed will be dillies."

"Yes, I'm afraid so."

"But what about my living expenses, rent and bills and all, in the meantime?"

"Technically, you are not supposed to give yourself any money from the estate even after you are appointed, not until the period of probate runs out; but you can keep records and reimburse yourself. If you are truly in need, we can petition the court to allow you maintenance."

But Ms. Devonshire obviously didn't like that idea. Penberthy reminded her that Crewel World Incorporated was not included in Margot's personal estate. As the new chief executive and store manager, she could write checks, and pay herself a salary that would let her stay in the apartment and buy groceries.

"Hey, I never thought of that!" she said, and was greatly comforted. Then she sobered again. "I'm afraid Mr. Mickels will continue to make trouble."

"You may be right. You may, of course, call on me when and if he does."

His pleasure at continuing to joust with Mr. Mickels showed in his voice, and she gave him another handsome smile. "Thank you, Mr. Penberthy. I will certainly do that."

• • •

Betsy came back to the shop to find Shelly sitting at the table working on a needlepoint canvas that looked, to Betsy, as if it were already finished. A customer was sitting close beside her, watching.

"You got your stitches all nice and even," Shelly was saying. "So I want to be careful to maintain the same tension." Her needle probed from below, came up and went down again. She looked up and said, "Hi, Betsy. My housework's done, so I decided to come in early. This is Mrs. Johnson; she wants this finished and framed."

"What are you doing to it?" asked Betsy.

"Looking for skipped stitches. Everyone has to do this. This is Mrs. Johnson's first big project and she has fewer than a lot of people."

Mrs. Johnson smiled, first at Shelly, then at Betsy, who wondered if that simple remark wasn't good for the sale of at least one more project to Mrs. Johnson.

Betsy nodded, then looked toward the big checkout desk where an exceedingly handsome young man was conferring with a middle-aged man in a black-on-gray houndstooth sports jacket. They both turned to look at her.

"I'm Godwin," said the young man, and Betsy recognized the name and voice as a part-time employee she had called. "I think Mr. Larson came prepared to write us a check." He added in a sweet drawl, one eyebrow raised a little too significantly, "It's a shame we haven't finished taking inventory."

"Yes, I'm afraid we're a little behind where we should be," said Betsy. "I'm Betsy Devonshire," she added, holding out her hand. "You must be Mr. Larson, from the insurance agency."

Taking Godwin's hint, she told the agent that they needed to complete the inventory before they could claim a loss honestly. He was understanding and left.

Two other part-time employees—one barely out of her teens, the other Betsy's age—came from behind the bookshelves where they'd already started counting things. They introduced themselves shyly and went back to work.

Betsy learned a great deal about Crewel World in the next few hours: about stock, about pricing, about storage, about record keeping. Godwin told her he was gay, accepted Betsy's indifference to it, and proved himself very knowledgeable about the workings of the shop.

They were all working in various parts of the shop when Godwin found Betsy's practice knitting in a desk drawer. "What's this?" he called out, holding it up as if it were a dead mouse.

"It's mine," admitted Betsy. "I'm still learning how."

That made him take a second look. He stretched it sideways, examining the stitches. "Not bad for a beginner," he said, "nice and loose. Have you been taking lessons very long?"

"Actually, that's my first try," she said, with less of an air of confessing to a misdemeanor than a moment before.

"Really? Then this is very nice indeed. But of course you're Margot's sister, so I guess a talent for needlework runs in the family. What are you going to make first?"

Betsy hadn't really thought about it. She'd been learning as a show of support for Margot.

"A scarf's easy and useful," Shelly suggested.

"Okay," she said. "A scarf."

They went back to work and continued until lunchtime, when Shelly went next door and bought sandwiches and an herbal iced tea in celebration of the return of mild and sunny weather. Betsy was suddenly hungry and ate quickly.

While waiting for the others to finish, Godwin brought her a skein of bright red wool and showed her a clever way to cast on using two lengths of yarn. Betsy discovered the doubtful pleasures of knit two, purl two, fifty times a row with an additional odd one at each end. Very soon she decided that it wasn't changing from knit to purl that aggravated, but the nuisance of moving the yarn from the front of the knitting to the back with each change. She felt she could make real progress if she could just knit or just purl.

"You could do that, and it would be faster," said Godwin. "But this way it will make such a pretty pattern. You'll see."

Betsy allowed a little additional time for gossip after Godwin and the others had finished their sandwiches. Shelly took out a length of off-white linen on which she was painstakingly cross-stitching an angel in shades of gold, wine, and moss green, consulting a pattern printed in Xs, Os, slashes, and other symbols. Godwin produced a rip-stop nylon sports bag, from which he took his own knitting: a half-finished white cotton sock, done on three small two-ended needles. He worked swiftly with a fourth needle, using tiny gestures, as if he were tickling a kitten.

He paused to look at Shelly's angel. "That is going to be really pretty," he said.

"Yeah, well I started it on forty-count aida, but only got the face done before my eyes crossed and threatened to stay that way if I didn't quit. This twenty-four count is much more comfortable, even if it is linen."

Betsy tried to imagine cross-stitching on fabric woven forty threads to the inch and her own eyes crossed in sympathy.

But soon the talk drifted to Margot.

About how scrupulous she was in sharing out part-time hours.

About how she paid only base wages, but allowed plenty of chat and personal project work—as long as it was needlework—in the shop while waiting for customers.

About how she insisted customers were the most important part of the place and that her employees must always go the extra mile to ensure customer satisfaction, whether it was special orders or returns or private lessons "just to get them started."

About the loyalty felt in return by her customers. "We have several customers who now spend their winters in

Arizona or Mexico, but who will buy a winter's worth of projects before they leave rather than buy them from someone else,'' Godwin said, to LeAnn's emphatic nod.

"And we have some real talented needleworkers in the area,'' said LeAnn. "For example, Irene Potter—have you seen her work?'' she asked Betsy.

"No, but I've heard it's wonderful.''

"She's a difficult person, but her work belongs in the Smithsonian, I kid you not.''

"Whereas Hud Earlie is a really easy person,'' said Shelly, exchanging a significant look with Godwin.

"What does that mean?'' demanded Betsy.

"He fancies himself a bit, that's all,'' said Godwin airily. "I mean, where *does* he get that hair dyed? And a matching brass cane, for heaven's sake, *and* a smile that says he's God's gift to the world.'' Godwin tossed back a lock of his own unnaturally blond hair and Betsy smirked into her knitting—maybe Godwin was miffed that Hud wasn't gay.

"Margot had his number, that's for sure,'' said the younger of the volunteers. "He never got away with anything when she was around.''

"Margot had all our numbers,'' Shelly put in gently.

The talk went on, and soon there were sniffles. "It was such a beautiful funeral.'' Godwin sighed. "Didn't you just love that reading about the woman who dresses her servants in scarlet and is always busy with business?'' He said to Betsy, "Her Christmas gift to her employees every year is something knitted; year before last it was red mittens, that same shade of red you're working with.''

Shelly said, "And that part about the sashes. Wasn't that amazing?''

"But everyone laughed during that!'' Betsy protested. "I thought it was a joke!''

"No, no, nooooo.'' Godwin looked at her, very surprised. "We had a Founders' Day parade last year and Margot made bright green sashes for the people playing the characters so the watchers would know who they were supposed to be. So when that psalm—''

"It was from Proverbs," Shelly corrected.

"Whatever," said Godwin. "When he read that, it was the high point of the whole funeral, if there can be a high point of a *funeral*. I mean, the whole thing was so *apt*. No one will ever forget that reading."

Betsy was working on the fourth row of knitting without seeing any sign of the pattern promised when the door went *bing* and a woman came in. She was tall, about sixty years old, slim, and wearing a heather-blue knit dress.

Betsy put her knitting down and stood. "May I help you?"

"I understand the owner has died," she said. "I had placed an order with her and I wonder what the status of it might be."

Betsy went to the desk. "What is the name, please, and what was it you ordered?"

"I am Mrs. Lundgren. Mrs. Berglund agreed to copy her needlepoint Chinese horse for me for one thousand dollars, to be picked up here before Thanksgiving Day. Since she obviously won't be able to fill that order, I am here to inquire if someone else has taken on the task."

Margot had told Betsy about the commission, and had remarked that Mrs. Lundgren was a longtime customer. Yet the woman standing at the counter did not indicate in the slightest that she was shocked or saddened by the death of Margot.

"I see the framed original has been taken down," said Mrs. Lundgren. "Do you know if it will be for sale?"

"*That's* what's missing!" shouted Godwin.

"What do you mean, it's missing?" Shelly asked. "It was here last Wednesday, I saw Margot matching silks with it. In fact, I hung it back up on the wall myself."

Godwin came around the desk to look on the floor under the wall where the horse had hung. "I wonder where it got to?"

"Broken; stepped on, probably," said Betsy. "Thrown away."

Godwin stared at her. "Did you throw it away?"

"No, of course not. Actually, I don't remember seeing it while we were cleaning up. I know I didn't throw it away. But somebody did. Or else why isn't it here?"

But everyone else emphatically denied that anyone would have thrown away Margot's T'ang horse. They all knew it was Margot's finest original needlepoint piece, that she had loved it. Godwin said there was not a flaw in it, and Shelly said it was very valuable, with a glance at Mrs. Lundgren. They all agreed that even if it had been broken out of its frame and dirtied, it would have been set aside to be cleaned and reframed, not thrown away.

"So it must be here somewhere," Betsy concluded. She began to look through the several boxes of things still waiting to be sorted. Everyone, except Mrs. Lundgren of course, began searching the whole shop.

The search took a long while; they even emptied and sorted through the trash bags. It continued long after Mrs. Lundgren had given up and gone away. But at last Betsy called a halt. "It's gone," she said. "I told the police I thought nothing was taken in that burglary, but it appears I was wrong. Margot's needlepoint T'ang Dynasty horse is missing."

12

"C'mon, Mike, at least think about it! Maybe she's got a point!" said Jill, trying to keep her tone light and not sound wheedling or pushy. Which was hard when Detective Mike Malloy was patently not interested in her— or Betsy Devonshire's—thoughts on the case.

"Ah, she's just upset over her sister being murdered by some piece of trash, that's all. Everyone thinks when someone important gets killed it's some kind of plot or something. Even when she's only important to them. But one of these days we'll arrest some druggie or a punk kid and he'll start in crying and tell us all about the store with yarn in it and the woman he offed in there."

Mike wasn't interested in hearing Jill's opinion for two reasons. First, he was sure what he'd just said was correct. Second, he was also sure Jill wanted his job. On a small force like this one, even with only two investigators there was barely enough to do. Uniformed cops with ambition to make detective grade generally moved on to some big city, where openings happened. Cross was ambitious, but she wanted to stay in Excelsior. So naturally she wanted to show she had some ideas of her own.

Mike was ambitious, too—but when he moved up it would be to chief, if not here then in some other small town. Or maybe to sheriff in some out-of-state county.

That meant protecting his turf here and now. Which included not letting some street cop give everyone the idea he was going about this wrong.

On the other hand, Cross was female, so he had to be careful not to give the impression he thought she ought to turn in her badge for a bassinet—though she'd make a better mother than a cop, in his not so humble opinion. She should have a kid balanced on those hips, not a gun.

Jill, watching his eyes wander and thinking she could read his thoughts, tried to stifle a sigh.

Mike saw the sigh and misread it. Sensing victory, he became magnanimous. "How's she doing, the sister?"

"Okay. Better, in fact. You going to talk to her again?"

"Not right now. I got my feelers out all over the area. Something'll turn up soon, you tell her that."

"Sure, Mike. Thanks."

Jill left to go on patrol. She'd done what she told Betsy she'd do, bring Betsy's notions to Mike's attention. Betsy had offered to come in herself if Jill failed to put them across. But if Mike failed to listen to a fellow cop, he'd be even less likely to listen to Betsy, who tended to get excited.

Besides, Mike was awfully sure about the burglar, and he'd busted a small dope ring running right under everyone's noses just last winter. So maybe Betsy was wrong.

"He's the one who's wrong," said Betsy.

"Who died and made you Sherlock Holmes?" asked Jill.

"It doesn't take Sherlock Holmes to see something's wrong," Betsy argued. "Did you do the other thing I asked you to do?"

"Yes, I did," replied Jill, with an air of confessing to a crime, which it probably was. "The preliminary autopsy report says she was struck one time from behind, near the base of her skull, with an instrument that was round or rounded and had a nail or spike on it.''

Betsy stared at her. ''Round with a spike on it? That sounds like one of those weird medieval weapons you see in museums. Or something Hairless Joe would carry.''

''Hairless Joe?''

''A character in an old comic strip called Li'l Abner.''

Jill shrugged. ''Never heard of it. But that's what the report said. I didn't write down the exact words, I was in a hurry in case Mike came back and caught me. But it was clear enough: she was hit once, with something that gave her a roughly circular depressed fracture with a hole in the middle of it. Killed her instantly.'' What the report really had said was that Margot had probably lost consciousness immediately and died soon after, but Jill didn't want to distress Betsy with that information.

Betsy sat silent awhile. They were in the shop, which Jill was glad to see was open for business, seated at the table. Betsy had begun knitting something in red yarn, probably a scarf, and while her hands seemed competent, she had the beginner's slow and careful movements. Unless she sped up, that scarf would be ready in time for the Fourth of July.

''They didn't find the murder weapon, did they?'' Betsy said, purling twice.

''No. And I can't think of anything in the store that would have made that shape of a wound. Can you?''

''No.'' Betsy thought awhile, then shook her head in confirmation. ''No,'' she repeated. And after doing that inventory, she knew every item in the store. She looked at her knitting, and knitted the next stitch.

''So he must have brought it with him, and taken it away again,'' said Jill.

''I remember reading in a book about putting something heavy in a sock and swinging it as a weapon.'' Knit again.

"Sand," said Jill. "A sockful of sand makes a really nice weapon."

Yarn over. "Yes, but sand hasn't got a spike in it." Purl.

"A long skinny rock can be a kind of spike. And all you have to do after is dump the rock out, run the sock through a washing machine, and nobody's the wiser."

They both glanced toward the store's front window and thought of the lakeshore, a stone's throw away.

Bing! "Have you had lunch yet, Betsy?" asked a man's voice from the doorway.

Betsy looked up from behind the desk. Hud was standing there in a spice-colored suit and vest, white shirt and no tie, which looked wonderful with his ruddy complexion and streaky hair. He was leaning elegantly on a brass-headed cane and sunlight coming from behind put him in a golden aura.

Betsy smiled, both in admiration and remembering Godwin's sarcastic description. "Well, hi, Hud. As a matter of fact, I haven't yet."

Godwin said, "Bring me back a sandwich. Any kind."

As they left the shop, Betsy teased, "What's that cane for? Did you sprain your ankle?"

He hoisted it, twirled it, set it down again. "What, don't you like it? Then I'll bring another next time. I have a collection." He held it out and she took it.

It was heavy; the shaft was of a dense wood whose color matched his suit, the head was an upright lozenge that on closer examination was seen to be an owl. The barely raised features made it pleasant to grip.

"Is it a sword cane?" she asked, pulling at it.

"Not this one." He took it back. "But I have one with a blade in it, and another that holds about four ounces of whiskey. They look exactly alike; can you imagine me trying to run off a mugger and instead offering him a drink?"

She laughed, then asked, "What are you doing in town?"

"Consulting you. We've been offered a seventeenth-century chatelaine, and I'm wondering if you can tell our European-art curator the uses of the implements in it."

"Why ask me? What's a chatelaine?"

"It's a metal holder for needlework implements. Scissors, thimble, needle pack, like that."

Betsy groaned softly. She was so ignorant!

Hud continued, "But this one has some other things in it that we're not sure of. A tool that looks to me like a really narrow guitar pick, for example. Everything's made of silver and everything matches, but I don't know if that pick really belongs or not."

"We have something like that in the shop. The package it comes in says it's a laying tool, but I have no idea what it's used for. I could ask my Monday Bunch: they know everything."

"No, never mind, one of my staff can look it up. A laying tool, huh? But hey, you want the truth? I've been thinking about you, and I've been looking for an excuse to come and see you. The chatelaine provided me with one." His smile invited her to join the conspiracy. "And now, having asked the question, I have both excused my absence from the office and made my lunch with you a deductible business expense."

"Glad to be of service, sir. Where are we going?" she asked as they rounded the corner that was marked by the post office. "Christopher Inn?"

"No, he doesn't serve lunch. I thought we'd go to Antiquity Rose's."

"Isn't that an antique shop?"

"It's also a very nice place to have lunch."

They had started up Second Street, going past the gas station. Antiquity Rose was just ahead. It had started life as a modest wooden house, and was now painted a blushing pink with maroon shutters. It had retained its front porch and a lawn full of cushion mums and late roses, but now Betsy noticed that the sign announcing its name and advertising antiques also mentioned luncheons.

In the front room were glass cabinets, tables, and shelves of glass dogs, china cats, odd silver spoons, antique jewelry, and collectible dolls. Hud led her to a small table in the next room, obviously converted from a side porch. The air announced fresh-baked bread and hearty soups.

Betsy was not an antiquer, but her eyes couldn't help wandering to the display on the wall over their table. An old poster advertising a black liquid that could cure both cancer and asthma hung between shadow boxes displaying old teacups and miniature Kewpie dolls.

"As the lunches get better here," said Hud, "the antiques get closer to plain secondhand stuff."

"I remember my grandmother sending me a Kewpie doll one Christmas," said Betsy. "I was disappointed that it didn't come with clothes to put on and take off." She smiled at the memory.

"You are looking very well," said Hud.

"Thanks," she said. But then turned to business of her own, for who better to ask about a medieval weapon than a curator?

"Hud, does the museum have antique weapons? I mean really antique, like medieval."

He glanced up from his menu. "No, why?"

"Is there a name for that thing that's a round knob with a spike through it?"

He offered a humorous look of suspicion. "Who are you mad at?"

"Nobody. I was talking with Jill earlier today, and somehow the subject came up. We were trying to think of the name of that kind of thing. Not morning star, not mace, but something in that family."

Hud shrugged and resumed consulting his menu. "Not my area of expertise, sorry. Or the museum's; we collect art, not weapons." He put it down again. "But talk of hurting someone reminds me. How's Sophie?''

"Just fine. She actually gets around despite the cast. They made it longer than her leg to discourage running or jumping, so she kind of paddles with it rather than walking on it. The vet's assistant calls it the square-wheel syndrome. Sophie goes along very smoothly on three legs and then the cast lifts her about two inches.'' Betsy moved her hand across the table, lifting and dropping it at intervals. ''Like a pull toy with one square wheel.''

Hud laughed so hard at the image of a cat with a square wheel he had to put the menu down. His voice was a splendid baritone and his laugh matched it; people turned smiling to see who was making that beautiful noise. Betsy wasn't sure whether to feel envied or embarrassed, and so picked up her menu and pretended to read it.

They had corn chowder with hunks of rosemary-flavored chicken in it, and the talk grew so friendly—Hud was familiar with San Diego, Betsy knew something about symbolism in medieval and Renaissance art—that by the end of the meal Hud had to remind her to order a take-out sandwich for Godwin.

Rather than going right to Crewel World with the sandwich, Betsy continued walking with Hud up Lake Street to his car. She had heard you could learn things about a man by the car he drove.

Hud's was a big old black convertible, highly polished but slab-sided. Betsy was startled—she thought Hud was the sports-car type—until she saw the peaked grille with the fey creature perched on top of it. ''Oh, my God, Hud; it's a Rolls-Royce! Wow! Say, what kind of salary do they pay you, anyhow?''

"Not enough to buy a car like this." Hud laughed, going to unlock the door. "I bought it seven years ago, used, at a government auction. It probably once belonged to a drug dealer. I paid eighty-two hundred dollars for it." He slid into the tan leather interior and vanished behind darkened glass. When he started the engine, it purred almost inaudibly. Then the passenger-side window rolled silently down and he leaned sideways to look through it at her.

"Like it?"

"What's it like to drive?" she asked.

"Smooooooth. Would you care to try it out sometime?"

"You'd actually let me?" Betsy had briefly dated a man who owned a Porsche. Nobody drove it but him; he wouldn't even use valet parking.

"Oh, I'm not married to my car like some people are," he said carelessly. "If it wasn't a Rolls, it would be just another ugly car. By the way, there's a dance this Friday, at the Lafayette Club. May I take you?"

She studied him, at first naturally then as a ploy, enjoying the hopeful look on his face. "Yes," she said. "I'd like that."

An order of alpaca wool came in that afternoon, and Betsy had to write a disturbingly large check to pay for it. She was comparing the contents of the box with the order placed by Margot when Irene Potter came in.

"They're rewiring our end of the plant," she said, "so the circuit breakers will stop turning everything off; and they told us to take today and tomorrow off. I decided to stop in and ask—"

"I'm sure we don't have any hours for you to work," Godwin called loudly from the back of the store.

Irene threw a frosty look in his direction and focused her attention more pointedly on Betsy. "—find out if you are getting along all right. I know it must be hard for you to take over a business without warning or preparation."

Betsy said candidly, "Well, it would be nice if I could put everything on hold while I take a semester or two of business courses. Godwin and the others are very helpful, but it's hard to be the boss under these circumstances."

Irene's thin mouth pulled downward. "Margot's death happened at a particularly bad time, just when we're going to be swamped with orders."

"We are?" Betsy noticed the "we"; Irene must still think she was going to own this shop someday.

"Yes, our inventory will be growing quickly toward its peak this month, in time for the holidays. This is when we spend the most, and hope to make it all back and more by the end of December. And, of course, utilities go high during the winter. That front window leaks heat as if it were screen instead of glass—Joe Mickels won't double-glaze it—and with people in and out, the heat just flows like a river through that door. And now, of course, you've got that burglary loss. Have you figured it out yet? How much?"

Betsy was staring at Irene as if she had never seen her before. And, in fact, she hadn't seen this Irene, the competent businesswoman. "Uh, we're pretty sure it's a little over seven thousand, mostly damage to fixtures."

"That's not so bad."

"No, it looked really terrible, but a lot of it we could just pick up and shake out, and there's more I think we can sell after it's been washed. I had wonderful help, they sorted thousands of beads and buttons."

"Getting good help is half the battle." Irene nodded. "I wish I could have been here, too."

"But you have a better job, one that pays more than I can offer."

"Ensuring a computer keyboard gets to Detroit by morning isn't as exciting the thousandth time as it was the first."

Betsy'd had that kind of job, once. Besides, she had a question she wanted to ask Irene. "Would you like a cup of coffee?"

"No, I rather hoped Rosemary would be here. I wanted to ask her about that Appleton wool she bought, if she liked it. Since she isn't, I think I'll just go home—"

Godwin sang "Good Night, Irene!" and this time it was Betsy who glared at him.

"Irene," said Betsy, trying at least to get her to come

back soon, "Margot said I should see some of your work, that it was wonderful."

"She said that?"

"People tell me you win prizes with it all the time."

Irene nodded, her dark eyes glowing. "Yes, I do. Very well, I'll bring some to show you, maybe tomorrow. Perhaps you should hire me to teach a course on needlepoint, everyone in the class would end up with a finished project."

"I'm sorry, I can't afford to hire another person right now. And if I could, the person I'd hire is someone to advise me, a consultant, someone to give me more advice like the kind you just gave me."

Irene's dark eyes glittered. "A consultant?"

"Someone like you, who knows how to run a small business, and also knows all about needlework. Look, are you sure you wouldn't like a cup of coffee?"

Irene said slyly, "A consultant's job would pay better than working the register, wouldn't it?"

"Much better, because it's more important. Do you take cream or—"

"Just black," said Irene.

"Fine, I'll be right back."

When Betsy returned, Irene was trying to convince a customer that she could use DMC floss rather than the silks she wanted for a small doorstop canvas, while Godwin made futile attempts to intervene.

"Irene," said Betsy, forcing the smile now, "here's your coffee."

"Just a minute," said Irene. "I'm consulting with this customer."

"Irene," said Betsy, allowing a warning note to creep in, "if you consult with the customers, then I will think you are on their side, not mine."

Irene turned toward her, mouth open, but changed her mind about whatever she was going to say. Instead, she turned back to the customer and said, "But perhaps I am

wrong. I think Godwin here can help you. Excuse me?''
and went to the table, where Betsy was setting down a pair
of pretty china cups.

After the customer left with her selection of silks, Betsy
remarked, ''I'm surprised Margot didn't think of you as a
consultant.''

''Oh, Margot thought she knew everything already,''
said Irene.

''Well, she did know a whole lot more than I do.''

''Naturally.'' Irene shrugged. Then she looked up at
Betsy and smiled without a trace of rancor or wickedness
in her eyes, and Betsy, with sudden compassion, realized
that Irene truly had no understanding of the human heart.

Betsy took a drink of her coffee. ''I hope they catch the
person who murdered her,'' she said.

''Well, they probably won't. It was an impulse thing,
I'm sure—a burglar who was startled and just swung without meaning to kill. And don't they need fingerprints to
solve a murder?'' Irene was doing a great deal of stirring
and hardly any drinking.

''I should think he'd be sick about it, unable to eat or
drink or sleep,'' said Betsy.

''Probably,'' agreed Irene, stirring.

Betsy leaned forward, seeking an aura of confidentiality.
''You know how you remember what you were doing
when something important happens?'' she asked.

Irene nodded.

''I was sorting socks from the laundry when the first
men landed on the moon.''

''I was working on 'Autumn Roses' in crewel for the
chair in my living room,'' said Irene.

''And I was sitting next to Jill Cross in the Guthrie
Theatre, watching *The Taming of the Shrew*, when Margot
was murdered.''

Irene's eyes slid sideways, then back. ''I was doing the
background of a Kaffe Fassett in basketweave,'' she said.

''At home?''

"Yes."

"All alone?"

"Yes. I was using Medici wool, which I think works better than Paternayan. That's one of the projects I'll bring in to show you; it came out rather well. Perhaps you'll want to hang it up where Margot's blue horse used to be."

Betsy turned to look at the blank wall behind the check-out desk. "You noticed it was missing?"

"Of course. Was it taken with the rest?"

"Rest?"

"Yes, the Designing Women angel and my Melissa Shirley Christmas stocking and that child-size Irish fisherman sweater. Margot usually kept three or four completed projects on display."

Betsy remembered the sweater, knitted in a beautiful cream-colored wool. "We found the sweater, trampled. I'm going to try washing and reblocking it." She raised her voice. "Godwin, do you remember the other things?"

"What things?" asked Godwin, coming out from behind the shelves where he'd been rearranging instruction books, his eyes suspiciously innocent.

Betsy glanced at Irene for confirmation as she named them, the Designing Women angel and the Melissa Shirley Christmas stocking. He shook his head. "I remember them in the shop, of course, but I don't remember seeing them when we were digging through the trash looking for the T'ang horse, and I think I would have."

"Me, neither." Her eye, too, had been set for finished needlework during the search; she would remember if she'd seen any.

So more than the T'ang horse was missing. What did that mean? She had no idea. She picked up the phone book to look for the police department's number. What was the name of the investigator in charge of her sister's case?

13

The Excelsior police station was a new, one-story building of brick and dark gray stone. It was on the south edge of town near Highway 7, next door to the McDonald's and across the street from an ice cream shop—perhaps, Irene suggested in a very dry voice, to make up for its being so far from the Excelo Bakery and its wonderful doughnuts.

A thin-mouthed man with dark red hair and a lot of freckles came to the tiny foyer and said he was Detective Sergeant Mike Malloy. He seemed to recognize Irene, and not with pleasure. But he took both of them back to a small office crowded with two messy desks and several filing cabinets.

On one desk was a large paper bag stapled shut, with a big red tag labeled EVIDENCE covering the staples. He pulled a metal chair from the other desk so each woman could sit down.

Malloy broke the seal on the paper bag with professional nonchalance. "I want you first, Betsy, to tell me if you recognize any of this." He upended the bag and wads of colored fabric mixed with the broken sticks of a wooden frame tumbled out.

"May I touch it?" she asked.

"Go ahead."

Betsy picked up a wad of dull green cloth, which unrolled itself into a Christmas stocking. She turned it around to find a needlepoint picture of children looking through a multipaned window at Santa and toys. The stitches were fancy; Santa's beard was done in long curls, his fur trim was really furry, and the toys were crusted with tiny beads. "I think this is ours," said Betsy, looking at Irene for confirmation.

Irene nodded, her eyes sad. "It's mine," she said. "Maybe it can be saved. I won't know until it's been washed and reblocked."

"I think it looks fine, just a little dirt here and there," said Betsy, surprised.

But Irene shook her head. "I don't know if it will ever be the same."

The angel, broken out of its frame, was in much worse shape. It seemed to have been pulled at its opposing corners, distorting the stitches along with the picture, and to have picked up some serious stains along its journey. "Oh, dear." Betsy sighed.

"Yes, quite ruined," said Irene.

Those were the only two pieces of needlework from the bag; there were also pieces of the mat that had enclosed the angel, and fragments of the wooden frame. There was also extraneous paper trash, and an empty plastic pop bottle.

"Is that all you found?" asked Betsy.

"Why, isn't that all that's missing?"

"No, there was also a needlepoint picture of a blue Chinese horse."

"It was in a plain wooden frame, quite narrow," added Irene. "Matted in very pale green."

"That's all that was turned in." Malloy sat back in his chair. "Were there price tags on these items?"

Betsy replied, "No, they weren't for sale. Although

there has been a customer who wanted to buy the blue horse. Margot had agreed to make a copy of it for her for a thousand dollars.''

Malloy's eyebrows elevated. "A thousand dollars?''

Irene said, "It's quite an art to make a needlepoint project from scratch.''

"Would these other two things cost that much if they were for sale?''

Betsy said, "I don't know. An unfinished canvas by the artist who did this stocking sells for three hundred dollars.''

Irene said, "If my stocking were for sale, which it is not, I would charge fifteen hundred.'' Betsy thought it possible that Irene made up that number on the spot, seeking to outdo the value of Margot's work. Certainly she beamed brighter when Malloy wrote that down.

Malloy said, "But people who don't know needlepoint wouldn't know the value of this stuff.''

"Probably not,'' said Betsy. "I didn't before I started helping my sister out in the shop.''

"So the fact that a framed horse is missing instead of the stocking tells me the burglar hasn't got a kid, but has got a mother or sweetheart with a birthday coming up.''

Betsy stared at him. Malloy laughed, but not unkindly. "Most people don't realize that crooks have a life outside their criminal activities. A lot of burglars are married or have steady girlfriends. And all of them, of course, have mothers. It's not uncommon for a burglar to take something to give as a present. Which is how we catch them, of course.''

Irene said, "You mean their own mothers will turn them in?''

Malloy laughed again. "Not very often. But Mom will show off the present, wear the ring or fur coat, hang the painting in her living room, and of course her friends will ask where it came from. 'My son gave it to me,' says Mom, and word gets around, and one of my informants

calls me. Then''—Malloy produced a pair of handcuffs—
''you're under arrest.''

Irene chuckled but Betsy frowned.

''Now, what if it wasn't a burglar who did this,'' she
began.

''I beg your pardon?''

''Suppose someone wanted my sister dead, and came to
see her the night I was out, and somehow talked her into
going down to the shop, maybe pretending he, or she,
wanted to see something. And then murdered her and
trashed the shop to make it look as if a burglar had done
it.''

''Where did you come up with an idea like that?'' Malloy asked, his tone patronizing.

''There are a couple of things. For one, the shop was
trashed *after* she was murdered.''

Malloy nodded. ''Yes, we know that. A very cold-
blooded individual did this.''

''Second, the shop was completely torn apart. Either the
thief was angry because there was nothing of value to steal,
or he was looking for something.''

''Looking for what?''

''I don't know. The blue Chinese horse? It's the only
thing missing.''

''But that was hanging on the wall in plain sight,'' said
Irene. ''And how do you know there's nothing else missing? Have you finished your inventory and compared it to
the last inventory and all the orders received since and
records of things sold?''

''That's in process. So far nothing important has come
up missing. But I don't think the murderer was looking
for a pair of bamboo knitting needles; I think it was something else.''

''What?'' Malloy asked again.

''I don't know. I may be wrong, but maybe he just
wanted to make you think he was a burglar, and got carried
away.''

"Maybe he was angry that he'd broken in and there wasn't anything worth his while to steal."

"You would think killing the owner would be revenge enough," said Betsy, and to her chagrin she sobbed just once.

Malloy sat very still, watching, until he was sure she wasn't going to break down. Then he said, "It's a stinking shame what happened to your sister. This is a quiet town, with a low crime rate. We haven't had a murder here in years. Everyone is angry and upset over it, and I want to assure you that I'm putting in a lot of overtime working the case. Your reporting the missing items really helped, because when someone rummaging in the trash for aluminum cans found this stuff, I got called and here we are. And I appreciate your thoughts as well. I don't want you to think I'm dismissing them just because you aren't a professional like I am." He smiled, stood, and held out his hand.

Betsy, following suit, shook it. Malloy only nodded at Irene, who nodded back. He opened the door to his office.

"I hope you don't mind if I keep working the burglar angle," he said. "After all, the calculator wasn't found in that trash barrel. Maybe he hasn't dropped out of school yet and needs a calculator. But it's that embroidered horse that will identify him as the thief when we catch him, and help us get a confession."

Irene asked eagerly, "You have a suspect?"

"I think I can safely say that significant progress is being made," he said, gesturing her out.

Betsy reluctantly followed. "Who's your suspect?" she asked over her shoulder.

"I don't want to say anything at this point that might jeopardize the case or put an innocent person in a false light," he said, dodging around them and leading the way down the hall. "I will keep you informed, I promise. What I need from you now is a little more patience."

And before Betsy knew it, she was alone with Irene in the little foyer.

Irene thanked Betsy profusely for "this most interesting experience," and went her way. Betsy returned to the shop.

When she walked in, Joe Mickels was waiting for her. "I've come to see who's paying the rent," he said. "Or are you going to make me put in a claim against the estate?"

"I can't do that," she said. "The corporation didn't die; it is an immortal entity." She remembered reading that somewhere and was pleased to note he was familiar enough with the concept to look a trifle diminished. In fact, as she approached him, she saw that he wasn't a whole lot taller than she was. Funny how she remembered him as a big man. Perhaps it was that fierce Viking face, with its bristling sideburns. And the fact that he was a landlord and the bane of Margot's life for many years. His legs, she noticed now, were very short and a little bowed. She wondered if there had been a shortage of milk while he was growing up.

"I assume you want the check sent to the same address where Margot sent it," she said, stepping around him to go behind the desk and opening the center drawer to get out the Crewel World checkbook. "Or, since you're here, shall I just give it to you directly?" She pulled a pen from a small basket of pens, pencils, foot rulers, and scissors and prepared to write.

"The September rent has been paid, so you have a month's grace," he grudged, and handed her a business card with his name and a post office box number on it. "Send October's rent here." Some of his arrogance returned. "And don't be late."

"I won't be," she snapped, and promised herself she'd live on milk and crackers if necessary to make that true.

He turned and looked around the store, nearly restored to its former state. "Not many customers," he noted.

"We're doing fine," she said. "By the way, I've just been talking to the man investigating Margot's murder."

"Yeah?" he grunted, but there was a flicker of interest in his ice-blue eyes.

"He told me he has a suspect in the case."

"Who?" The word came sharply.

"He wouldn't say. I told him—say, would you like a cup of coffee?"

His eyes narrowed suspiciously. "What for?"

She feigned exasperation. "Because I'm having one, and it's only common courtesy to offer. Do you take cream and sugar?"

Wordlessly, he nodded, and wordlessly took the pretty cup when she brought it to him. His fingers were too thick to fit even one through the small handle.

"It was so horrible about Margot," she said, stirring her own sugared cup. "I didn't think things like that happened in small towns."

"It's a city."

"That's right. Margot told me. Something about a law that every town had to reconfigure itself as a city or go out of existence. So why didn't Excelsior make its boundaries city size?"

Mickels shrugged his heavy shoulders. "The town council had a big fight over where to set the borders, either city size, way beyond where the town already was, or just where it was then. They figured that if they expanded the borders, they'd get stuck with high taxes bringing water and sewage to everyone, so they chose to limit the borders. They're still arguing over whether or not it was a good idea."

"What do you think?"

He shrugged again. "It doesn't matter to me. It saved downtown, I guess, but the tax base is too small. There are other towns that had the same choice, and most of them stayed small, too. Then once their borders were settled, Shorewood took the rest. So anytime you're not sure what city you're in out here, you're in Shorewood."

Betsy smiled. "Are you from Excelsior?"

He nodded.

"Do they have a good police department?"

He frowned. "Why do you ask?"

"Because I want to be sure they can find out who murdered my sister, Mr. Mickels."

"I thought you said the police have it solved."

"I said, the detective thinks it was a burglar. But if he has a suspect, why isn't he under arrest? And what if it wasn't a burglar at all?"

His bushy eyebrows met over his nose. "Not a burglar? Then who?"

"Someone who had a reason for wanting the owner of this shop out of the way. Someone, perhaps, like you, Mr. Mickels."

He stared at her for a long moment, then put his cup on the desk, turned, and started for the door.

"Where were you the night she was murdered, Mr. Mickels?" she called after him.

He stopped at the door and there was another long moment of weighty silence. "I was at a business meeting in St. Cloud," he said at last. "Not that it is any business of yours."

"Of course it's my business! She was my sister." Betsy felt her eyes start to sting, and turned away. "Just go," she said, but the door had already closed.

That night up in the apartment, she remained furious at herself for openly accusing Mickels before finding out if he had an alibi. Of course he'd claim to have one, asked the way he had been! And she wasn't sure how to go about proving it false.

She opened a can of soup for supper, watched the early news, then convinced herself she was tired and went to bed.

But she couldn't fall asleep. She got up and dragged on

her robe and wandered the apartment for a while, wondering if she might be hungry. But a look in the refrigerator convinced her she wasn't.

Finally she found a radio station that played classical
music, sat down in her sister's chair, and took up her knitting.

To her surprise, after ten minutes of it, she felt her mind,
like a pond that has been disturbed and then left alone,
settle and grow clear.

Mickels's remark notwithstanding, Crewel World had
had a good day, saleswise. But there had been more deliv-
eries—most of them, fortunately, with an invoice that gave
her thirty or more days to pay. But even ninety days to
pay was shorter than the five or six months it was going
to take to close the estate. She hoped she could do enough
business to make those payments.

Shelly had come back in soon after Joe had left, and
said it was time to plan the Christmas display. Shelly and
Godwin—who were going to be essential to the continu-
ance of the shop, Betsy was already aware—put their
heads together and came up with a design for the front
window that looked okay to Betsy.

Later both of them, having apparently discussed it between taking an order for a thousand dollars' worth of silk
and metallics for a woman doing an enormous canvas of
an Erté-like portrait and explaining the use of an eggbeat-
erlike device for twisting yarn into braid to a woman who
bought two as gifts, had come and sat her down and
wanted to know what her plans were. It was obvious they
wanted her to keep Crewel World open. She'd been nearly
as touched as alarmed. She hadn't agreed—it felt too much
like a trap for someone of her ignorance to promise to stay
and run a small business in a state notorious for fierce
winters. Didn't blizzards close the stores and schools
around here for great hunks of the winter?

Hey, she didn't even have a winter coat. And she didn't
know how to knit a pair of mittens. She looked down at

the red scarf, which was now over a foot in length. She'd put another inch on it sitting here musing, and there was not an error in it, amazingly. So maybe she could do a mitten.

No, wait, mittens had that thumb sticking out. How did one do a thumb? She recalled Godwin knitting his sock. He'd been using four needles, three of them stuck in the project and the fourth used to make and lift off the stitches, around and around, so there was no seam. One set of four to do the hand and another set of littler ones to do the thumb? No, wait, she remembered her mother's hand-knitted mittens. The thumb's stitches weren't smaller than the rest of the mitten. She smirked a little at being able to figure that out. She was learning.

But her ignorance wasn't the main problem. There were people who knew how to run the shop, and they were eager to help. But Betsy needed to decide if she was going to stay, and if not, to decide where she was going to go. And to start making plans to do one or the other.

She turned her knitting around and started back across the row, purl two, knit two. The first three inches of the scarf didn't have the promised welts or ridges or whatever in them, and she had figured out all by herself that when she began a new row, she should do the opposite of what she'd done; that is, where she'd knitted, now she should purl, and vice versa. In two more rows, there were the ribs, boldly standing up. And now that it was long enough to really see, the pattern was very attractive. She had thought about tearing out the beginning, but decided it made an interesting edge, kind of lacy. She'd make the same "mistake" at the other end, if she ever got that far. Shelly had said a good scarf was at least six feet long.

She looked at her knitting. Where was she? Ah, knit two.

First of all, was she going to stay in Excelsior at least until her sister's murder was solved? Yes.

Well then, she'd better make a success of the shop, because she was scared how swiftly the Crewel World bank balance was draining out. She was down to the dregs of what she'd brought with her, and her credit cards were near their limit. It was great that Margot had left so much money, but Betsy couldn't touch any of it for months, according to Mr. Penberthy. And while today's sales were good, Godwin had remarked on the amount that had come in, which meant it was unusual, which meant tomorrow and the day after might not be good at all.

So, maybe she should go ahead and hold that going-out-of-business sale and try to live over at Christopher Inn on the proceeds until Detective Mike Malloy arrested the burglar with a mother who had a birthday coming up.

Because she was not leaving Excelsior until Margot's murderer was behind bars.

But suppose it wasn't a burglar? Suppose she was right and Detective Mike Malloy was wrong, and Margot's murder had been a personal matter? Since her body was found in Crewel World, she probably had been murdered by someone with a connection to the shop. Then, since the motive involved the shop, if Betsy closed the shop, her contacts with people connected with the place ended. And if Joe Mickels's alibi checked out, she might have to look elsewhere for the murderer.

So the shop had to stay open, at least for now.

But on the other hand, Betsy still didn't know what she was doing at Crewel World. Okay, she could write up sales slips, she could read and understand invoices. And she could knit, embroider, and just today she realized she could tell silk from perle cotton from wool at a glance. Just as she could tell at a glance that she had knitted one and needed to knit another. Purl two.

But what about payroll? When were paychecks issued? And in what amount? And how did one figure withholding taxes? And what did one do with the money withheld? She felt the familiar despair come over her. How in the world did she think she was going to do this? She was a fool—an *old* fool! Her fingers cramped and she realized she was gripping the needles too tightly. She forced herself to open them, wriggled them a bit, then slowly knit and purled her way across the rest of the row, waiting for her mind to settle and clear again.

When it did, a memory rose up. Years ago, right out of the navy, Betsy had worked in a small office, and had helped the office manager do payroll. She remembered it hadn't been all that hard.

And Jill had said that Margot kept all her business information in her computer.

It was time to have a look. Betsy put down her knitting, careful to stick the pointed ends of the needles into the ball of yarn to keep the stitches in place, and marched into Margot's bedroom.

Everything was as it had been, the bed smoothed rather than properly made, Margot's makeup still on the dresser, the scent of her perfume still lingering in the air.

Betsy nearly fled, but told herself not to be an idiot, and went to sit at the computer. She found the power switch and turned it on. The screen flickered, the computer grumbled, and then came the chord of music: ta-dah!

At first Betsy just explored, noting the AOL icon, finding games (FreeCell solitaire and something called You Don't Know Jack, which made her smile wryly) and the word-processing program. Margot had Windows 95, which Betsy had had on her own computer, so it didn't take long to get comfortable.

She began looking for a business program and found Quicken. But when she tried to get into it, it demanded a password. She tried Margot and Berglund and Crewel and World and Crewelworld, and then all the needlework terms she could think of, to no avail. She sat back, frustrated.

She remembered her own computer, and the list of her assets she had kept in a file that required a password. She had used "Margot." She looked at the screen, its cursor

flashing impatiently. She typed "B-E-T-S-Y" and hit Enter.

And she was in.

And there she found the business courses she needed to
run Crewel World, Inc. In Payroll was a list of employees,
their pay scales, their hours (none entered since Margot
died, of course, but Betsy knew where the time sheets were
kept, so that was all right). Also Social Security paid, and
withholding for state and federal income tax, for herself
and for each employee. ("That's my first business deci-
sion: as CEO, do I get a raise?" she muttered.) The inventory file had a list done in January. And another done
a year ago January. And another, and another, going back
five years. Taxes, paid and due, the special account it was
paid into. A list of suppliers and what was ordered, when
it was due, the amounts owed, the amounts paid.

She printed out much, read more. Hours later, heavy-
eyed, she could no longer make sense of anything. She
shut down the computer and went to bed. She could do
this, she was going to stay in business, paying her workers
and herself. But she dreamed for the remaining four hours
of the night of audits and penalties and bankruptcy.

14

Late the next morning, she left the shop in Godwin's hands and went to the First State Bank of Excelsior. She found a seat in the little waiting area, feeling important. She was wearing a light gray skirt, white blouse, and jacket-cut gray sweater; she carried an attaché case she'd found in Margot's closet, now weighty with printouts.

The magic word, she had learned, was *line of credit*. Margot had had one, a nice big one. When someone has considerable assets, a bank can issue a line of credit, which is sort of like getting a preapproved series of loans. Betsy was sole heir to two and a half million dollars; surely that was an asset worthy of a considerable line of credit, even if the asset hadn't paid its taxes yet. She had called earlier and gotten a very prompt appointment with the vice-president—okay, *a* vice-president—of the First Bank of Excelsior.

When her name was called, she rose with the air of someone who is about to do a banker a big favor and allowed herself to be shown into a small but nicely decorated office.

And left it half an hour later greatly humbled. The vice-president had read with interest the notes Betsy had written about Margot's estate—but then pointed out that since Margot had banked with First State, the bank was even more cognizant of Margot's financial status than Betsy was.

However.

Bankers were, according to this one, reluctant to make a loan based on an estate that was in the process of being settled. "There is occasionally a slip between the cup and the lip," quoted the vice-president, not quite accurately.

Perhaps when Betsy had been officially named as personal representative, they would consider making a loan against the assets of the shop in order to buy more inventory, because of the fact that the business was of long standing. Perhaps the loan would be as much as one hundred percent of the value of what she was purchasing. They might also lend her money based on the insurance settlement for the burglary.

Even this was not usually done, the banker concluded, but after all, it appeared that Betsy would be coming into a lot of money one of these days, and the bank would love to do business with her, as they had with Margot.

With an effort, Betsy refrained from leaping across the desk and watching the vice-president's pink complexion turn to mauve as she throttled him. Instead, she pointedly snapped the attaché case shut, shook his hand perfunctorily, and left the bank.

First State was on the corner of Water and Second, where she'd almost missed the turn the first time she'd come into Excelsior. She walked toward the lake and reached the tavern, but couldn't make herself turn down Lake Street toward Crewel World. She dreaded going back to the shop. She had been so sure she'd come bursting back in with the glad news that their troubles were over, the shop could keep running, and everyone would be paid. Now . . .

She dithered awhile, and finally crossed Lake Street and

walked down to the wharves. They barely met the defini-
tion of the word, since no actual ship tied up here, only
excursion boats. Still, the boats were large, multidecked
objects, painted white, made of Formica. Or was it fiberglass? *Queen of Excelsior*, one was named. Beside them,
the streetcar boat *Minnehaha* looked very odd and old-
fashioned. Betsy walked out on the wharf it was tied next
to.

The *Minnehaha* was made of wood painted a brownish
red with mustard-yellow trim. A black metal chimney
stuck up from its midsection. Its stern sloped sharply away
from the rear, like a warship back in the days of the Great
White Fleet.

The lake twinkled in the sunlight. Betsy looked down
into the clear water. She could see three good-size crappie
swimming among the waving water weeds, into and out
of the shadow cast by the *Minnehaha*. How much was a
fishing license? Maybe it would be a savings to invest in
one, and a cane pole. If she ate fish a few times a week,
it would cut back on her grocery bills.

Sophie would probably like that, too. She thought of
Sophie, curled on a cushion in the shop, injured leg up-
permost so everyone would see her cast and offer sympathy and treats. Sophie, regaining weight almost hourly,
had not stopped purring since she'd returned from the hos-
pital.

Some way would have to be found to pay the vet.

She went back up to the corner of Lake and Water. A
short block away was Second Street, a little way up that
was the entrance to that big parking lot with City Hall on
the other side of it. No wonder Margot walked over to the
meeting and then home again. It wasn't very far. That's
also why she had been wearing those sensible low-heeled
pumps instead of her flashy high heels.

Betsy started up Lake Street toward Crewel World. Margot had come home this way on the last night of her life.

Had the murderer been waiting in the shadows for her?

Did he come out and introduce himself and find some reason for her to take him up to her apartment?

When did he strike Sophie? Because the vet said he doubted if Sophie had been hit by a car. There was a deep, narrow bruise over the break in Sophie's leg, he said, as if someone had hit her with a rock or club. That confirmed that Sophie and Margot had entered the shop together, where the murderer struck both of them. Perhaps the murderer swung first at Sophie, and Margot could not help crying out, because Margot never struck, nor would she allow anyone else to strike, Sophie. But if he had hit Sophie with the weapon, why didn't Sophie have a hole in the middle of her bruise?

Why wasn't it Sophie who was dead and Margot walking around as if she had a square wheel?

Betsy wished suddenly she had turned down that invitation to go out that evening. She would have been at home with Margot, and the murderer would not have dared to try anything with both of them there.

Say, there was a new thought. Was it possible the murderer knew Margot was home alone?

Who knew Betsy was going out that night? Jill did, Margot did, Shelly did. Did one of them tell Joe?

Without thinking, Betsy put a hand out and opened the door to Crewel World.

"How'd it go?" came Godwin's eager voice.

"Oh!" said Betsy, who, amazingly, had forgotten she was the bearer of bad news. "Not good, I'm afraid. I can borrow against the inventory, he said; and we'll have the insurance money from the burglary claim. And Margot had a life-insurance policy, Mr. Penberthy mentioned it, but I guess it's not very large. We're going to have to work very hard and make this shop pay, not only for itself, but for me, too."

She looked at Godwin's disappointed face. "Sorry," she said, and then she noticed the dark-haired lady standing beside the desk. Irene Potter.

"I brought you something to look at," she said, and unrolled a piece of cloth across the desk.

Betsy came to look. It was a picture of the sun coming up over hills and a river.

"You should get that framed," said Godwin.

It was a stunning work of art, with many subtle changes of color. "Incredible," breathed Betsy. "Tell me, how did you get that misty effect?"

Godwin said over her shoulder, "Oh, my God, she did the *entire thing* in half cross!"

Betsy looked closer; it was true, instead of the X of cross-stitch, here Irene had used only one leg of the cross—and in places, less than that, half of one leg. The colors shifted constantly, it even appeared that some of the stitches contained more than one color.

"Didn't you get headaches?" asked Betsy.

"Sometimes," Irene admitted. She turned and stared at Godwin until he walked away, then leaned toward Betsy and muttered, "I hear Mr. Mickels told you he was at a business meeting the night your sister was murdered."

"Who told you that?"

Irene hesitated, then lied badly. "I don't remember, exactly. But if that's true, he must have held the meeting on his rowboat. *And* had a for-real battle with his board of directors."

Betsy stared at her. "Why do you say that?"

"Because I saw him walking up Minnetonka Boulevard that Wednesday night with a broken oar in his hand."

Betsy frowned at her. Irene nodded several times. "That's the street that goes out past the old Excelsior Park restaurant—where the Ferris wheel is?"

Betsy nodded wordlessly. You could see the Ferris wheel a long block away from the front porch of Christopher Inn, which was itself barely more than a block from Crewel World.

"What time was this?"

Irene thought briefly. "I'd say around ten-fifteen."

"Could it have been earlier?"

"I don't think so. I started out from my house right about ten, and it usually takes me about ten minutes to walk to the lake. I wasn't walking fast, as I was enjoying the weather. It had stopped raining, and was dark and cool and misty, and as I was coming up the street, he kind of loomed up under a streetlight. He was wearing one of those old-fashioned black rubber raincoats and his hat had the brim turned down, and he was carrying a broken oar. I thought for a second I was seeing a ghost, but then I saw the silver whiskers and I realized it was just Mr. Mickels. I think he saw me the same time I saw him, because he suddenly ducked into the parking lot and went behind this big car."

"A broken oar . . . ?" Betsy prompted.

"Yes, you know." Irene nodded. "The paddle part was gone."

"So how do you know it was an oar?" thrust in Godwin, back like a bad penny. "Without the paddle, it's just a stick, isn't it?"

Irene drew herself up. "The oarlock was still on it."

"Oarlock?" echoed Betsy.

"Yes, you know, oarlock." Impatiently, Irene took up a phone message pad and drew what looked like a capital *U* with a stem growing out of the bottom of it. "You stick the bottom part into a metal holder on the boat so you can row." She looked at Betsy without seeing her, thinking. "Or maybe it's the holder that's the oarlock. Whatever, that's what he was carrying, the handle part of an oar with that metal part dangling. And the paddle part broken off."

Godwin sniggered. "I bet that was a hell of a meeting with his board of directors. I bet they still have headaches."

Betsy cast a quelling look at him and asked, "You're sure this happened last Wednesday?"

"Yes, I'm sure. It had been raining off and on that evening and there was a light fog. Just the right kind of a night to see a ghost. But it wasn't a ghost I saw; it was Mr. Mickels.''

"Maybe he didn't duck out of your way," said Betsy. "Maybe he just went to his car." She turned to Godwin. "What kind of car does Joe Mickels drive?"

"Some big old yacht, like a 1973 Cadillac or something."

"See?" said Betsy.

"Is it one of those old cars that has fabric on the roof?" asked Irene. "An imitation convertible. Because this car was like that. And it had a hood ornament, too."

"N-no," said Godwin. "It's a real dark green, I think. And not two-tone, just one solid color."

"This car wasn't two-tone," said Irene. "And it might have been green, though I thought it was black. Those streetlights make it hard to see colors."

Godwin gave Betsy a triumphant look over Irene's head.

"But it did have fabric on the roof," she said. "I know it did. I was there, I saw it."

"Wait a minute, I thought you were at home all that night," said Betsy.

Irene's triumphant glare at Godwin faded abruptly, and her breath snagged in her throat with a sound almost like a snore. "What?"

"I said, I thought you told me you were home, working on a needlework project."

"I was, I was home all evening. But I got hungry, I hadn't had any dinner. And I just love to walk when it's all misty and foggy, so at about ten o'clock I decided to walk to McDonald's and have a hamburger, and I was almost there when I saw Mr. Mickels. And he ran away and hid when he saw me coming."

Betsy looked at Godwin, she couldn't help it. And his face showed he was thinking what Betsy was thinking: I, too, would have ducked into a parking lot rather than encounter Irene Potter. Her face must have shown her thoughts as well, because Godwin simply bloomed with amusement, and he turned quickly and walked away.

"That man is so rude!" said Irene.

Betsy got her face under control before Irene turned back. She said, "Did you see anyone else while you were out walking?"

Irene thought. "Not close up. And not anyone I recognized. Not many people were out that night. And I wasn't looking around, I was just enjoying the misty night air. I came down Water to Second, and up Second to Excelsior and up Excelsior to McDonald's." She paused in the act of rolling up her wonderful cross-stitch picture. "You know, if I had gone one block more, down to Lake, and come up that way, I might have seen the open front door of this shop, and it might have been me who found your sister's body. Isn't that interesting!" She tucked the roll of cloth under her arm. "You will let me know if you want to display this, won't you? I'll get it framed if you do."

"Thank you, yes, I'll do that," said Betsy, and watched her march out. That woman, she thought, has no instinct for self-preservation at all.

The next day, Jill, Shelly, Godwin, and Betsy sat at the worktable in Crewel World. Betsy was knitting—her fingers moved more swiftly now, but not so swiftly that people might suspect her needles were getting warm from the friction. Shelly, who was supposed to be at a teachers' conference, was needlepointing an angel as a Christmas gift; and Godwin was doing some very elaborate needlepoint stitches on a sampler.

Jill was in uniform, on duty, and so didn't have anything to work on. She was drinking coffee and tickling Sophie under the chin. Sophie, purring loudly, was draped in luxurious ease over a cushion on what Betsy had come to realize was *her* chair. Jill had come in to have a private conversation with Betsy, but the other two were determined to miss nothing and Betsy couldn't think of a task that would take them to the back of the shop, out of ear-shot.

"I heard someone saw Joe Mickels near the store carry-ing the murder weapon," said Shelly.

"Who told you that?" Betsy demanded.

"Heard it at the Waterfront Coffee Shop; that's where you go to get the good gossip."

"But it's not true," Jill said firmly. "In the first place, no one knows what the murder weapon is. In the second place it probably isn't an oar."

"A *broken* oar," corrected Godwin, who had decided this fact was of great significance. "If you could have seen the way Joe behaved toward Margot, you wouldn't be so quick to dismiss Betsy's suspicions—or the story Irene came in here with. She said he saw her coming and he ran and hid behind his car so she wouldn't see who he was."

"What have you got against Joe Mickels, Goddy?" asked Jill.

"Me? Nothing, but he was downright mean to Margot, you know that. He was very angry about her thwarting his big-time plans. He bought the two lots behind this build-ing, you know, so whatever he wanted to build here was going to be big, really big. Probably another condo." His expressive blue eyes glanced out the front window, toward the gray condo complex across the street, then at Betsy. "Margot just hated that thing, you know," he said softly.

Betsy said, "So you think it was in part to keep Joe from putting up another condo that made her glad she could thwart Joe's plans?"

"I don't think anyone knows what Joe plans to put up on this site," said Jill.

"Well, that's true," Godwin conceded. "It could be a business block. It could be a vertical mall. But whatever it was, it was going to be a lot bigger than the current building."

"How do you know Joe bought the property behind this building?" asked Betsy.

"Because my sister's brother-in-law owned the gas station up behind here. Joe bought his place nearly two years ago, and is renting it back to him on a month-by-month basis, so he's been planning this for at least that long."

Shelly remarked, "You know, holding on to all this property all this time may have given Joe cash-flow problems. I mean, he was all set to start building this spring, but Margot wouldn't vacate."

"If Joe is going to put up a big building on this site, he can't be short of cash," said Jill. "Besides, he's collecting rent from all three shops—and the other two don't have leases, so he's getting more from them."

"But big-time financiers are always getting into trouble when they have to delay their plans," Shelly argued. "It has something to do with cash flow."

Jill made a dismissive noise. "Like you know anything about big-time financiers."

"I may not be rich, but I read," Shelly retorted. "And the *Strib* has stories all the time about big companies and rich people who get into trouble because they bite off more than they can chew, or they start in doing something big and there's a delay or a glitch. It's like one day they're rich and the next day they're bankrupt."

There was a cozy little silence as everyone contemplated Joe Mickels filing for bankruptcy.

"How far would someone like Mickels go if all that stood between him and making a lot of money was Margot?" asked Godwin, serious again.

"And if not doing what he planned meant going broke?" added Shelly.

The sober mood was broken when the shop door opened. Standing in the door was Mike Malloy in a brown tweed suit too warm for the seventy-five-degree weather. "What are you doing off patrol?" he said to Jill in a hard voice.

Jill stood, flushed a faint pink. "My coffee break," she said.

"Hit the road," said Malloy.

"Yes, sir." Jill glanced at Betsy, but Betsy was keeping her wary attention on Malloy. Jill brushed by the detective and he closed the door after her.

"I need to talk to you, Ms. Devonshire," said Malloy in that same hard tone. "Alone," he added with dramatic emphasis, just like on television. He even shrugged a little bit inside his coat as if to adjust, or loosen, the gun in an armpit holster.

That worked a lot better than Betsy's hints; Shelly and Godwin immediately put down their work and went to make busy noises in the back of the shop.

Malloy yanked out a chair—the one Sophie was in. She half fell, half jumped out of it and went square-wheeling off to join Shelly and Godwin, giving Malloy a look over her shoulder that made it clear *she* wasn't afraid of him.

Malloy sat down, leaned toward Betsy, and said in a deadly monotone, "What the hell do you think you are doing, accusing Joe Mickels of murder?"

"What makes you think I accused him of anything?" Betsy managed to keep her voice cool and calm, but she knitted when she should have purled.

"He came in and told me. I asked him if he wanted to file a formal complaint, and he said no, not if you stopped spreading it around that he's a murderer."

"I haven't been spreading it around. As a matter of fact, I didn't accuse him of anything. All I did was ask him where he was the night my sister died." She looked Malloy right in the eye. "And he lied to me, he said he was at a business meeting in—"

She tried to think. Some town with a funny name, like a fake saint.

"St. Cloud," came a voice from the back of the shop.

Damn and bless Godwin's sharp ears!

"St. Cloud," she confirmed. "But Irene Potter told me just a little while ago that she saw him in town about ten o'clock that night, and that he hurried into a parking lot when he saw her coming. She said he was carrying a broken oar with an oarlock attached to it.''

"I thought you just told me you haven't been accusing Mickels of murder.''

"I haven't. Irene was the one with the information. And she came in all on her own and volunteered it. If you want to accuse someone of spreading rumors about Joe Mickels, I suggest you talk to her. But I suggest you also talk again to Mr. Mickels.'' Again Betsy dared look the cop in the eye. "I haven't accused anyone of murdering my sister, Detective Malloy. But just because Joe Mickels is a rich man doesn't mean he's also an innocent one.''

"Mr. Mickels was out of town; if Irene Potter says she saw him, she's lying.''

"No, she isn't,'' said Shelly, loudly, from behind the shelves at the back of the store. "She's a little bit off center, but she doesn't lie.''

"All right, so she saw him down by the lake with an oar in his hand. How does that make him a murderer?'' demanded Malloy.

Betsy went back to her needles, purling where she should be knitting. "It means he hasn't got an alibi, Detective. He wanted my sister to relocate her shop so he could tear down this building and make a million dollars selling space in a new and bigger one. And when she refused to move, he started looking for legal ways to evict her, harassing her, not holding up his end of the lease. Talk to Mr. Penberthy, her lawyer, about the times Mickels hauled Margot into court with some stupid writ. Maybe he just got tired of it, maybe there was some kind of time limit he was operating under. You can find these things out. Why don't you go do it?''

Godwin spoke, startling them both. He was standing by the edge of the table, having come on noiseless feet up to it. "And it seems murdering Margot didn't fix things for him, Detective Malloy. Because Margot had incorporated her business, and named her sister Betsy as an officer of the corporation. So guess who stands between Joe Mickels and his big plans now?''

Betsy gulped and dropped a stitch. She hadn't thought of that.

But Malloy turned on Godwin. ''In my opinion, Joe Mickels is an honest man. You can think whatever you want, you even have the right to speak up about it. But if Mickels is what you two think he is, quick to use the law for his own ends, then you maybe should worry about the libel and slander laws in this state. He was sure enough breathing fire about you, Ms. Devonshire, when I last saw him. If I was a Jeannie-come-lately thread peddler or her''—Malloy hesitated just long enough—''employee, I'd bite my tongue.'' He stood and suddenly his attitude gentled. ''You're an amateur, Ms. Devonshire, and you're new around here. You have no idea what you're getting into, messing with Mr. Mickels. I think it's interesting that he doesn't have an alibi, and I'll check into that, but I don't think it will turn out to be important. I repeat, you would be wise to stop making accusations against him without real proof, okay?''

All Betsy could reply to that was, ''Yes, sir.'' Malloy nodded sharp approval of her meek tone, and left.

When the door had closed on his brown suit, Godwin huffed, ''He'll be sorry if he finds you dead in the middle of another fake burglary!'' He sat down with a snort to resume work on his sampler.

Betsy started to laugh; she couldn't help it. When Godwin looked up at her with that innocent, limpid gaze, she laughed even harder.

But she couldn't make Shelly understand what was so funny.

15

"I apologize for the short notice," said the voice of Mayor Jamison in his heavy Midwestern twang, "but things got bollixed up when Margot died. So now we have to get really moving on this thing. Can you come to Christopher Inn this evening? You'll get a free supper out of it again."

"Yes, I think so," said Betsy into the phone. "What time?"

"Seven o'clock. See you there."

Betsy didn't know of what use she would be to the committee; Margot was the driving force, she was only one of the driven. But it did occur to her to ask Shelly to stay awhile after closing and help her find the slash jacket Margot had promised to donate, since Betsy wouldn't have known a slash jacket if it jumped up and bit her. Which from its name it might.

Betsy found a big box of donated items: a table lamp, a gift certificate, a framed print. But no jacket. Shelly was the one who unzipped a garment bag in Margot's closet. "Here it is," she announced.

At first, Betsy thought it was knitted somehow, with lots

of ends left loose to make it look shaggy. But no, it was some kind of red-orange cloth with small black figures printed on it, and short, multicolored fringe in curves all over—no, that wasn't it, either. "What the heck is that?" she asked, coming closer.

"It's the slash jacket," said Shelly.

"No, I mean, how is it made?"

"You take six, eight, ten different fabrics, layer them, cut out your jacket, and sew the layers together in lines, like . . . like"—she cast about for a simile—"contour farming." Her hand described curves. "When the jacket is finished, you cut through the layers between the contour lines. You line it, then you wash it over and over, until the cut edges stand up and fray. See how she used a layer of navy blue among all the reds and yellows? That gives a really interesting effect."

"It sure does. Who in the world dreamed up the idea?"

"Beats me. I've wanted to make one for a long time, and Margot told me it's easy to do, but I never got up the nerve. I mean, to take a razor to a finished garment! I'd probably chicken out and just call it quilted."

"Here, let me see it." Betsy took it off the hanger and tried it on. It fit a little snugly, and when she looked at herself in the mirror, she made a face and shrugged it right off again. "Makes me look fat."

Shelly looked as if she wanted to disagree, but honesty won out. "That *is* a drawback," she said. "And it's not as warm as a down coat would be."

"I suppose I could just hang it on the wall, like a work of art." She backed off and cocked her head, studying it. "Yes, that would be really effective on the right wall."

"Are you going to bid for it, then?"

"I don't know. How much do you think it might go for?"

"Three or four hundred, maybe more."

Betsy sighed. "Well, I guess not."

"Yeah, me neither."

"Shelly, can I ask you something?"

"Sure, what?"

"Who would you consider to have been Margot's enemies?"

"Now, that's an ugly question. But I guess the right answer would be, nobody."

"Come on, Joe Mickels has to go on the list."

"Okay, Joe Mickels."

"And Irene Potter?"

"Oh, Irene's just a little crazy, not dangerous."

"She came over here after the funeral wanting to buy Crewel World."

"Of course she did, she's wanted to open her own needlework store for years."

"So she wanted Margot out of the way, didn't she? How badly?"

Shelly was smoothing the slash jacket on the hanger. "Oh . . . pretty bad, I suppose. But she's the kind of crazy that would make a little doll and stick pins in it. I can't imagine her coming after Margot with a real weapon."

"All right, then, who would?"

Shelly hung the jacket on the closet doorknob. "I told you, nobody. Margot was a good person. She organized charity events, and got people excited to start working on them."

"There's a silly old joke: she lives for others; you can tell the others by their haunted look. Was Margot one of those, always poking into other people's business? Trying to reform people who maybe didn't want to be reformed?"

Shelly frowned. "No, that wasn't her at all. All I ever heard from people she helped were thank-yous. She was a busy lady, and she liked getting other people up off their butts. She got so much more done in a day than normal human beings, I used to wonder if she slept four hours a night or something. She kept the store going, she was involved in her church, she did a lot of volunteer work, yet she never complained about being tired. Or not a whole lot, anyway. She inspired me, so now I teach and I work part-time in the store and I'm on this one committee.'' She grinned, a little embarrassed. ''I will say, once this committee's work is done, so am I. Christmas is coming, and there's enough work in that for me.'' She consulted her watch. ''Oh, gosh, I've got to get home and feed the kids.''

Betsy said, surprised, ''I didn't know you had children.''

''That's what I call the dogs. My husband got the boat, the Miata, and the condo in Chicago; I got the summer home here in Excelsior—which was my grandmother's to start with, so big deal—the Caravan and 'the kids'—two goldens and a miniature schnauzer bitch who bosses us all. Still, I figure I came out way ahead; he has the Cubs to contend with.''

While the dogs were wolfing down their evening meal, Shelly dialed Hud Earlie's home number.

''Today Detective Mike Malloy came in and read Betsy the riot act. Remember you told me you heard she thinks Joe Mickels did it? Well, you were right. And Mr. Mickels complained to the cops and the cops are leaning on Betsy, hard.''

''Yeah, well, if Betsy had said something to me, I could have told her Mickels casts a long shadow in Excelsior.''

''Shoot, any of us could. But you know something? Even after he said he'd arrest her if she didn't lay off, she was asking me who Margot's enemies were.''

''So you think she won't lay off?''

''You can't stop a person from thinking about something, but I don't know if she'll go around accusing people anymore. You could ask her tonight.''

''What makes you think I'll see her tonight?''

''Aren't you coming to that fund-raising committee meeting tonight?''

''Oh, that. Was she invited?''

''Sure, she's on the committee, isn't she?''

"I thought she was only an add-on of Margot's. Not really official."

"Hmmm, well, I was there when Jamison called, and he asked her. Maybe they'll try to put Margot's mantle onto her."

"It won't fit."

Shelly sighed. "Nothing of Margot's will fit anyone else. That's the really sad thing about this business. I bet if it was Betsy who got murdered, Margot would have the murderer wrapped up in floss and delivered to the jail by now."

The Dick Huss vase Hud brought to the meeting at Christopher Inn was eerily beautiful. It was black glass, about fourteen inches high, shaped like a jug, down to a little neck just the right size for a cork. But it was covered with a three-dimensional flowing pattern of tiny triangles, circles, and dashes. It cried out to be touched, and Betsy complied.

"How does he get that effect?" she asked.

"He puts little pieces of tape all over it, and sandblasts the spaces away," Hud replied.

"It's beautiful," said Betsy. "Here's the slash jacket," she added, putting it on the table beside the vase. Its bright color only made the Huss vase stand out more.

"Can I talk to you?" asked Hud.

"Sure, what about?"

He led her to a back parlor. "I hear the cops are close to making an arrest."

"Where'd you hear that?"

"I also hear the perp is a burglar."

"Detective Malloy *says* he's on the trail of a burglar. But I don't think he'll arrest anyone, because I don't think it was a burglar at all."

"Of course it was a burglar, the store was trashed like only a burglar does."

"No, it was trashed way beyond that, like someone was angry at Margot."

"Angry about what?"

"I don't know. But I'm going to find out."

He looked down into her unwavering eyes. "I wish you wouldn't," he said as sincerely as he could, putting all his concern for her into the words, and he could see a bit of wavering set in.

And her reply was defensive. "But I can't just take everything Margot left behind, all that money, the shop, all her good friends, and not try to do anything in return!"

"Silly kid," he said very fondly, and pulled her into a warm embrace.

Which she immediately began to struggle out of. "Let me go," she said, and he did. She straightened her jacket and ran a hand over her hair. "Don't ever do that again," she said, and walked out of the room.

"Well, then, let me help," he said ninety minutes later, walking her home.

"How can you help?"

"I don't know. Ask me something you want to find out."

"Who hated Margot?"

"Ha!" he said, surprised. "Nobody. I don't think anyone was even mad at her."

"Joe Mickels was." How could people keep forgetting that?

"Joe Mickels was caught up in a business disagreement with her. He was doing everything he could think of to make her move out of that store. He wasn't treating her any differently than he'd have treated anyone who was in his way like that. It wasn't personal."

"You mean he'd have murdered anyone he couldn't evict legally?"

He stopped and took her by the upper arms. "Joe Mickels has been around for years. He is a very accomplished, very patient, very persistent businessman. He has never found it necessary to murder anyone before, and I doubt if his situation with Margot was any different.''

But Betsy was remembering the look on Joe's face when she asked him where he was the night Margot was murdered, and the oddly long wait for his answer. There had been fear as well as fury in that face. She shrugged free of Hud's hands and continued down the sidewalk. "Who else?" she asked.

"Who else what?"

"Was mad at Margot?"

"Nobody."

"Not even Irene Potter?"

"Hey, her problem is envy, not anger. She thinks she could've run that store better than Margot."

"Hud, if Margot hadn't incorporated, what would have happened to Crewel World?"

"It would have gone out of business, I guess."

"You don't think Irene would have taken it over?"

"No. Well, she might have tried, but it wouldn't have worked, not for long. She's not a people person, which you need to be to run a successful store. And I think she might not even have tried, because on some level she must be aware that she has no people skills."

"I have people skills."

"Yes, you do. For which I am grateful. Are you going to stay in Excelsior?"

"At least for now. I kind of think I like it here."

He took her hand. "It's an even nicer place now that you're in it."

She freed her hand. "Who else?"

He sighed. "You seem to be the one with the list. Who else do you suspect?"

"Where were you the night Margot was murdered?"

"Me?" He put both hands on his chest, fingers splayed. His eyebrows were actually up under his forelock. "You're kidding!"

She had been, but his astonishment was so overdone that she frowned up at him. When she spoke, there was a crisp edge to her voice. "I know you think I'm an incompetent fool for looking into this, but I am not kidding."

He dropped his hands and sighed. "I don't think you are a fool, but I do think you are asking for trouble."

"So help me, get me into trouble. Where were you that night?"

He cocked his head at her. "I took my secretary out to dinner at the Green Mill, then went up the street and rented a movie, then went home and watched it. I put it in the car the next morning so I'd remember to take it back, and on my way to work I heard on the radio about Margot. The only part I can prove is the dinner—well, I suppose the video place will have a record of my renting *Men in Black*."

"I loved that movie."

"Me, too, but I'll never watch it again without remembering. Who else is on your list?"

She had nobody else, but didn't want him to know that. "Who is the person who knew Margot best?" she asked instead.

He drew twin lines from the corners of his mouth to his chin with thumb and forefinger. "Probably Jill Cross. Those two have been thick as thieves from the day they met."

"I'm going to repeat Mike's warning, Betsy. Stay out of this. You could get arrested. Mike's very territorial about his cases." Jill looked tired. They were at the coffee shop on Water Street; Jill was on another coffee break; Betsy had found Jill's beeper number on the kitchen phone list and arranged this meeting.

"You were Margot's best friend," Betsy persisted. "Who was mad at her? Who was jealous? Who hated her?"

"Nobody hated her. She was an extraordinary lady with

a kind heart and more energy than a dozen of the rest of us put together. You'd think, with all her activities, that someone would at least envy her, but no one did. Her loss is the whole town's loss.''

''Irene envied her.''

''Yes, she did. But she's crazy.''

''That can be enough to set off the mob. So why aren't people out with torches demanding Irene's head? Or Joe's?''

''Because Minnesotans don't march with torches. They prefer to let the police do their job. That means Mike. He'll do it right, come up with the proof that will stand up in court. You should just get on with your life and be patient.''

Betsy said, ''I don't have a life. And if I did, I couldn't get on with it knowing Margot's murderer is free.''

''Don't be so melodramatic!'' There was a definite snap in Jill's voice.

''Then help me.''

''I am helping you; I'm keeping you out of really serious trouble. I told you she had no enemies.''

''Okay, then tell me what she did on the last day of her life.''

''I don't know, the usual I guess—ran errands, went shopping. It was her day off. I know she went to Minneapolis, to the art museum. Check her calendar.''

''Where is it?''

''I don't know. I know she has one, she called it her nag and said she'd be lost without it. But I bet when you find it, all it will have on it for that day is that trip to the art museum, and the city-council meeting that night.''

Betsy nodded; she didn't remember an appointment book in Margot's purse, but she hadn't been looking for one; she'd check again as soon as she got home. Meanwhile: ''Who did Margot have a fight with lately?''

''How lately?''

''Jill . . .'' Betsy made two tired syllables of the name.

"Forever, okay? Who had she ever been really mad at?"

Jill sighed. "Godwin, for making fun of her. That was years ago, when he thought she was just messing around with her committees. Shelly for gossiping. And Hud, of course."

"Why 'Hud of course'?"

"It's a long story. He never was a big fan of hers, you know. Maybe because she was on the board of directors of his precious museum, and she disagreed with him at board meetings once in a while. She took her position on the board very seriously, you know. And she was very bright. Hud likes women who flirt with him and let him have all the ideas. Especially if they're rich."

"Like me, I suppose?" Betsy heard the edge in her voice but couldn't help it. She was tired, too. It was late and she'd had a busy day.

"Well, maybe it's more that he gets along better with women who don't have any power over him," Jill conceded. "Because I think he likes you, so he must like some women with brains."

"But he really didn't like Margot," Betsy persisted, "just because she was on the art-museum board and therefore his boss?"

Jill took a deep drink of her coffee; she was working a double shift because a colleague was ill. "That's not all of it. Hud's second wife used to be Margot's best friend, and when he dumped her for the woman who became the third Mrs. Earlie, Margot was furious. Eleanor—that's the second wife—moved away, and Margot was depressed about that. And when the third marriage broke up after only six months, she was even madder at Hud. Every so often he'd try to be friends with Margot, and she'd get mad all over again at him."

"I suppose she thought it might have been better if Hud had just had an affair," Betsy heard herself say, and was surprised at the defensive tone. Did she like Hud that much? She rubbed the underside of her nose with a forefinger and caught Jill's sardonic look. Or was she amused? Betsy still had trouble reading that enigmatic face.

Jill said, ''I think this time she was mad because he and you seemed to have hit it off.''

Later, in bed, waiting to fall asleep, Betsy thought the conversation over. Margot had been furious with Hud for dumping his wife, Margot's best friend. That was interesting, but it didn't seem relevant. If anything, it might have been a motive for Margot to murder Hud, rather than for Hud to murder Margot. But not all these years later. Of course, it spoke ill of Hud, behaving that way. Hud's face, that confidence man's grin all over it, swam up before her, then Margot's face appeared, with a disapproving look. So Margot had spoken to Hud about her? How dare Margot think Betsy couldn't take care of herself!

She rolled away from the faces, seeking sleep—and after a bit, found it. In a few minutes she was dreaming that she and Jill were in a sinking boat, and she was frantically knitting a new paddle for the broken oar while Jill bailed.

16

Betsy woke with a start. Something energetic was playing on the clock radio, Groucho Marx being greeted as Captain Spaulding by the gritty sound track from the old movie. Betsy had first heard that song as the theme from Groucho's TV show, *You Bet Your Life*, and had been surprised when she heard it in the movie *Animal Crackers*. Or was it *Cocoanuts*? Never mind, it was a delightfully silly song to wake up to.

She had been surprised by KSJN's *Morning Show* because that radio station played classical the rest of the day, which in Betsy's opinion was the genuine, authentic, real stuff for easy listening. Still, she left her clock radio set to wake her to the *Morning Show*, because she was rarely annoyed by the music they offered. On the other hand, she never knew what they would play next. In this case, it was Glenn Miller's "Pennsylvania 6-5000." Betsy smiled; she could remember her parents dancing to this; it had been one of their favorites.

What was more, the sun was slanting brightly through the window, it looked to be another pretty day. On those two happy notes, she began her morning stretches. Pennsylvania stretch, stretch, stretch!

The song ended. Dale and Jim Ed began one of their faux commercials—this being public radio, and they apparently felt a need to make up for the lack of real ones. They touted a company that, for a price, thought up weird excuses for why you could not come to work. Their current offering involved a rare mildew infection, and included a scientist who would call your boss to confirm the infection and give the recipe for the powerful cleaning solution needed to wipe down anything you had touched. "This way," concluded Dale, "when you go to work the next day, not only have you convinced everyone you had a legitimate excuse for being off work, you will find your work area spick-and-span!"

And Betsy had thought California had a lock on weird!

Stretches completed, she relaxed for a bit. She felt the mattress jiggle, then lean into big-cat-size footfalls as Sophie came up alongside her. The cat fell weightily against her hip with a combination sigh and purr. The cat enjoyed these slothful morning minutes as much as Betsy did. Betsy closed her eyes and let her fingers wander through the animal's fur until she came to the special itchy place under Sophie's chin, where she paused to scratch lazily. Sophie put a gentle paw around Betsy's hand in case Betsy had any notion of moving it away. The purr became richer, deeper, deeper, deeper. . . .

Betsy was brought back from a doze by a gentle but insistent tugging at her hand. She resumed scratching.

But when Betsy tired of scratching and tucked her hand back under the covers to try for another nap, Sophie turned the movement into a game of Mouse Under the Blanket, which finished that notion.

Then, thumping along on her cast, Sophie led the way into the kitchen, where she sat pointedly beside her empty food dish. But Betsy started the coffee first. It was her sole victory in the mornings nowadays and she was determined to hang on to it.

When it was a little before ten Betsy went downstairs to open up, eager for customers.

But by noon she had added another four inches to the knitted scarf (including errors unraveled and reknit properly) and nothing to the till. Only two people had come in. One wanted something the shop didn't carry. "Try Needle Nest in Wayzata," Godwin said, adding to Betsy, "They send people to us." The other person was merely curious about Betsy's sleuthing, and she firmly put him off. As she told Godwin, perhaps he was on Detective Malloy's list of informants.

At last Betsy announced she was going to call the part-time help and tell them not to come in for the afternoon shift.

Godwin, taking down some outdated announcements on the mirror by the front door said, "Don't do that. Take a half day yourself. Margot always took Wednesdays off."

"I don't have anywhere I need to go," she objected, thinking perhaps she should give Godwin the half day and save his salary, too.

"Yes, you do."

"Like where?"

"First, you should go back upstairs, have a little lunch, and find Margot's sketchbook, the one with the red cover. I can do the needlepoint, if Margot did a graphed drawing of it. I'll work it like counted cross-stitch, only in needlepoint. It's a thousand dollars for the shop."

"Less what I'd have to pay you to do it."

"I'll do it for nothing. For the sake of the shop. For Margot."

"Oh, Goddy . . ." Betsy felt guilty for even thinking of shorting Godwin's paycheck.

"Now don't get mushy. Besides, here's where you really need to go this afternoon," he added, bringing a new flyer back to her. "Look, there's a Kaffe Fasset exhibit just opened."

"Who's Kaffe Fasset?"

He sighed and rolled his eyes. "Only one of the best needlework designers in the world. Needlepoint to cry for, knitting to die for. People who see the exhibit or read about it will be coming in to buy his patterns and it will help if you can talk intelligently about him."

He put the flyer in her hands. The front flap had a color photo of a magnificent sweater, knit in a pattern of subtle, earth-toned stripes under an Oriental-looking pattern of flowers.

"Hmmm," she said. "This is at the Minneapolis art museum. Yes, you're right, I think I need to go see this."

"Upstairs first. Go on, go right now."

Because it had been Shelly who found the slash jacket and Irene who had noticed the T'ang needlepoint horse missing, Betsy considered she, perhaps, was not the one to be looking for the sketchbook.

But she told herself sternly that since she obsessed about Margot's murder, and was therefore the sleuth, however amateur, she had a responsibility to prove herself capable of sleuthing.

Unlike Betsy, Margot had been a neat and organized person. (Already the apartment shows that, Betsy thought, and sighed.) Presumably there was a place she kept such things as the notebook she used when designing pieces. Betsy had been living in the apartment long enough to know that if the notebook were kept outside Margot's bedroom, she would have come across it by now. And she hadn't.

Therefore (Betsy smiled to herself, this was rather like a syllogism, and she'd been rather good at syllogisms), the notebook was in Margot's bedroom.

She stood a quiet moment inside the door, feeling suddenly that her sister was quite close, that this was an important moment. She stopped the shallow breaths she'd been taking and instead took a deep one, letting it out slowly.

If I were Margot, she thought, where would I keep a

sketchpad on which I was designing a copy of the blue horse?

Filed away under *T'ang*, came the prompt answer.

She went to the wooden file cabinet and slid open the bottom drawer, labeled M-Z. Under *T*, she found T'ANG HORSE. The file folder was slender, containing only the handwritten note about the order for the copy Mrs. Lundgren had placed. No, wait; in the bottom of the folder were two sets of three slim packets of Madeira blue silk embroidery floss, each held together with a rubber band. They were numbers 1005, 1007, 1008, 1712, 1711, and 1710. One packet was dark, medium, and light shades of midnight blue; the other, silver blues.

By now Betsy had seen enough of needlepointers to know that a needlepointed rose was often four or more shades of red. So why not a horse six shades of blue? She started to put the folder back, but changed her mind and kept it out.

There was no sketchbook in the file cabinet, of course; she had realized as soon as she opened it that the sketchbook was too big to fit in the drawer—Betsy had seen the sketchbook, it had a thick red cover with spiral binding across the top. Any other notes Margot had made on the original horse she'd either thrown away or taken with her to the museum, where she'd probably added a few new ones. And she'd never gotten a chance to put them back into the folder.

They were probably with the sketchpad.

Which wasn't in the closet. It wasn't tucked behind the file cabinet or the dresser, either. Or under the bed. Or under the comforter pulled across the bed.

Betsy searched the other closets, cabinets, bookshelves in the apartment with equal lack of success. She went out to the kitchen to spread a dab of peanut butter on a slice of the Excelo Bakery's excellent whole-wheat bread and do some thinking.

Betsy had overheard some conversation between Margot

and a customer about using a computer to design patterns. Margot had sounded knowledgeable on the topic; maybe she did that herself.

Betsy put down her bread half-eaten and went back to the bedroom. She booted up and looked for a publishing or artwork program. The first one she found didn't have anything connected to needlework in it. The second one was for designing needlework, but there were no files in it. She searched around for a while, found no other design program, and finally summoned the word-processing program.

The computer burped and gurgled at her, and instead of a screen ready to accept text, offered something called *What Are You Supposed to Do Today?* It had a list under it, beginning with some general notes: *Betsy's birthday, October 15,* for example. Under that were specific dates. *Wed, Aug. 19, 11 am—See Hud at museum,* read the first of those entries. Under it, indented: *2 pm, Penberthy, sign papers;* and under that: *7 pm, City Hall, bring report on art fair.*

Betsy smiled. She had not been able to find a physical date book because Margot kept her appointments on her computer.

Thursday, Margot was supposed to see if Eloise was back in town and ask her if she would run the food shelf this winter. Friday asked, *Told Betsy yet?*

Betsy sat frowning at that. Tell Betsy what? She thumped the screen with a knuckle. Tell me, she thought at the screen, as if it had ESP and would respond. But it didn't.

Betsy scrolled down the screen. Margot had a date with Mayor Jamison for the Last Dance of Summer at the Lafayette Club on Friday. The date of the fund-raiser, also at Lafayette Club, was noted, and there continued a steady stream of things to be done, running right through the end of this year and into the next, including that spring art fair she'd gone to talk about at City Hall.

She pressed the exit button and the computer wanted to know if it should save the calendar, noting that no changes had been made. Betsy punched *N* for no, and on getting a blank screen asked to see a list of files.

The contents were mostly letters, including one to Mrs. Lundgren about the T'ang-horse needlepoint, saying that it would be ready Tuesday of Thanksgiving week and reminding her that the one-thousand-dollar price was due on delivery.

But there was nothing else about the T'ang project in the files.

Betsy shut down the computer and finished her sandwich before going back down to the shop, frowning with discontent.

Godwin was no help; he had no idea what might have happened to the sketches or any other notes Margot might have taken about the needlepoint project. Or what papers Margot was to sign at Penberthy's office.

"You could call and ask," he suggested.

Feeling a little foolish, she went behind the desk and phoned Mr. Penberthy. He was out, but his secretary remembered Margot coming in. "She was here to sign the incorporation papers."

Well sure; Penberthy had told Betsy that! And of course that was what Margot had meant to tell her, that she was an officer of the new corporation.

Betsy said, "Margot had this big sketchbook, a kind of tablet with a red cover. She didn't by chance leave it behind when she was there, did she?"

"Now, funny you should ask," said the secretary. "Because she did leave it behind. I had to run out of the office to catch her and give it back to her. We had a nice laugh about it, like she was getting real absentminded lately. Which of course she wasn't."

"Do you know where she went from your office?" asked Betsy.

"No. Home, I guess. She sort of waved that big pad at

me and said, 'Thanks for this, I've got some work to do now,' or something kind of like that."

"She didn't say she was going straight home?"

"She said something I didn't quite catch. I said, 'Are you going home now?' and she said—well, you know how you hear something all wrong? I heard her say, 'I mean to putter around the mix,' which I know is wrong. I heard it wrong. I remember that I tried for an hour to figure out what she really said, because it kind of bothered me. Then when she was killed, I thought about it some more, because it might be important. But the police never came around asking, thank God. I'm thinking maybe I missed the last word, so it's the mixed something."

Betsy thanked her and hung up.

" 'I mean to putter around the mix'?" echoed Godwin, when she repeated it to him. "What does that mean?"

"Irene Potter is next," said Betsy. She had opened her mouth to say she had no idea what Margot meant, and instead that came out.

Godwin stared at her.

"Margot was my sister, Godwin," she said. "I can understand her better than some secretary, even if she's not speaking to me."

"You are *good*! So, are you going to go see Irene instead of going to the museum?"

Betsy hesitated. "Both," she said. "The museum first, because it may be hard to get away from Irene." She picked up the file folder. "Is there anything odd about this?" she said, spilling the silk onto the desk.

Godwin came for a look. "I don't know. I'd think they were the colors for the horse, except these two families are so different."

"Would they be like samples?" asked Betsy. "I mean, there isn't enough here to do the entire horse, is there?"

"Probably not, although you get more loft from silk and so don't need as much of it as you'd need of cotton. These are more likely samples, to see which family came closer to the actual horse—Margot liked to match colors as closely as she could. But then why not a selection of yellows for the mane, or whites for the saddle? The ground was a light tan, I remember, but that wouldn't matter as much, since she wasn't matching a real wall or drapery.'' He checked his watch. ''If you're gonna visit the museum, *and* flirt with Mr. Earlie, you'd better get a wiggle on.''

''Goddy!''

''I know, I'm incorrigible.''

Betsy got directions from Godwin and set off. She was halfway there before it occurred to her that she wasn't exactly dressed to kill. Oh, well, she thought, better he learns now that I'm not the clotheshorse Margot was.

The museum was perhaps a dozen blocks south and west of the Guthrie, in what had once been a neighborhood of wealthy families, and was still a long way from crumbling. Some of the fine old mansions had been converted to offices, but others held the line, stubbornly insisting that the 1880s would be right back.

The museum was built in the classical style, with lots of steps leading up to a row of massive pillars, flanking bronze doors. The new main entrance, around the corner, was a modern addition, and wheelchair-accessible.

The inside had been thoroughly renovated, too, though here and there was a room that still showed signs of having been built the same time as the beautiful old houses in the neighborhood.

The Fasset exhibit was in two rooms, one very small and the other not really large. Betsy was disappointed to discover that Kaffe Fasset was a man. She had never considered herself much of a feminist, but needlework is *so* traditionally female that while it was nice to see a woman's homely craft at last recognized as art, it would have been equally nice to have the artist be female.

On the other hand, Mr. Fasset was indeed an artist. There were gorgeous sweaters, some so enormous only an

NBA star gone to fat could have worn them. Is that what makes these art? wondered Betsy. They are clothing no one can wear? Mr. Fasset favored rich earth tones of gray, mahogany, green, and gold.

The artist also did needlepoint; Betsy was intrigued by a red lobster on a checkerboard ground. His work was perfectly smooth, unmarred by errors, fancy stitches, or beadwork.

Signs everywhere warned patrons not to touch, but this was a weekday morning, and the exhibit had few visitors. Betsy took a quick peek and discovered that Mr. Fasset was not fastidious about the backs of his works. Betsy hadn't been either, when she was doing embroidery. Would it be worth her while to work really hard and gain artistic status so she might escape the criticism the Monday Bunch leveled against messy backs?

Betsy studied a knitted shawl inspired by the arum lily, row upon row of perfect curved shapes, each marked with a narrow tongue, in a harmony of colors that made her sigh with envy and covetousness. No, she would never be this good. Better to learn to be more careful with the back-side of her work.

She left the exhibit and went looking for the Asian art section. One wide hallway was lined with European sculp-ture from the last century, which Betsy only glanced at— until she saw a small white bust of a young woman wear-ing a veil held in place by a circlet of flowers. She slowed, stopped. She could see a hint of eyes, nose, and mouth behind the veil, and almost instinctively reached to touch it. But her eye was caught by a hand-lettered sign asking her not to. Smudges on the veil showed not everyone pulled their fingers back as she did. Not that one could move the veil, of course; the entire thing was of marble, a three-dimensional *trompe l'oeil*. She looked for and found the brass tag naming the genius who had done this: Raffaelo Monti. When I am rich, she thought, and went on.

Her feet were tired before she found the Asian art section, up on the third floor. It was cramped between two areas being noisily renovated, and was disappointingly small. The centerpiece was a massive jade mountain carved into paths, brooks, bridges, trees, houses, animals, and people. But in the few surrounding glass cases there was no pottery horse of any color from any dynasty.

Betsy went down to the information desk on the main floor, which was manned by two middle-aged women whose manners were so open and informal that they had to be volunteers. One of them called Hudson Earlie's office, and permission given, a guard was summoned to bring Betsy up four flights to him.

She was shown into a small anteroom where a secretary said Mr. Earlie was on the phone. Hud stayed on the phone a long time—but Betsy didn't mind. Chat was better than "music on hold," and Hud's secretary was personable, as well as young, trim, and pretty. Doubtless Hud had taken her out to dinner any number of times, though Betsy was careful not to ask.

Hud's inner office was quite grand, with tall windows on two walls and an Oriental carpet on the floor. He came out from behind his desk to take her hand in both of his, pleased she had come calling.

"Nice of you to come into town especially to see me," he said.

"Actually, I came to see the Kaffe Fasset exhibit."

He smacked himself on the forehead. "Oh hell, where is my head? I should have realized that you'd be interested in that and seen to it that you got a ticket."

"It was only five dollars, Hud."

"Yes, but you're not on Easy Street yet."

"True, true." She looked around. The shelves flanking the windows held small, exquisite examples from Hud's specialty, Asian Art, and the books were also on that topic, except one called *Art Crime*.

"Do you get thieves or see a lot of fakes?" Betsy asked.

"Not a whole lot," he said. "Asian art sometimes has the same problem as art from third-world countries: provenance. Because some of it is stolen or smuggled, provenance can't be given—you know what provenance is?"

She nodded. "The paper trail of owners tracing a piece of art back to the artist."

"Or the place where it was dug up," he agreed. "So what we get sometimes is an authentic piece of ancient art with a fake provenance. It's my job to authenticate pieces that we acquire, and I've learned to look beyond the paper to the piece itself."

"Hud, where's the T'ang horse?"

If she hoped to startle him with that question, she didn't succeed. "In storage. Most of our collection is in storage, because we're renovating the Asian art exhibits, giving separate galleries to India, Korea, Islamic countries, Himalayan kingdoms"—he was counting on his fingers—"Southeast Asia, China, and Japan. Plus new lighting and better alarms. It's going to be spectacular. I take it you went looking for the horse?"

"Yes. Margot was going to redo her needlepoint picture for a customer, who offered a thousand dollars for it—a sum the shop can use, badly. I've got an employee who thinks he can do the needlepoint, so maybe we can still get the money. I was curious to see what it looks like—I don't remember more than glancing at Margot's original."

"You want me to show it to you?"

"Can you?"

Hud glanced toward his desk, where papers waited. Then he smiled at her like a schoolboy plotting to play hooky. "This will have to be quick, okay?"

"Thanks."

But as they turned toward the door, Betsy saw the one non-Asian note in the room, an umbrella stand made from an elephant's lower leg, standing by the door.

"Let me explain," Hud said with upraised hands, when her questioning gaze came back to him. "I needed something to hold my walking sticks, and they were going to de-accession that. Somehow, it ending up in a Minnesota landfill seemed worse than keeping it, though of course we can't display it. So don't look at me like I killed the elephant myself; that happened a hundred and thirty-odd years ago."

Betsy approached the object gingerly. She had heard about such things, but to actually see one was horrible— it even had the toenails—so she changed focus to the seven or eight walking sticks and the one umbrella it held. Most had brass heads, including the umbrella, which was tightly furled. "Is this your collection?" she asked.

"Part of it. I'm always taking one or another home and then coming in with a different one. I don't even know what's in there right now."

The flat-faced owl was, and another shaped like a snail. "Which one's the sword cane?"

He pulled out an ebony cane with a standard curved handle. Apart from some copper-wire inlay, it was undecorated. Hud had to pull fairly hard to get the handle to separate, which he did with an overhead flourish, and suddenly there was a length of gleaming steel waving under Betsy's nose.

"Cute," said Betsy, taking a step back. "I'm glad it was the sword or I'd be covered with whiskey."

Hud laughed and put the cane back together, and they went out of his office. "I'll be back in a few minutes, Dana," he said to his secretary as they swept by.

They took the freight elevator, a big, padded box so old-fashioned it had a human operator—a retarded man from a local group home, who loved this vehicle like Hud loved his Rolls. As it slowly clanked its way down, Hud said to Betsy, "How do you like our Guthrie Theatre?"

"Very impressive. How did you know I went?"

"You're a new face in a small town. Everyone's paying attention."

"I didn't know you lived in Excelsior."

"I don't, I live next door in Greenwood. But I eat breakfast every so often at the Waterfront Café."

Betsy chuckled.

They went up a broad hall lined with huge eighteenth-century religious paintings to an unmarked wooden door that opened with a key.

The door let into a long narrow hall, at the end of which was another door, which opened into an enormous room full of stacked wooden crates, a big stone statue of Shiva, and glass cases containing golden Buddhas, Chinese watercolors, Japanese robes, and enigmatic stone heads. "Wow," breathed Betsy, "it's like Christmas at Neiman Marcus."

Hud laughed. "Here, this way." He led her through a labyrinth formed by the rough wooden cases. At last he led her around an immense crate and pointed. "There it is."

The blue horse was inside a glass case with a brown horse and two human figures. Hud said, "As you can see, it's part of a set. They are funerary figures from a tomb in China built early in the eighth century."

He watched as Betsy slowly approached the case. The figures were on a stepped base, the male figure on the highest point in the center. But Betsy only glanced at him and focused in on the blue horse. This was so typical, thought Hud, that he was going to suggest at the next board meeting that they discontinue the postcard showing all the figures and make one of just the horse.

High but directly above the case was an air vent; it blew a chill draft down on them. He saw Betsy shiver and stuff her hands into the pockets of her blue cardigan as she moved around the case. Suddenly she stooped as if to see it from a child's angle. He could see only the top of her head, and was surprised at the amount of gray in her hair. Her face was young; she could get away with a dye job. Doubtless when she came into that money, her hairdresser would suggest it. What was it, three million? He would himself suggest some improvements to her wardrobe—that cardigan was positively shabby.

He waited, but she showed no signs of being finished. At last he cleared his throat, and when Betsy straightened he was looking pointedly at his watch.

"Sorry," she said, and they retraced the labyrinth out of the storage room.

Back in his office, she asked, "May I ask why Margot came to see you the day she died?"

"She had some idea about a proposed fund-raising campaign. She felt it was too ambitious, that we wouldn't meet our goal. She wanted me to support her at the next meeting when she voted against it."

"Did you agree to?"

"No, I told her I thought the goal was achievable. We agreed to disagree and she went off to see the T'ang horse."

"But the door was locked. Or did she have her own key?"

"No, she borrowed mine. There was talk among the board members about getting their own keys, but the staff argued successfully that the hand of authority is not the same as the hand that knows how to handle fragile artifacts."

"Yes, of course. So why, when she brought the key back, was she all upset?"

He looked at her slantwise. "Have you been talking to my secretary?"

"That's what you get for making me wait while you chat on the phone," she said archly. "But why was she angry?"

"She wasn't all that angry. Every time she went into that storage room, she snagged a stocking or her good wool skirt. She wanted to know when we'd get the renovations finished; most of our artifacts have been in storage for over a year. I told her it might be another six months;

we're short of money to complete the renovations." Hud grinned at her. "I think that might have changed her mind about voting against the fund-raiser."

Betsy smiled back. "Do you remember about what time she left here that Wednesday?"

He had to think. "I'm not sure. Wait; I had an appointment at two and I made it, so it must have been fifteen or twenty minutes before that."

"Did she tell you her plans for the rest of the day?"

"No. Why?"

"I know she had an appointment with her attorney to sign the incorporation papers, but that only took half an hour. Yet she didn't get home until after I'd closed the shop. We hardly had a chance to talk, I was getting ready to go out when she came in, and I left her changing to go to the meeting at City Hall."

"Maybe she went to a movie," Hud suggested. "It was her day off, after all." He took her by the upper arms and gave a gentle shake. "I wish you'd let this alone," he said.

"I can't, Hud. It's on my mind all the time, like one of those dumb songs that start in and won't go away. I can get busy in the shop or figuring out Margot's computer, but if I stop for just a minute, it starts in: Who murdered Margot? Who murdered Margot?"

He embraced her, and this time she let him. "Poor kid," he said. He felt her lean into him and tightened his embrace just a little.

But that only made her pull back. She said, "Hud, I understand you and Margot were not exactly friends."

"Who told you that?"

"Is it true?"

He grimaced. "Well, she was kind of mad at me, but that was a long while ago."

"Because you dumped your second wife for your third."

"I see my secretary has really been dishing the dirt." He didn't bother to sound amused this time.

"It wasn't her, someone else told me."

"You don't think *I* hated Margot, do you?"

"No, it seems to have been the other way around. What happened?"

He sighed. "I got to know Margot through my wife Eleanor. We used to go out as a foursome, Eleanor and me, her and Aaron, and we all got along swell. Then I hired Sally as an assistant and thought I'd found true love. It was like Fourth of July fireworks." He made an upward spiral with his hand. "Whoosh, whee, bang!" He dropped the hand. "Darkness." He sighed. "I was the world's greatest jerk, but by the time I found that out, Eleanor was dating a banker in Kansas City and not inclined to listen to anything I had to say. And Margot had been named to the board of directors of the art museum, which I thought for a while she maneuvered herself into as a way of getting at me. But while she never really forgave me for what I did, she was too interested in what was good for the museum to damage it in order to hurt me."

"Was she alarmed about you flirting with me?"

He felt a little alarmed himself. "Did she say something to you?"

"Kind of. Hinting that you weren't altogether one of the good guys."

He nodded. "That's fair. Because I'm not, you know."

She smiled up at him. "Yes, I suspected that from the start." He wanted to go back to that embrace, but she moved out of range, saying, "I'm keeping you from your work. Thank you for being patient with me."

"Don't forget Friday. I'll pick you up at seven-thirty, if that's not too early. I want to show you the lake at sunset."

"I look forward to that," she said, and continued toward the door. Then, just like Columbo, she turned with one last question. "Oh, how long was Margot in the storage area looking at the horse? We can't find her sketchbook, but I'll stop looking for it if I know she didn't have time to make a graph of the pattern."

He shrugged. "An hour, maybe? I'm afraid I don't know how long it takes to make a graph."

He frowned worriedly at the closed door for a moment after she left, but as he dug into the paperwork he had to work on he began to whistle. Someone was going to get kissed very thoroughly on Friday.

17

Betsy retraced the route back to Lyndale and went up it, toward the towers of downtown. In a couple of stoplights she was driving past the Hennepin Avenue Methodist Church, with its circular nave and crown-like steeple, then past the Gothic St. Mark's Episcopal Cathedral, and saw ahead the entrance to 394, next to St. Mary's Roman Catholic Basilica, built in the Baroque style. If I'm going to live in this part of the world, maybe I need to start going to church, she told herself.

In another minute she was on 394, which curved around sharply and headed west.

What did it all mean? What was Joe Mickels doing in an Excelsior parking lot when he was supposed to be an hour away at a business meeting? Had he come back in time to murder Margot?

Irene Potter said she saw him, which meant she'd contradicted her own alibi of being at home doing needlework at the time of the murder. Was she so innocent she didn't realize that? Or was she astute enough to realize that someone might have seen her, and so was getting in ahead of that witness?

Hud drove a car that at first glance or in the dark looked like an American model from back in the sixties. Why hadn't she thought to ask his secretary if in fact he had taken her to dinner that fatal night? Not that there wasn't time to have gone from dinner to Excelsior and parking his convertible in a parking lot only a couple of blocks from Crewel World.

And Hud was the Asian art curator, responsible for the T'ang horse, the needlepoint representation of which was mysteriously missing.

The question was, why? Hud had no motive.

Still, it was interesting he was keeping abreast of her comings and goings. Or should she be flattered by his interest, rather than concerned?

She continued west to 100, south to 7, west to Excelsior. There, she drove around looking for Irene Potter's house, whose address she had gotten from employee records.

Irene lived in a brown clapboard house that had not enjoyed the meticulous care of the houses around it. When Betsy reached the door, she saw a clumsily crayoned sign in the window indicating that this was a rooming house with a room for rent. She knocked on the door and an elderly, sad-faced man answered it and she asked for Irene Potter.

"She ain't here," he said.

"Is this her house?" asked Betsy.

"No, it's mine. She just rents from us."

"Who is it, Father?" called an old woman's voice from the back.

"Someone wanting Miss Potter!" His voice, when he raised it, quavered.

"Let me talk to him."

A plump woman with a face like one of those dried-apple carvings came to stand beside him. She wore a faded blue dress under a clean white apron, and her dark eyes were bright with intelligence.

"You're not a policeman!" she said indignantly.

"No, I'm Margot Berglund's sister. I've taken over her shop, Crewel World. Irene sometimes worked for my sister, and I wanted to talk to her."

"She's gone out."

"So your husband was telling me. Do you know when she'll be back?"

"Not much longer, I don't think. She's at church, one of the volunteers who helps cook Meals on Wheels."

"How nice of her to do that. Do you know her very well? I take it you're her landlady."

"Yes, that's right. But I don't know her that well, though she's been with us for years. She's not one of the friendly ones."

"Yes, I'm afraid that's true. But she is very talented at needlework."

The woman smiled. "She tried to show me how, but I just didn't get it."

Betsy smiled back in kind. "Me, too. Irene isn't a very good teacher."

"Won't you come in?"

"Now, Mother—" said the old man.

"Shut up, Father." The old woman led the way, saying, "It was terrible what happened to your sister. We don't have murders in Excelsior, so this was a terrible shock. And of course it was even more terrible for you, being her sister."

"Yes, it's been a sad time." The living room had too many couches and chairs, all well used. The woman gestured Betsy to an easy chair.

"Would you like a cup of tea?"

"No, thank you," said Betsy. "Irene told me that she was out walking in the rain the night my sister was killed. In fact, she was near the shop about the time it happened."

"I know. That's why I thought it was a policeman at the door."

Betsy said, "From here to the lake is quite a walk in bad weather. Does she do that sort of thing often?"

The old man cleared his throat, clearly disapproving of the direction this talk was going. His wife shot him a look that made him decide he'd be more comfortable elsewhere. He tottered out without saying a word, but she waited until she heard a door close before turning back to Betsy.

"Miss Potter is a great one for walking. Part of it is necessity, of course; she never learned to drive. But part of it is plain contrariness. The worse the weather, the more she likes to be out in it. But I must say it agrees with her, she never gets so much as a sore throat."

"So you saw her go out that night? Do you know what time she left?"

"No, I was out myself, at my granddaughter's house. They just bought this place out in Shorewood, and it's a wreck. Needs everything, from paint to plumbing. So I was out there scrubbing and painting and watching the great-grandkids." She drew herself up a little. "Got three of 'em now."

"Congratulations," said Betsy.

"You're the one who thinks the police are barking up the wrong tree with their burglar theory, aren't you? Do you really think Miss Potter might have done it?"

"Right now I suspect everyone."

"Yes, that's probably smart, though I don't think your sister had many enemies. What were you going to ask Miss Potter?"

"If I could see some of her needlework. I've seen one or two pieces, but I keep hearing how wonderfully talented she is."

The old woman frowned in puzzlement.

"You see, I'm not trying to prove Irene murdered my sister, I'm trying to find out the truth. If Irene is innocent, I want to make use of her expertise. She's already given me some intelligent suggestions about running the shop. And my sister kept some of her work on display as an inspiration to her customers."

"I could loan you something of hers. Wait here a minute.'' She left the room and soon Betsy could hear heated conversation, cut off by a closing door. Then the woman was back with a square pillow. ''Is this the kind of thing you want to display?'' she asked, and handed it to Betsy.

The face of the pillow was divided into quarters, each containing a picture of the same house in a yard with a tree. Each quarter represented a season. In spring, a robin sang in a tree branch and tulips glowed in the yard. In summer, a child skipped rope in the yard. In fall, the leaves on the tree were a gorgeous mix of red, yellow, and orange, and a jack-o'-lantern sat on the porch. In winter, a Christmas tree decorated with tiny beads glowed in a window. The snow was done in white yarn, which had been brushed to make it fluffy. In each, the sky had been done in fancy stitches that Betsy knew had names like gobelin and Victorian step, though she did not know what names to call these skies.

There was not a misstep in the stitching that Betsy could see, and the overall effect was lovely. ''This is really nice,'' she said.

''Her room is full of this kind of thing,'' said the woman. ''She has a quilt stitched all over with angels. You can borrow this, if you want.''

''I don't want to take it away from you. What if someone stole it?''

''Oh, likely she'd make me another. She's good about that kind of thing, though she can be very unfriendly right to your face, too. Of course, if you hit on the right subject, she'll talk your ears off.''

Betsy nodded. ''So I've heard. Did she ever talk to you about my sister?''

''No, not once. But your sister came to see her the day she died.''

''She did?''

''Let me think. Maybe it was the day before she was killed I went to my daughter's. No, the day of because I didn't hear about the murder till the next evening, on the television news. My cousin Emily came over that Thursday, and sore as I was from the day before, we went out, so it wasn't till evening that I learned about it. It was a terrible shock, and it wasn't till the next morning it occurred to me that Miss Potter must've been one of the last people to see her alive. And it was a shame, a real shame.''

"Why a shame?"

"Because Father says they went at it hammer and tongs, the two of them. He says he was in the kitchen—Miss Potter's room is over the kitchen—and while he couldn't hear any of the words, they was at it for quite a while. Then he says he heard someone coming down the stairs and he went to see, and it was Mrs. Berglund. Miss Potter, he says, stayed at the top of the stairs and hollered after her, 'You'll be sorry you talked to me like that! You'll be sorry!' But Mrs. Berglund just went on out, never looked back.''

"Could I talk to him about this?"

"No, I'm afraid not. He's mad at me for not promising not to repeat what he told me to you. Says it's none of your business. He's talked to a police detective about this, and is waiting to be interviewed by him.''

Joe Mickels glared up at Betsy. He was trying hard to keep hold of his temper, because angry as he was that she had come, he was more afraid of what she was going to ask. But he'd told his secretary to show her in, because he did not dare let her know of either his anger or his fear.

She came in looking tired, and he sensed at once that she was nervous, too. That made him feel he could handle her.

"I take it you are still stirring up trouble over your sister's murder," he said bluntly.

She drew herself up a little. "I am asking questions the police should be asking." He did not offer her a chair, though she seemed a little footsore. He remained seated behind his desk.

"What kind of questions?"

"For one, if you were in St. Cloud that night, as you claim, how did you manage to be seen ducking into a parking lot in Excelsior?"

"Who says they saw me?"

"Irene Potter."

"She's a loon, likely to say anything."

"Her description is a little too detailed to be a hallucination. She said she saw a man with big whiskers, carrying a broken oar and wearing a black rubber coat and a hat with the brim turned down. Do you own a black rubber coat and a brimmed hat? Is your boat missing an oar?"

Bad questions, worse than he thought. He knew lying was a mistake, so he didn't say anything at all. But she was content to let the questions hang there, being answered by his silence. At last he stood and went to the window. The sun was shining, people were going about their business. Old Mrs. Lundgren came out of the Excelo Bakery with a white paper bag in her hand.

"I should get these whiskers cut off," he said. "Not many people wear them anymore." He turned to find her looking at him with a pretty good poker face. "It was me," he said.

"Why a broken oar?" she asked.

"When I've got something I need to think over, I like to do it on the water. Bad weather don't bother me, so long as it's not a thunderstorm, and it wasn't. So I went out in my rowboat. It was so damn foggy out there that I lost my way and rowed right onto some mudflats. I didn't want to get out—you can sink up to your, uh, backside in that stuff. So I stuck the oar in and started pushing. I was stuck pretty good, I was prying hard, and the thing snapped. It's an old oar—hell, I've had that boat since I was nineteen, and that's the original set of oars. But I finally got loose and I paddled with the other oar till I found a dock I could tie up to, near the Park Restaurant. I was walking home when I saw Irene coming, the old witch. I thought I got out of her way quick enough.''

"So you weren't in St. Cloud at all.''

"No, that was the night before. That night I went to supper at Haskell's, then I took my boat out and rowed around. It helps me think.''

"What were you thinking about?''

"You want the truth? Margot Berglund. That woman was the bane of my life till the day she died.'' He glared at her. "And now you've taken over, worse than her, talking about me behind my back, and all.''

"I haven't been spreading rumors about you. I don't know who is repeating what I say in confidence, but they seem to be putting their own twist on it. All I'm doing is wondering out loud who murdered my sister. What time was it when you saw Irene?''

He glared harder, but she didn't back down an inch. "Sometime around ten, or a little after,'' he answered grudgingly. "I remember it was about twenty past when I got in the house.''

"It must not have taken you long to drive home,'' she remarked.

"I didn't drive home, I walked. I live in Excelsior Bay Gables.''

"You mean, you live in that condominium right across the street from Crewel World? I didn't know that.''

"No reason you should.''

"Why were you so anxious to get my sister to break the lease and move out?''

"Because it's time Excelsior had a really decent building. Are you going to insist on staying to the end of the lease?''

"I haven't decided. Did you murder my sister?''

"No, I did not. And I don't appreciate you siccing that cop detective back onto me.''

"Did he come and talk to you again?" She was surprised.

"He did, said you were the one who broke my alibi."

"You shouldn't lie to the police."

"Especially in a town where everyone keeps track." He nodded.

She asked, "Did you recognize Irene when you saw her?"

"I was pretty sure it was her. That's why I ducked out."

"Tell me your version of what happened."

He did; it didn't vary much from Irene's story, so she thanked him and left.

After she was gone, he told his secretary he did not want to be disturbed, then locked the door and went into his strong room for a silver restorative.

When Betsy got back to the shop, it was going on four. Godwin was completing the sale of Marilyn Leavitt-Imblum's *Song of Christmas* counted cross-stitch graph and the yarns to complete it. "You'll need bugle beads for the candles on the tree," he was saying, leading the customer to the big metal box that held little drawers full of beads.

And Shelly was talking with a customer who was interested in using DMC floss instead of Paternayan three-ply persian on a project. "Let's see what Fiber Fantasy says is the equivalent color of Paternayan 501," Shelly was saying.

Betsy stood near the doorway a moment, thinking she really ought to go to church and thank God for competent help. And while she was there, she could apologize to Reverend John for thinking badly of him. Which reminded her, she needed to call Paul Huber at the funeral home and apologize to him, too.

The door went *bing* and she hastened out of the way. Jill came in with, of all things, an oar in one hand. She went right past Betsy, saying over her shoulder, "Follow me.'' She was wearing old jeans and a sweatshirt, but was nevertheless exuding cop authority, and Betsy obediently followed out the back door into the hall that led to the back entrance.

''What, what's the matter?'' asked Betsy when Jill at last stopped and turned around.

''This is an oar,'' said Jill.

''Yes, I can see that.'' It wasn't broken, and so wasn't Joe Mickels's oar.

''Look at the oarlock.''

Betsy obeyed, and even reached out to note how the thing was attached, which was through the oar so that it could swivel. ''I can see how it might be difficult to swing it so that the spike is driven into someone's skull,'' said Betsy.

''And, that spike is too thick and too long to have done that injury,'' said Jill.

''Interesting. But I already don't think Joe murdered my sister.''

''You don't?'' Jill put the oar down. ''What changed your mind?''

Betsy explained, concluding, ''Still, it's interesting about the oar. You're sure the spike is too big?''

''The autopsy report said the spike was not more than an inch and a half long. And the injury to Margot's skull was fairly small, only an inch or so across. But that doesn't mean the weapon was that small. It depends on whether or not the weapon sank to its full diameter.''

''Ugh!'' said Betsy. ''The things you know.''

''These are things you encounter when you investigate homicides. I think Hud's right, you aren't cut out for this sort of stuff.''

''Hud? When did you talk with him about me?''

''He didn't tell me, he told Shelly. Shelly told me. Didn't I warn you about her? She's the most terrific gossip I've ever known.''

''And in this town that's saying something,'' said Betsy.

"So she's the one who told Hud you and I went to the Guthrie."

"Yes, she told me he told her he wished it could have been him taking you out. Those two talk on the phone a couple of times a week."

"Hud's a suspect, you know."

"*Hud?*"

"You're the one who told me they quarreled."

"That was *years* ago!"

"Actually his motive has nothing to do with the quarrel; it's that T'ang horse. Margot went to see it on that Wednesday, and then went to see Hud upset—he says because she snagged her stockings again in that storage room and wanted to know when they'd get the new exhibit set up. That night she was murdered, the shop was ransacked, and the only things still missing are the T'ang needlepoint and her sketchbook in which she was making a new copy of it. What's more, not only does he not have an alibi, a Rolls-Royce was in an Excelsior parking lot that night."

Jill stared at her. "How do you know that?"

"Irene said she saw Joe Mickels ducking down behind a big dark car, an imitation convertible with a hood ornament. I remember those imitation convertibles, and none of them had hood ornaments. In fact the only car with a hood ornament I can remember is a Rolls-Royce—and Hud owns a Rolls that has a beautifully made convertible top, so perfectly fitted you might think it was one of those cars with the fabric top. And Joe Mickels remembers the hood ornament looked like a fairy, which pretty much describes the Rolls ornament."

Jill thought a minute. "You know, Betsy, Hud doesn't own the only Rolls-Royce in the state. Or the county, for that matter. Probably half of their owners don't have alibis. You can't go around saying this kind of thing without more proof than that!"

"I wonder how many Rolls-Royces there are in Minnesota?"

Jill frowned at her. "I don't know. I've seen a few."

"How many?"

She thought. "Two, maybe three, right in this area."

"I bet it would be interesting to call their owners up and ask them where they were that Wednesday night. If all of them but Hud have an alibi, then we'll know something of value. Say, Jill, can you really find out how many there are? Who their owners are? Where they bought their cars? Hud says he bought his at a car auction, but I wonder—could we find out where he bought it?"

"You're serious!"

"You bet your sweet bippy I am."

"The Minnesota Department of Public Safety keeps those kind of records. You can ask their computer to do sorts to get that kind of information. Like a friend of mine on the Minneapolis force was investigating a ring of snowmobile thieves. They were breaking them down for parts, but now and then they'd take the leftovers and make a new snowmobile and sell it. Jay asked them to sort out all the reconstructed snowmobiles registered in the past two years and broke the case that way."

"Can you ask for a sort of Rolls-Royces, even though you're not a detective?"

"Sure, but it will go through Mike and he'll ask me why and I'll tell him you want to know. Better you ask them yourself."

"How? Pretend I'm a cop?"

The cold look Jill gave her made Betsy wonder how she had ever mistaken any of Jill's earlier looks for chilly dislike. Jill obviously did not approve of impersonating an officer. But she replied courteously enough, "No, of course not. Automobile registrations are public information. Car salesmen line up to get lists of people who've bought more than one sports utility vehicle in the past four years, or are driving a Cadillac more than three years old. The state charges for the information, but you can get the name and address of every Rolls owner registered in the state."

Betsy started back into the shop. "Where is this department? How long does it take to get the list?"

Jill followed, the oar in her hand. "It's in downtown St. Paul. Are you really going to go and ask?"

"That's not the broken oar," Godwin observed.

"Duh-uh!" said Jill.

"What were you two talking about?" asked Shelly.

"Why do you ask?" asked Betsy. "Are you out of things to tell Hud?"

Shelly said in a hurt voice, "What do you mean?"

"I mean, it was wrong of you to tell him everything I— or anyone else—told you." Betsy flashed a look at Godwin, who had the grace to look abashed.

"Hud?" said Shelly. "But you're in love with him!"

"I am not in love with Hudson Earlie. I was indulging in a flirtation with him. He's very attractive, but he's not one of the good guys—you should see what he has in his office. And I think maybe he murdered my sister."

Shelly said in a faint, appalled voice, "Why do you think that?"

"Because he stole the T'ang horse from the museum and Margot found out about it."

Godwin said, "You mean, when you went to the museum today it was *gone*?"

"Oh, no, there's a horse there all right. But it's not the same horse."

Jill asked sharply, "Are you sure?"

"Pretty sure. I mean, I took those Madeira silks with me, all six of them." She fumbled in her pockets and pulled them out. "Godwin pointed out that they are really two different families of blue, one of them kind of grayer than the other. Well, the 1710, 11, and 12 are the colors that match the horse I saw. These others don't. But Margot had all six in the folder labeled T'ANG in her file cabinet."

Shelly said, "When Margot was laying out the colors, she said 1008 was the right shade of blue." They looked at her. "I'm positive, I remember it distinctly. She was putting the colors beside the framed picture and saying she remembered it was 1007.''

''There, Jill; there's your proof!'' Betsy said. ''The horse Margot used as a model for her canvas and the horse I saw are not the same color. I think that when Margot went down there to look at the horse last Wednesday, she took the 1007 colors with her. And they didn't match the horse in the case.''

Jill said, ''And of course she went to tell Hud. He's responsible for the Chinese stuff.''

''And Margot was murdered that night. I suspect Hud told Margot not to tell anyone else until he checked into it. But what he did was come out here and murder her. And he stole the needlepoint horse and the sketchbook, because they're evidence. Then he trashed Crewel World to make it look like a burglary.''

''Wait a minute,'' said Godwin. ''Wait just a minute.'' Then he himself waited until they all turned to look at him. ''About those different families of blue. I've been to the museum, and I know how carefully they light those exhibits. I have a feeling they don't light the storage areas like that.''

Betsy flashed on the warm lighting of the Fasset exhibit and then on the big chill storage room with its harsh overhead lights. ''No, they don't.''

''Well, how many of us have put on an outfit that matches beautifully in your bedroom, but when you get to the office it's like you got dressed in the dark?''

The women, frowning, nodded doubtfully.

''So of course the silks didn't match the horse! On exhibit, in storage, different lights, different colors.''

Betsy stared at him, her heart sinking. What if she had made a terrible mistake?

18

Hud arrived Friday evening, right on time. He paused inside the door when he saw Jill and a very tall and well-built man waiting with Betsy for him.

"I'm so sorry, Hud," said Betsy, "but Lars's car broke down this afternoon and Jill's is in the shop, too, so I said you wouldn't mind giving them a lift."

Hud looked for a moment as if he did mind, but then he shrugged and said, "Sure, why not." He was wearing a beautifully cut tuxedo—or perhaps it fit so well because he was the shape the designer had in mind.

Jill had said the dance was "dressy," and turned up in a short cocktail dress of ice-blue silk, her escort in a dark suit and tie. So Betsy felt right in her little black dress and the garnet earrings and necklace her mother had left her.

"How 'dressy' is this dance?" asked Betsy. "I mean, am I all right?"

"You look wonderful," said Hud sincerely, so she let him wrap her in her black silk coat and followed him down the stairs.

Hud put Jill and Lars into the big back seat of the Rolls and pushed a button that rolled up a window between it and the front seat—which sent the two of them into gales of laughter.

"What's so funny?" Betsy asked Hud.

"Beats me." He handed her into the car and they started off.

The drive to the club was along a back road that wound among the bays of Lake Minnetonka, through small towns and past modest cottages and the beautiful new mansions that were quietly replacing them, all set in rolling land covered with big old trees. The sun was a glowing red ball—Betsy caught herself trying to decide which shade of perle cotton would be closest and decided she was carrying this needlework business too far.

The Rolls was big and comfortable, and as smooth to ride in as Hud had said it was. "Yeah, I really lucked out with this car," said Hud when she remarked on that, and on the powerful but quiet engine.

"You said you bought it at a police auction?" asked Betsy. "How did that happen?"

"I was in Las Vegas for our annual convention about six years ago." He showed his wolfish grin. "What, you think curators should meet in Chicago? In February? Anyhow, I took an afternoon off from the doings and got lucky at the craps table. A fellow curator told me about the auction. He said there would be sports cars—he was going to bid on a Porsche 928S. I went along to see if he'd get it—he didn't—but right at the end, when most of the people had left, this Rolls Corniche came up. A cop with a great big grin bid five hundred dollars, so I bid eight, which surprised him. Then he bid a grand, and I bid twelve hundred, and we kept going up until I bid everything I'd won, which was eight thousand, two hundred dollars. Silence from the cop, who wasn't grinning anymore. So I packed my bags and started driving for home, because you don't want to be in a town where you've wiped the grin off a cop's face. And you know how you hear about how crummy English cars are? Well, this one sure isn't. It has never given me any trouble at all. It gets terrible mileage, of course, because it's so heavy. But it's like sitting on a leather couch and watching the road come at you on a big TV screen.''

"Nothing like being at the right place at the right time," said Betsy. "I didn't recognize this as a Rolls-Royce until I saw the grille. I remember seeing them in England back in the sixties, and they had kind of a roll of front fender that swooped down along the side to the back fender. Very distinctive.''

"I think someone around here has one of those," said Hud. "But I'm glad this is a later model. Unless people notice the hood ornament, they think I drive an older American car.''

"If you don't like the hood ornament, why don't you take it off?''

"Because then it would be a Bentley, and that's not quite the same thing.''

Hud laughed and Betsy joined in, because it was true, Bentleys are Rolls-Royces without the hood ornament. Once upon a time, Rolls dealerships would not sell a Rolls to just anyone. Rich commoners had to settle for Bentleys.

Interesting that Hud knew that, too.

Lake Minnetonka is big and has a complicated shoreline so the drive took a while. The lake showed itself in tree-lined bays, or in glimpses through evergreens, and even occasionally came boldly right up to the road.

They were running alongside a particularly wide bay into which the sun had nearly sunk when Hud slowed and flipped his turn signal on. They turned away from the water, past a self-consciously quaint little brown church and across a railroad line. The other side of the road was lined with a golf course. And there, awash in white lights, was the Lafayette Club.

It was not at all the modest place Betsy had expected, but a 1920s stucco palace, with an arched arcade, faux-Moorish windows, and a forest-green canvas marquee at the entrance. And a valet in a dinner jacket waiting to park their car.

The lobby was huge, with a red tiled floor and a big old antique bronze fountain. A large, live band was playing somewhere, and the three couples ahead of them checking their coats were in tuxes and long dresses.

"Oops," said Betsy, and turned to Hud. "Why didn't you say black tie?" Her glance took in Jill, who widened her eyes innocently.

"What?" said Hud. "I told you, you look wonderful."

Fortunately, when they got to the ballroom there were a number of other women who either hadn't read Miss Manners on "Proper Attire for Black-Tie Events" or didn't care. Hud took her around, introducing her to people. Some of them she already knew, such as the chief of police, whom she'd met only yesterday. His wife was an ardent counted cross-stitcher.

The band was good. It played a mix of big-band, soft rock, and standards, mixed with waltzes and, once, a polka. She danced first with Hud, who made her think she was a better dancer than she remembered, then with Mayor Jamison and attorney Penberthy, who taught her that Hud was the kind of dancer who made his partners look good.

It was a slow dance with Penberthy, and as they box-stepped around the floor, she asked, "Were you a friend of Margot's, as well as her attorney?"

"I'd like to think so," he replied, a little dreamily. He hummed a snatch of the melody.

"Did she talk to you about anything the last time you saw her?"

"Hmmm? No, I don't think so."

"Are you sure? You saw her the last day of her life. Surely you remember what people said to you when they turn up dead right after."

He loosened his hold to lean back and look into her face. "What's this all about?"

"The police are here, they're going to make an arrest," she said.

"Arrest who?" he asked, alarmed.

"I'm not supposed to say, but it's the person who murdered Margot."

Penberthy tried to look around and dance at the same time and stepped on both of Betsy's feet. "Sorry, sorry," he said. He regained his rhythm. "Is that Joe Mickels over there?" The landlord was holding a highball in one hand and gesturing sharply with the other to a trio of men.

"Yes, and there's Detective Malloy. Jill's here, too, and her date is a Shorewood cop."

"Jesus God," murmured Penberthy. "When is it going to happen?"

"I don't know, but don't worry, they won't do it in front of everyone. They're supposed to let me know when everything's set up."

"Why you?"

"Oh, I'm going to be in at the kill. In fact, I get to take the first bite."

"Jesus God." The dance ended; Penberthy assumed a patently false look of indifference and escorted her back to her date.

During a break, the mayor came by and suggested to Hud that so long as he was here he might take Betsy around and show her the features of the club, since they would be using it for the fund-raiser next month. Hud seemed pleased to get out of the ballroom, which was a trifle warm. He showed Betsy the enormous fireplace lounge (two, count 'em, fireplaces), the long screened porch that overlooked yet another bay, the dining room, the intimate café, and the indoor pool.

Betsy's opinion of the Lafayette Club racheted up another notch with every feature. The suggested cost of a ticket to the fund-raiser, she remarked to Hud, was not high enough.

"Yes, but if they pay a lot for a ticket, then they won't

feel a need to buy anything at the auction."

"Oh. Yes, I suppose you're right." They were back in the café, which was deserted and dimly lit, lined with semicircular booths in red tufted leather. There was the warm smell of coffee in the air. "Here's where they make the greatest coffee in the state," said Hud. "They'll start serving it soon."

"Minnesotans sure drink a lot of coffee."

"We're probably near the top per capita," said Hud, but with an air of intimacy that did not match the topic.

She looked up at him, his smiling face, the bright hair, the broad shoulders. "Hud, did you really have to murder my sister?"

He stood perfectly still for several long seconds. "What are you talking about?" His voice was still soft, as if he hadn't understood.

"Is the T'ang horse the only thing you've stolen from the museum?"

That caught his attention. "Stolen? I haven't stolen anything!"

"Yes, you have. The Asian art collection is almost completely in storage, and has been for over a year. What better time to replace some of the artifacts with replicas? People are less likely to notice any differences when they haven't seen the originals for a long time. But Margot noticed, didn't she? She made two trips to that storeroom, the first to do her original canvas and then only a few months later to do the second. And she saw the difference right away. You said she kept snagging things while she worked on that horse, that's what made me realize that both times she saw it was in the storeroom. So it wasn't a change in lighting that made her think the horse was a different shade of blue."

"What are you talking about?"

"The T'ang horse in your collection, the one Margot made a needlepoint copy of. The horse she saw originally matched the one-thousand series of Madeira blue silks, while the horse she saw the second time matched the seventeen-hundred series. She realized it wasn't the same horse.

"And what does one do when one suspects there has been a theft? Why, one reports it to the person responsible—that was you, wasn't it, Hud?"

He made a little noise in his throat, but no words came out.

"And you said you'd look into it right away. You probably asked her not to tell anyone until you'd checked it out, right? Then you came to her apartment that night, saying you needed to see the proof. So she got her sketchbook and took you down to the shop because that's where the original needlepoint hung. And you hit her with your cane—was it the one with the head shaped like a snail? I remembered the way the slinky little head came out of the shell on the head of your cane, and it made me wonder. But maybe it was the one shaped like a bird. What kind of a bird is that, with the pointed beak?"

"Who have you told this fairy tale to? You're going to have some explaining to do if you've told anyone, because you're making a horrible mistake."

"Whatever cane it was, you hit Sophie with it, too, but with the side, and you broke her hind leg."

"I didn't hit anyone with a cane. Anyhow, I thought you said Joe Mickels did it. Or Irene Potter. They both were near the store, weren't they?"

"Yes, but they couldn't have done it, either of them, Hud. Margot left City Hall pretty close to nine forty-five. It took her six or maybe seven minutes to walk home, so she got in before ten, but not by much. The murderer was waiting for her, but he had to talk his way into her apartment, convince her to come down to the shop, murder her, and then trash the shop. There wasn't time to do all that and still be down by that parking lot by ten-fifteen."

"Maybe Irene saw Joe on his way to the shop, before the murder."

"No, because I made that call to 911 at three minutes after eleven. Say five minutes to the shop from the parking lot, persuade Margot to come down into the shop, murder her and injure the cat, then wreck the shop, and get away before I got there at eleven—not enough time, Hud. Even if he was still in the place when I saw the open door, there wasn't enough time. The shop was *really* trashed; you must have spent a long time breaking and tearing and kicking and smashing. It must have taken you at least half an hour to do that, and more likely forty-five minutes, or even an hour.

"Both Irene and Joe described your car as the one they saw in that parking lot at a little after ten. You really should have taken that hood ornament off. Ask me how I can prove it was your car."

"You can't prove it was my car."

"The department of public safety can make up lists of Minnesota car owners broken down any way you want. Did you know there are only seventeen Rolls-Royces in the state, Hud? And only two of them are convertibles. And guess how many owners of Rolls convertibles don't have alibis?"

"Bitch," Hud muttered. "You *bitch*!" He grabbed for her, but prepared, she ducked away.

"Jill!" she shouted, and Jill stood up on the other side of the gleaming-empty salad bar. Beside her were Lars and two more uniformed officers, one with his gun drawn.

"Hold it right there, Mr. Earlie," the cop with the gun said in a deep, calm voice.

"I tried," said Betsy. "But he wouldn't confess."

"Close enough, I think, Miss Devonshire," said another man's voice, and a heavyset man who looked like every B-movie plainclothes cop came out of the kitchen. He was the chief of Excelsior's police department. With him was Mike Malloy, handcuffs in hand.

Jill, Lars, and the uniformed cops ducked under the salad bar and approached.

"You're under arrest, Mr. Earlie," said Malloy. He reached for Hud's right arm and snapped the handcuffs onto his wrist. "For the murder of Margot Berglund. You have the right to remain silent. . . ."

Betsy had always wanted to hear the entire Miranda warning, but all of a sudden her head was swimming and someone grabbed her and the next thing she knew she was sitting sideways at the end of a booth and the room was empty, except for Jill.

"Hey," said Betsy. "Where did everyone go?"

"Down to the police station," said Jill. "They want to talk to you some more, but it can wait until tomorrow."

"That's good, I think I'm kind of talked out. Did Hud go quietly?"

"Yes."

"Too bad, I would have liked him to feel a billy club or two."

"Want to go back to the dance?"

"Oh, gosh no. But oh, and how am I going to get home? Hud brought me!"

"Want a ride in a squad car? I can arrange for you to ride in the front."

"Can I play with the lights and siren? No, sorry, I don't mean that. I think I'm still light-headed. Riding in the front—is that what you and Lars thought was so funny about riding in the back of Hud's Rolls?"

"Yes, when he rolled up that window we started reciting the Miranda warning to each other." Jill chuckled.

Betsy said, "We got him, didn't we?"

"You bet we did. Mike has a whole lot more respect for you than he used to."

"Did he order up the the list of Rolls-Royce owners like I asked him to?"

"Yes, he did. How did you know there were only seventeen of those cars in the state?"

Betsy stared at her. "There are? I just pulled that number out of the air. Wow, do you think I'm psychic?"

"No, I don't. But I do think you are damn quick on your feet. Now come on, let's go phone for transportation."

Hud wisely invoked his right to silence. And the indictment did not mention a motive when he made his first appearance in court Monday morning. So the *Strib* put the story on the first page of its Metro section, below the fold, without a photo.

But when an Asian art expert came up from Chicago on Wednesday to look at the Minneapolis art museum collection, two employees of the museum resigned without notice. They were arrested and one of them began negotiating a deal.

A week later Jill sat at the table in Crewel World. She was in uniform, drinking coffee with one hand and stroking Sophie with the other. She didn't seem too concerned that Mike Malloy might come in and run her off.

Betsy was grumbling over a piece of twelve-count aida, blunt needle in her hand threaded with scrap yarn. "I just don't get it, Goddy."

"I know, I know; but it's like purling. Just listen and be patient and all of a sudden you'll wonder what you were complaining about. Now, where do you go next?"

"I haven't got the faintest idea."

"You're about to go up, so go down here."

"See what I mean?" she demanded. "I'm going up, so I go down."

"Yes, that's right. Here," he said, pointing, and Betsy obediently stuck the needle through from the back.

Jill said, "You'd think anyone who could figure out the clues that pointed to Hud Earlie could figure out a simple thing like basketweave."

"Yeah, you would, wouldn't you?" Betsy said crossly. She stuck the needle back in again on the diagonal. "Now where?"

"Here."

"Ah, this part I get." Betsy finished the angled row and said, "Now where?"

"Now we're starting down again, so go across, here."

"Ahhh!" Betsy growled, tossing the canvas down. "To go up you go down, to go down you go across. It gives me a headache!"

"But it isn't hard," said Godwin, picking it up and putting it back in her hands. "You're saying it right, that means you know it. Just do it."

Jill said, "How's business?"

"Crazy," said Godwin. "Everyone wants to meet the person who figured out a murder. And thank God they're ashamed to admit it, so we're selling every starter kit in the place."

Betsy said, "That knitting class Margot had on the schedule is overbooked; I may have to hire Irene to teach."

"Don't do that, you'll lose all those potential customers," said Jill. "You teach it."

"Me? I can't do anything more than knit and purl. Those crossovers and knots and all are a mystery to me."

"But you're so good at mysteries," said Godwin with his famous limpid look.

"And the students will be more interested in how you solved a murder that baffled the police than they will be in how to do crossovers," said Jill.

"Are you upset that I solved it?" asked Betsy. "Is Detective Malloy?"

"I'm not upset. And I think Mike has decided you're a special kind of informant. After all, you came to him at the end."

"Of course I did! I'm not V. I. Warshawski."

"Some people think you are," said Jill. "They'll be really disappointed not to meet you at knitting class."

Betsy laughed. "You teach it, Godwin," she said. "I'll sign myself up as a student. That way we won't disappoint our clients in any way."

"Well—"

"Thanks. I'll make up the poster tonight. Say, do either of the rest of you subscribe to that newsgroup rctn?"

"No," said Jill.

Godwin said, "Aren't they fun?"

Betsy nodded. "And long-winded. It takes forever to download their messages, but they had this thread about coffee stains on a needlepoint—"

The door went *bing* and talk stopped. A young woman wearing a maternity top she barely needed came in with an older woman who looked enough like her to be her mother. Betsy stood and asked, "May I help you?"

"My daughter may have to spend the last part of her pregnancy in bed. She can knit and wants to make a bed jacket, but she can't do complicated stitches. Can you suggest something?"

Betsy said, "Here, let me show you something." She reached beneath the worktable and lifted a wood-framed folding canvas holder up onto its surface. She pulled out a pair of knitting needles to which was attached a pale gold length of knitting. It caught the light in a very attractive way when Betsy draped it over her hand.

"Oh, that's beauti—why, look at that, Mama, it's ribbon!"

"Yes." Betsy nodded. "It's mine, and I'm just learning. If you can knit and purl, you can do it. Isn't it pretty? We have the ribbon in stock in a wide range of colors, and there are pattern books that show you how to knit with ribbon."

The older woman fingered the knitting. "You know, that *is* beautiful. It makes me want to take up knitting again myself. Do you have any alpaca wool?"

"We just got a shipment in. I've never seen such wonderful colors. We have bone and bamboo knitting needles, if you need needles. But first, let me show you the ribbon selection." Betsy started to lead them toward the back. "Oh, and do you know we have classes here? Our regular knitting class is full, but there's going to be a second one starting soon, if you're interested. Or if you want to wait until spring . . .''

Over at the worktable there was a lot of winking and nodding going on. No one had wanted to ask, but if Betsy was talking about spring classes, she wasn't going to be holding a going-out-of-business sale anytime soon.

Turn the page for your free
T'ang Horse needlepoint pattern.

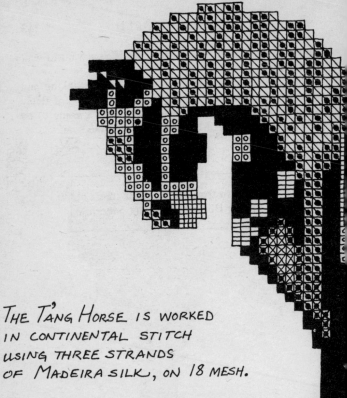

THE T'ANG HORSE IS WORKED
IN CONTINENTAL STITCH
USING THREE STRANDS
OF MADEIRA SILK, ON 18 MESH.

BLACK	◉	0305	◿
1003	⊠	0402	◩
1005	◪	0401	◣
1007	■	1910	⊟
1912	⊞	2014	◉
0306	◢		

Denise E. Williams

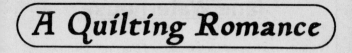

A Quilting Romance

Patterns of Love
by Christine Holden

When Lord Grayling Dunston appears on Baines Marshall's doorstep asking for her only quilt, she sends him on his way. But Baines discovers that Mary's Fortune is no ordinary quilt—its pattern reveals the map to a treasure Gray desperately needs to pay off his debts. When the quilt suddenly disappears from her home the two embark on a journey that deepens their attraction and changes their lives...

❏ 0-515-12481-8/$5.99